REAWAKENED

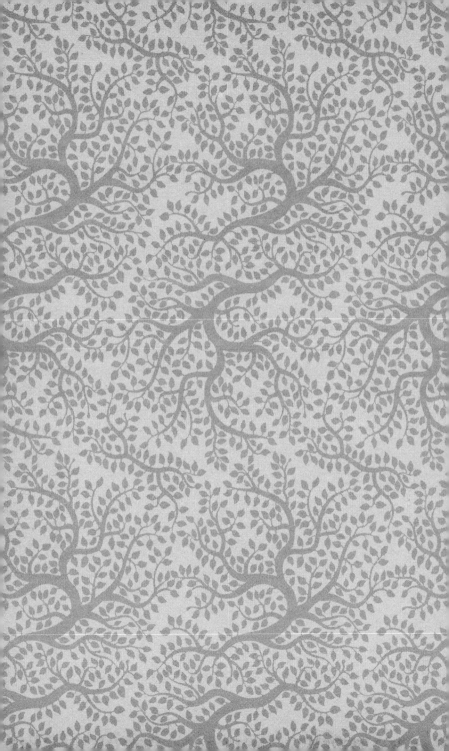

REAWAKENED

A
ONCE UPON A TIME
TALE

Odette Beane

TITAN BOOKS

A Once Upon a Time Tale: Reawakened
Print edition ISBN: 9781781169063
E-book edition ISBN: 9781781169070

Published by Titan Books
A division of Titan Publishing Group Ltd.
144 Southwark Street, London SE1 0UP

First edition: July 2013

1 3 5 7 9 10 8 6 4 2

Book design by Karen Minster

To receive advance information, news, competitions, and exclusive offers online, please sign
up for the Titan newsletter on our website: www.titanbooks.com

A CIP catalogue record for this title is available from the British Library.

Printed and bound in Great Britain by CPI Group UK Ltd.

Did you enjoy this book? We love to hear from our readers. Please email us at
readerfeedback@titanemail.com or write to us at Reader Feedback at the above address.

To the extraordinary fans—
you are the fairest of them all

CONTENTS

CONTENTS

REAWAKENED

PART ONE

WANDERING
HEARTS

CHAPTER 1

WELCOME TO STORYBROOKE

HE HAD BEEN HUNTING RYAN MARLOW FOR nearly three weeks now, since he'd emptied his family's bank accounts and fled New York, embezzlement charges hanging over his head. Why he had decided to stop off in Boston for a little online dating was anybody's guess, but Emma Swan didn't care much about why the bail-jumpers she tracked down did what they did. She wasn't paid to know their stories; she was paid to find them, to catch them, and to bring them in.

She stood and watched him, uncomfortable in her high heels.

Marlow hadn't seen her yet, and she studied him for a moment. Handsome, just like he was in the pictures, but there was something smarmy about him as well. Which fit the bill, of course—arrogance and wantonness seemed to be the norm with these banker types. There was something about his cool confidence as he waited—it made her sick to her stomach, actually.

She went to him.

"Ah, you must be Emma," he said, rising as she approached the table, and she smiled her best nice-to-meet-you smile and held out her hand. She frowned at her own fingernails. She had forgotten to paint them.

He smiled broadly, lasciviously. Like a wolf. They shook, and he kept his eyes locked on her.

"Ryan?" she said.

As she sat, Emma, after seeing something in his eyes, smiled at him and said, "Well. You look relieved."

"I'm sorry," he said, chuckling nervously. "You just never know how a person will look when you meet them online. For real, I mean." He went to his seat and sat. "And you are—well, you're very hot. Online and in real life."

She did not blush. She looked down, pretended to be flattered. What had his online profile said? Divorced, no children, enjoyed yoga and pickup basketball? Right. Emma knew the real "real life" story. Back in New York, he had three kids under ten years old and a wife with a part-time job, trying to get by alone. Right now the wife was sorting through a welfare application. Devastated. Broken. Explaining where Daddy was. That was real. And here was Ryan Marlow, who had it in him to date after doing that to someone.

"So," said Ryan. "Tell me something about yourself, Emma." Emma smiled her sexiest smile.

"Well," she said. "First off, I'm an amazing judge of character." Ryan Marlow looked surprised.

She was going to enjoy taking this one down.

. . .

IN ANOTHER WORLD, in another time, Snow White stood hand in hand with Prince Charming in the Royal Castle's ballroom.

All the kingdom's subjects surrounded the couple. The

two looked into each other's eyes as the bishop asked Snow if she would have Charming forever.

There was no hesitation. She said that she would, and the two smiled at each other nervously and lovingly as the bishop pronounced them man and wife. The court's musicians began to play, and Charming and Snow leaned together to kiss once again.

It had been something of a miracle. Charming had awoken Snow from a cursed sleep brought on by her stepmother, the Evil Queen. And they were not, it turned out, free of her yet.

This time, just as their lips touched, a tremendous clap of thunder overwhelmed the music, and many in the room cried out. The assembled guests all turned at once to the ballroom's great doors, where the sound had originated, which flew open with great violence, striking the walls on either side of the entrance.

There, in the doorway, stood a figure all in black.

The Evil Queen.

Again.

Wonderful, thought Snow. More of this.

Guards rushed her as she began to stride toward Snow and Charming, who stood in the center of the room, clutching each other. The Queen sent a half-dozen guards flying through the air with a flick of her wrist—her magic was still powerful, there was no doubt.

When she was near, Snow pushed Charming back, grabbed the hilt of his sword, and unsheathed it before he could stop her. Snow White pointed the blade at the Queen, eyes aflame.

"You are not welcome here," she said, and her strong voice echoed through the great room. "Go. Now."

The Queen stopped walking, kept smiling.

"Hello again, Snow White," she said.

Charming, his hand on Snow's, slowly pushed the sword down until its tip touched the stone floor.

"She has no power," he said to Snow quietly. "We've already won."

He was right, she knew—after Charming woke Snow from the Queen's sleeping curse, the two of them united the kingdom against the Queen, driving her from power and allowing love to reign.

"Leave us," said Charming to the Queen. "You've already lost, and I won't let you ruin this day. Not another one. Let us have our happiness. You've been defeated."

"On the contrary," said the Queen, "I'm not here to ruin anything. I've come to give you a gift."

"We don't want it," said Snow quickly. It didn't matter what it was.

"And nevertheless, I shall give it to you," said the Queen. She raised an eyebrow. "Generous of me, don't you think?" The Queen was beautiful and terrifying all at once. Her features were severe, her hair black as onyx, her eyes piercing and ice-cold. Perhaps once, long ago, she had been an innocent young maiden herself, the fairest of the land, but now all could see that hatred and bitterness had pulled the warmth from her face. Snow had known her for a very long time, and every time she saw her, the Queen had become more embittered. Snow didn't understand how one person could hate so much.

As the Evil Queen spoke, more guards poured into the room, surrounding her, but her gaze did not waver.

"My gift to you is happiness," she said. "This happiness. Today."

"What do you mean?" asked Charming cautiously.

"I mean that tomorrow, good prince," said the Queen,

"I will begin my life's work. To destroy your happiness. Permanently."

At this, Charming had had enough, and he threw his sword in one quick, lightning-fast maneuver. It sailed toward the Queen, tip forward, bearing down on her heart.

Just before it reached her, the Queen disappeared in a cloud of inky black-and-purple smoke.

The sword disappeared as well.

Snow White, her hand on her new husband's arm, watched the cloud swirl and fade.

· · ·

EXHAUSTED, Emma walked down the hallway to her apartment, holding her red heels with the fingers of her left hand and a bag of groceries in the other hand. Taking down Ryan Marlow was not as satisfying as she had hoped, and now she had a headache.

Her hand also hurt.

He had tried to run, of course. The men all tried to run. He'd made it to his car, only to find it booted. Not a difficult thing for her to set up. That's when she had rammed his head into the car.

These things—the hunt, the chases—had all become a bit predictable. What else did she know how to do, though? And where else would she go? Something was off, but she didn't let herself think about it too much. Nothing a little sleep and scotch wouldn't cure.

Inside the apartment, Emma dumped the groceries on the counter, turned on some music, and removed the birthday cupcake she'd purchased for herself. She fished out the candles she'd bought, removed one from the package, stuck it in the cupcake, and lit it. It wasn't much of a party, no. But it was something.

She watched the candle glow for a moment. Another year, another year alone.

She closed her eyes.

Please, she thought, don't let me be alone on my birthday.

It sounded depressing there in her head, ringing around, but it was her wish, she had to admit.

She was not one to indulge in self-pity. Plenty of people had worse pasts than she had, and she was strong enough to contain the ache of her blank history. That didn't mean she didn't get lonely, no, but it meant she could handle loneliness. She just also needed to wish it away sometimes.

Just as she blew out the candle, the doorbell rang. Emma frowned at the door, ticking through the various fugitives she'd hunted down in the last few years, trying to recall if any of them had recently been released from prison. Probably, she thought. One of these days she was going to open the door to a sledgehammer falling down on her head.

She went and looked through the peephole and thought: What in the hell?

When she opened the door, a small boy—a stranger—stood looking back at her. He had shaggy brown hair and was wearing a sagging, full backpack. He stared up at her, eyes wide.

"Hello?" Emma said hesitantly.

"Hi," said the boy. "Are you Emma Swan?"

"I . . . am?" said Emma. "Can I help you?"

The kid smiled, held out his hand. "I'm Henry Mills," he said. "I'm your son."

Emma stared. She didn't take his hand.

"I don't have a son," she said flatly.

The boy seemed to ignore this. Instead of responding, he pushed past her, looking at the kitchen.

She was too shocked to do anything, to stop him. "Ten years ago," he said casually, looking around. He turned back to her. "Did you give up a baby for adoption?"

Emma again said nothing. Some of the color had drained from her face, though; she noted it when she looked in the mirror.

"I'm him. The kid. Are you gonna eat that cupcake?"

"I—"

It could be him. Emma didn't think he was lying, and she could see her eyes in his eyes. But if he was the son she had spent so many years burying and forgetting, to see him here, so casually asking for a cupcake, sent her into fight-or-flight mode. She felt dizzy. She felt—

She didn't know what she felt.

(She never knew what she felt.)

She closed the door and turned, trying to think of something to say.

"You can have it," she said, distracted. "Have the whole thing."

This seemed to please him. Emma put the cupcake on a plate, removed the candle, set him up on a stool, and excused herself.

In the bathroom, she stared at her face in the mirror, steadying herself, holding the edge of the sink. How different she looked from ten years ago, when she was only eighteen and all alone. She remembered looking in the mirror then, too, in the last days before the birth, when she'd been holed up in a dusty jail simply waiting, not a soul to help her. Loneliness. She remembered feeling it then, and realizing that the baby she was about to give up would have meant the end of loneliness had she kept him. But she didn't.

She took a few more breaths.

"Get ahold of yourself, Swan," she said out loud.

At the sound of her own voice, a more reasonable, skeptical, and stronger part of her mind stirred and snapped to life. Old Emma. Tough Emma. Bail-bond Emma. The real question: Who was this kid, really? He was certainly not her son. Here she was getting bent out of shape, and for all she knew he was rifling through her things in the other room, or he was the front end of some con that involved a number of large men bursting into her apartment just as she was beginning to open up. . . .

It was a con. That was it. Someone knew her past. Someone knew her past and someone knew how to get under her skin. She hurried back out to the kitchen, ready to start shouting.

The boy was sitting at the table, eating the cupcake. He looked up, and his eyes disarmed her.

"Hi," he said. "How was the bathroom?"

"Hi," she said, frowning again. She walked over to him, put her hand on the table, took it back. This little kid was making her unsure how to behave.

"So. I'd like to ask you a few questions," she said finally.

"Okay," he said. "Go."

"How . . . did you find me?"

"I'm resourceful," he said. He seemed bored by the question, more interested in studying her reaction than anything having to do with his own feelings. "This isn't going how I thought it would go."

"What's 'this'? This conversation?"

"Yes."

"How did you think it would go?"

"More like Oprah. You know? With crying and hugging."

"I'm not the crying type, kid."

"I can tell," he said, agreeing.

If she didn't know better, she would have guessed he was making fun of her. Or chiding her, at least.

"We should get going," he added.

Emma smiled skeptically, lowered her brow. She did like his audacity, whoever he was. "I'm sorry, I didn't know we were going anywhere," she said. "You were just leaving. I was just going to bed. We were just about to never see each other again."

"We are going somewhere," he said, nodding. "You have to come home with me. You have to give me a ride, at least."

"And where's home?"

"Storybrooke."

Emma looked at him. She looked at the book he'd taken out of his backpack. Ah. I see. This kid, she thought, is in the middle of some kind of psychological "event."

"Storybrooke?" she said finally. "Are you kidding me?"

"No. What?" he asked innocently. "That's what it's called."

"Okay, kid," she said. "This has been fun. But one, I don't have a son. And two, I'm calling the cops now. I don't have time for this and you're obviously a runaway. Do your parents not know where you are? I'm calling the cops." Emma went toward the phone, realizing she had said it twice.

"No you're not."

She glanced up, phone in hand. "I'm not?"

"No," he said, taking another bite of the cupcake. "Because if you do, I'll tell them you kidnapped me."

Emma thought it through. The doubts trickled back. If he was really her kid, it was a good plan. The cops would suspect her of having a motive for taking her biological son, and at the very least, she'd get tangled up with red tape for hours, possibly days. Calling the cops would be a lot more trouble than it was worth, even if she was in the right.

But still, something was wrong with this whole thing. He couldn't actually be her son, could he?

"Listen, kid," she said. "I like to think that I have one superpower. One thing I can do. You know what it is? I can always tell when someone's lying. Always. And you, kid, are lying."

She wasn't sure if she believed it, but she let it sink in. She was good at sussing out lies, but the truth was that he seemed to be telling the truth. Which meant she didn't know what to think.

He swallowed the last of his cupcake. "I'm good at telling when people are lying, too," he said.

"Are you? Spit it out."

He nodded slowly. She could see that his confidence was starting to wane; he looked upset. He's just a little kid, she thought.

And then that softhearted other Emma popped up again, and she thought: No, Emma. He's your kid.

It was the little things. His ears were the same as his father's ears. The shape of his eyes—she could see her own there, just a little bit, just a flash of I am looking in the mirror right now. Emma could even hear something in the pitch of his voice. Of course it would have been nice to be able to compare his ears and his eyes and his voice to her own father's, her own mother's. But that was another thing altogether. She'd never known her parents.

This isn't a con, Emma thought. You know it.

"Please don't call the police," he said. "Okay? Just come home with me."

Emma took a breath.

"To Storybrooke," she said. What else could she do? "You

need a ride home to Storybrooke? That's what you're asking. That simple request, is it?"

"Uh-huh."

Emma sighed. There was no fighting this kid.

"Okay, then. Let's go to Storybrooke."

She couldn't believe the size of his smile.

. . .

SNOW WHITE, belly amply swollen with both new life and anxious anticipation, hurriedly followed the jailer through the dark corridor. She and Prince Charming were on their way to speak with the one man in the realm who could answer their question. Snow had not been able to find peace since the Queen's threats; she had to know the truth.

The jailer, a bulky and dyspeptic man, did not like this idea one bit.

"Don't give him your name, and here, wear these cloaks," he said knowingly, passing two heavy hooded cloaks back to the couple. "Your best line of defense is anonymity."

Charming took the cloaks, put his on, handed one to his wife. "Why did I let you talk me into this?" he said to her.

Snow kept pace beside him. She put her cloak on, too. "It's the only way," she said. "You know I'm always right."

"He is right to be wary, m'lady," said the jailer ominously. "None is filled with more regret than he who's spoken to Rumplestiltskin."

Charming and Snow shared a look: They were both a little worried at the man's words.

"I'll do the talking," Charming said simply.

Far down the long, dark corridor, the three reached the final cell. No light came from within, and the fire of their torches was the only thing that allowed them to see the ragged bars.

The jailer said, "Rumplestiltskin! I have a question for you."

"No you don't," came a bemused voice from the darkness. "They do. Prince Charming and Snow White would like to know whether the Queen's words should be heeded. Am I right?"

"How did you know that?" the jailer demanded. "Who's been down here speaking to you?"

"No one, my good man!" came Rumplestiltskin's voice. Snow could not see him, but it seemed as though he'd stood quickly. She knew how catlike he could be when he chose. Charming put his hand on his sword.

"Let's drop the game," Snow said, pulling back her hood and stepping forward. "Tell us what you know."

"I will," said Rumplestiltskin, stepping nearer to the bars. "If you'll give me something in return, sweet Snow White."

Charming stepped forward as well, putting himself between the bars and his wife. "You're not getting out of here. There is no chance. So don't even try it."

"No, not now," said Rumplestiltskin. "Of course not. I will be out later. When we're all gone. What I need is assurances. For then. For later. Eh?"

"What do you mean?" Charming said. "What would—"

"Just tell us what you want," said Snow. "We don't have time for this."

"The name of your unborn child would be . . . quite lovely."

"Absolutely not!" cried Charming.

"Deal," said Snow White, ignoring her husband. "Now tell us. What does the Queen have planned for us? How will she take our happiness? I know she has a real plan."

Rumplestiltskin was at the bars of the cell now, and they could see his scaled face. His nose was twisted and warted, his teeth yellow spikes. Some foul magic had done this to him, but Snow didn't know exactly how and didn't care to.

He smiled, his grotesque tongue wagging out of his mouth. "The Evil Queen has created a powerful curse," he said quickly. "Or at least gotten her hands on one. And it's coming. It won't just affect this land. It will touch all the lands. . . . Soon you'll all be in a prison. Just like me. Only worse. Your prison—all of our prisons—will be Time."

"This is foolish," said Charming. "Come on."

Rumplestiltskin ignored him, and his voice grew grave. "Time will stop. We will all be trapped, suffering for eternity. The Queen will lord over us, enslave us. We will be lost, confused. Hopeless. No more happy endings." He waited, let this sink in. "None of us can do a thing to stop it."

Snow looked at him grimly. Rumplestiltskin was full of trickery, but he never actually lied. Which led her to buy it, that they were in great danger, just as the Queen had promised. "Then who can?" she said.

"The child," said Rumplestiltskin, looking at her belly. "The child will be able to stop her."

"You must get her to safety," he said finally. "Away from here. When she reaches the age of twenty-eight, it will begin. She will save . . . us. All of us." This last line he delivered simply, as though it were only a matter of course.

"She?" said Charming, turning to Snow. The jailer was motioning for them to leave. "But it's a boy."

"Is it?" said Rumplestiltskin. "I don't think so, Mr. Prince!" he sang this last line.

"We have to prepare," Snow said to Charming. "Come, my love. His prophecy is correct. I know it."

"Wait!" cried Rumplestiltskin. "The child's name! I need it! We had a deal!"

Snow turned, looking at the monster of a man.

"Emma," she said. "Her name will be Emma."

• • •

THE ROADS WERE QUIET and empty. Soon they were out of Boston.

Emma glanced over at the boy, who had the book open in his lap. Based on the illustration, it looked like he was reading about Snow White—or someone who resembled Snow White and liked to hang out with bluebirds, at least—but it was a part of the story she didn't know—the heroine was down in some kind of dungeon, talking to a goblin. Emma looked back at the road and tried to remember the story. Wasn't it about a bunch of dwarfs? Singing? They were all jumbled up in her head. One set of foster parents had pushed the Disney movies on her, and she'd loved them, but to her, they'd all been the long string of one fairy tale, and she tended to get them confused.

"You like that book, huh?" Emma said.

Henry didn't respond, and she looked over, expecting to see him too engrossed in his story. But he was looking up, eyes wide, smiling. "We're here," he said.

She followed his eyes and saw the sign: WELCOME TO STORY-BROOKE.

"Great," she said. "Welcome to Storybrooke. Here we are. Fantastic. How about an address?"

"It's a really small town," he said. "It's really simple."

"I'll bet it's simple," Emma muttered, slowing the car as they began to pass the first houses and buildings. It was like any town in any part of America, really—shops and houses, some of them new and bright, some of them beat up and dusty. Probably complicated and not so cute when you looked past the surface. She had never heard of Storybrooke, but she knew this town like she knew every town.

"Really," she said. "Where do you live?"

"I'm not telling."

Emma rolled her eyes, pulled over. Kids. Hilarious. The intensity of the feelings from her apartment had worn off. Now she was just tired and confused. She wasn't going to figure this out now. All she had to do was get him home and not get arrested. Make that your goal, Swan, she thought. Keep it simple.

There were few cars parked anywhere nearby, and it was late enough that all the shops were closed. The place looked deserted. She looked up at a clock built into what looked like a library. "It's already eight fifteen," she said. "Let's quit the games."

"That clock always says eight fifteen," Henry said.

"What?"

"The Evil Queen did it," Henry said. "Stopped time. She sent everyone here from there. From the Enchanted Forest. So everyone is trapped here. And trapped in time, too. They don't even know."

"Why don't the people just leave and go to where time works, then?" Emma said.

"Bad things happen whenever anyone tries to leave."

"Oh yeah?" Emma squinted. "What kind of bad things?"

Before he could answer, Emma was startled by a light tapping on the passenger-side window. A thin, harmless-looking man stood beside the car, adjusting his glasses, looking down at her passenger. He was holding an umbrella, even though it wasn't raining.

"Is that you, Henry?" he said.

Henry turned and looked up at the man. He rolled down his window. "Hi, Archie," Henry said.

Archie adjusted his glasses again, looked over at Emma. Emma smiled.

"Who's this?" he asked. Friendly but skeptical, Emma thought. I would be, too.

"It's my mom," Henry said.

"I don't—" Emma started.

"My real mom," Henry added.

Archie looked at Henry for a long moment, then at Emma. "I see."

"I'm just trying to get him home," Emma said, pleading innocence with a look. "Can you point me in the right direction? He showed up at my house in Boston. I don't know where he lives; he won't tell me."

"Sure thing," said Archie, apparently relaxing. "He lives at the mayor's house, of course. Regina Mills. The mansion right up Mifflin."

Emma, eyebrows raised, glanced over at Henry, who gave an innocent shrug. "The mayor?" she said. "Really? You're the prince of this town?"

"Was there a reason you missed our session today, Henry?"

"I was out of town," Henry said. "On vacation."

Archie gave him a friendly, understanding look. "Okay. What did I tell you about lying, Henry?"

"That it only hurts the person who does the lying. In the end."

Archie nodded.

"I'll get him home, Doc," Emma said. "Thanks."

She pulled away, watching the strange man in her rearview mirror. "So that's your shrink, huh?" They were always weirdos.

"Sort of," Henry said. "But he's also Jiminy Cricket."

"Excuse me?"

"Everyone here," Henry insisted. "I told you. Everyone here is a fairy tale character. Weren't you listening? From the book."

He pointed.

"All of the stories in this book are real."

Emma glanced again at the man, who was growing smaller and smaller in her mirror. She cocked her head. He did walk a little funny.

"Sure, kid," she said. "Whatever you say."

. . .

THEY DROVE IN SILENCE as Emma kept a lookout for the mayor's house. She had distracted herself with the task of bringing Henry home and had not let herself think too much about what he'd told her. All she remembered was a baby she'd only been allowed to hold for a moment—a warm, soft, crying thing who'd looked up at her with cloudy eyes from a stiff bed in a jail hospital ward. After that: just the devastation. Months of it. Years. It was funny that anything that small could grow into a walking, talking thing. That was almost the craziest fantasy story there was.

Nothing in her life had hurt more than when the nurse pulled him away from her. She was so exhausted that she couldn't even cry out. She remembered the baby's delicate face and tried to keep herself from glancing over at Henry to compare him to her memories.

She saw Mifflin and turned. It was only a cul-de-sac, and it was obvious which house was the mayor's mansion.

"Home sweet home?" Emma said as she stopped the car. "I'm sure your parents will be glad to have you back."

"It's only my mom," Henry said, looking down at his hands. "And she's evil incarnate."

"I know it feels like that sometimes."

He looked over. "No," he said lightly. "You don't understand. She's actually evil. Like for real. Evil. Satan? All of those guys?"

She didn't want her voice to crack, but she didn't know what to say to him. Was it her job to comfort him? How did one even . . .

"I don't think—" she started.

"Henry! Henry!"

Emma looked over. A woman—dark-haired, beautiful, sharply dressed—was rushing from the house, toward the car. Her eyes were locked on Henry. "Are you hurt? Where have you been?"

"I'm fine, I'm fine," Henry complained. "I found my mom."

The woman froze when she heard this, and looked at Emma for the first time. Emma felt coldness in her heart.

"You . . . are his birth mother?" she said eventually.

Emma nodded, trying to look surprised and innocent. "Apparently," she said. "Nice to meet you."

Emma couldn't tell what to make of the look the woman gave her next. Eventually she said, "Well. I see. And would you like to come inside for some apple cider?"

Henry looked over, hopeful.

Emma said, "You got anything stronger?"

. . .

AFTER THE MEETING with Rumplestiltskin, the knowledge of the curse settled over the castle like a gloomy, cold fog. Snow White urged action. After many meetings among the leaders of Fairy Tale Land, it was decided that steps had to be taken in order to protect the realm.

The Blue Fairy laid it out plainly: If it was true that the Evil Queen soon planned to unleash a curse that would trap them all, and that Snow White's unborn daughter was the only one who would be able to free them, then the girl would need to be protected.

The Blue Fairy's plan was simple. Using the last available tree in the Enchanted Forest, Geppetto would build a wardrobe that could protect Snow White from the curse and transport her and the child to a safe place. From there, Snow White would raise the girl and guide her to her twenty-eighth birthday. When she reached that age, she would fulfill her fated role and save them all.

As Geppetto readied the wardrobe, Snow White's pregnancy came closer and closer to its conclusion. Snow White and Prince Charming, knowing they would be separated, did their best to prepare themselves. It would only be temporary, they told each other. Little Emma would grow up to save them all. Somehow.

If only it were so simple.

One evening, a plume of green fog appeared on the horizon. It seemed to be gathering itself and growing, cascading up out from the trees as though it were exploding from a volcano.

This was it. The curse. It was happening now.

Grumpy began to yell. "It's time," Charming said to his wife. "Prepare yourself."

But Snow White, on the bed, couldn't speak. She had felt a contraction earlier in the day and had said nothing, hoping for it to fade. Now, though, another one—more intense— gripped her body, and she closed her eyes, breathing deeply.

"The baby is coming," she said.

She opened her eyes. She couldn't hold back her tears. Charming, surprised, looked at her from across the room.

"The baby is coming now, my love."

. . .

EMMA SAT in the mayor's study, holding a glass of cider, self-consciously hunched, staring at a painting of an apple tree.

"I've been keeping the same apple tree alive for a very long time," said Regina, watching her study the painting. "It's just off Main Street." She was sitting across from Emma, immaculate legs crossed, having regained her composure. "I feel as though there's a certain value to consistent, long-term support. Don't you?"

Emma could think of a lot of things to say in response. Instead, she just nodded, turned to Regina, and said, "Your tree is very nice."

"I'm sorry he dragged you out of your life," Regina said. "I really don't know what's gotten into him."

"Seems like he's having a hard time," Emma said, taking a sip. "I guess. Then again, what do I know?"

"Ever since I've been mayor, the balancing act has been difficult. You must understand. You have a job, I assume?"

"I have a job," Emma said, ignoring the condescension.

"Well, when you're a single mother, it's like having two full-time jobs. And so yes, I do push for order. I'm strict with him. But it's for his own good. I want him to be successful; I don't want him to feel like he was handed everything. But I don't think that qualifies me as evil, exactly. Am I crazy?"

"He's only saying that because of the fairy tale thing."

"What fairy tale thing?"

"You know, his book. He thinks everyone is a cartoon character from the book or something. I mean, the kid thinks his shrink is Jiminy Cricket. So."

Emma, who'd been staring at her drink, looked up at Regina and was surprised to see her looking rather alarmed.

"I'm sorry," Regina said. "I really have no idea what you're talking about."

Christ, she doesn't know about the book, Emma thought. She was crossing way too many lines. She had to get out of here before she found a way to blow up the whole town.

"You know what?" Emma said. "I'm just going to go back to Boston, I think. I'm in your way here. I'm glad he's safe."

Regina stood as Emma stood. "I am, too," she said, holding out her hand to shake. "I appreciate what you've done. I do. I'm glad he's back home and safe. Thank you."

Emma didn't think she could bring herself to say good-bye to Henry, and so she went directly to her car. She opened the door and almost made it in without looking back and up toward the bedroom windows.

She saw him there, briefly, before the light in the window went out.

She was leaving him again.

You'll get over it, she told herself as she drove to the end of town, heading back toward Boston. The feelings would pass. And besides, now she knew where he was, knew that he was safe. That was something. Surely the mayor would let her come by now and then to say hello? She should have gotten her contact information. She should have—

Emma's eye caught something sitting on the passenger seat. She squinted and turned on her interior light. It was his book. You sneaky bastard, she thought. She couldn't help but smile. She had an excuse to come back now, at least.

Still smiling, distracted by the book, she almost didn't see the wolf standing in the middle of the road.

Emma gasped, braked, and twisted the wheel all at once. The last thing she saw was the animal, unmoved, casually watching as her car skidded out of control. It didn't even blink its bright red eyes.

. . .

WITHIN THEIR CHAMBERS, as the billowing clouds of ghostly fog spread throughout the land, filtering through the forests and surrounding the castle, Snow White screamed through her labor while Doc attended to her.

Charming hurried to her side and took her hand. He had tried to convince her to get into the wardrobe during the early stages, but she had refused, and in turn had convinced him it was too late. Now the plan would not work.

"She's close!" Doc cried. "One more push!"

And then Charming heard the cries, and saw the baby in Doc's arms.

He turned to Snow, who looked exhausted, but who smiled nevertheless.

"Now," she said. "Take her."

Charming frowned. "What do you mean?"

"Take her," Snow White said. "Take her and put her in the wardrobe. It's the only way."

"No!" he cried. "We have to all stay togeth—"

"It's the only way," she insisted, and she pushed Emma to him. He took her. He looked down at her soft, beautiful young face.

He looked at Snow. She had a bad, bad habit of being right.

"Keep her safe," Charming said to Doc, getting to his feet. "I won't be a minute." He ran out of the room, the baby tucked into his arms.

. . .

EMMA CAME TO and spent a moment staring at a concrete wall, wondering why she was not in her apartment, wondering why she was dressed, wondering why it was light outside, wondering what the hell had happened. She thought of the dream—the dream of her son, the dream of the town . . .

She rolled her head and saw the bars.

Oh.

She was in jail.

In Storybrooke, Maine.

A lean man, evidently the sheriff, stood over by his desk, looking at some papers. When he saw that she was up, he nodded to her. "Good morning," he said. "I'm Sheriff Graham. And you're under arrest."

"Why am I in jail?" was all she said.

"You had a bit too much to drink last night, it seems." He made a phantom tipping motion.

"I crashed because of the wolf. It was an accident."

"The wolf?" Graham said, and he seemed genuinely amused. "Do tell. I've heard some good ones, but that takes the cake."

Before he could continue to chide her, Regina Mills burst into the station, eyes wide. She went directly to Graham.

Emma, groggy, sat upright.

"Henry's run away again," Regina said. "We have to—"

She saw Emma in the cell. "What is she doing here?"

Before waiting for an answer, Regina strode over to the cell. "I see. This is not a coincidence, is it? Do you know where he is?" she demanded.

"Lady, I haven't seen him since I left your place," she said. She found herself much less interested in civility than she'd been the night before. She looked at Graham. "I got an alibi. Two, actually. This guy and a wolf."

Graham nodded. "Well, I can vouch, at least. She's been here all night."

"He wasn't in his room this morning," Regina said, and Emma could hear the real concern in her voice.

"How about his friends?" Emma said. "You tried them?"

"He doesn't have any."

Emma frowned. She didn't like to hear that piece of information. It reminded her a little too much of herself.

"Every kid's got friends. What about his computer? Did you check his email?"

"And you know this how?"

"I find people, lady, that's my job," Emma said. "Don't get all worked up. Let me out of here and I'll find him. Free of charge."

Regina and Graham shared a look.

"Then I'll go home," she added. She looked at Graham for a long time, making sure he understood the deal.

"Computers aren't exactly my specialty," Graham said. "And she does seem to know what she's talking about."

Regina, frustrated, turned on her heel and headed for the door. "Fine. Bring her. I just want to find my son. I don't care how."

They drove back to Regina's house, Emma in the back, looking out at the town, none of them speaking. Once inside, Regina led them up to Henry's room, and Emma went directly to the computer.

"Kid's smart," she said, after a moment. "He cleaned out his inbox." She dug out her key ring and held up a little flash drive. "Lucky for both of you, I'm smart, too. Little hard-drive utility I like to use." She inserted it into Henry's USB port and watched as the mirrored files detailing his recent activity transferred onto her drive.

"Does Henry have a credit card?" Emma asked.

"He's too young," Regina said, apparently irritated that she was making progress. "Of course not."

"Well, he used one," said Emma, reading from the screen. "That's how he got his bus ticket. Who is ... Mary Margaret Blanchard?" she asked.

Regina, arms still crossed, looked furious. "His teacher," she said. "I'm going to kill her."

"Aw, I'm sure he stole it from her," Emma said. She stood up, closed Henry's computer. "Come on. Let's go to the school, then. Maybe she knows something."

. . .

AGAIN THEY RODE in silence; only this time Emma couldn't wait to get home, get back to her normal life. She looked at the back of Regina's head, her hair perfectly sculpted and trapped in place. You can't just insert yourself into someone else's life. Maybe this woman was a bitch, sure, but she had raised Henry.

Emma owed her respect. She owed her space. She had been out of line. Find him, get out—that's what she would do.

She had nearly said something to this effect when Graham chirped up. "Here we are, then," he said. They'd arrived at the school.

Mary Margaret Blanchard looked, somehow, exactly like Emma had expected her to look based on her name: petite and pretty, with close-cropped dark hair, at once both demure and—judging by the sparkle in her eye—potentially somewhat feisty. They arrived just as her class was filing out of the room, and when Regina asked her about her credit card, she paused for a moment, thinking. Emma could see that she was remembering the precise moment Henry had tricked her and stolen it, even before she went to her purse to check. She nodded, looking through her wallet. "Clever boy," she said. "I never should have given him that book."

"What is this book I keep hearing about?" Regina said.

"It's a book of stories I thought might help Henry," she said. "He's a creative boy. He's special. We both know that. He needed stimulation."

Regina seemed to have heard enough, or to have detected an insult in what Miss Blanchard said. She huffed, shook her head, and turned to Graham. "Come on, let's go find Henry. This is useless." She turned back to Mary Margaret. "What he needs, Miss Blanchard, is a reality. Facts. Truth. He doesn't need stories."

Mary Margaret said nothing, merely raised her eyebrows. Regina stormed out of the room, followed by Graham.

Mary Margaret smiled kindly at Emma. "Welcome to Storybrooke?" she said, and this time it sounded more like a joke, and Emma smiled. Feisty was right—she liked this woman.

"I'm afraid this is partly my fault," Mary Margaret said, crossing the room and beginning to organize her desk. "He's been so alone lately. I just thought he needed stories." She thought about this for a moment, then looked at Emma. "What do you think stories are for?"

"Burning up some time?" Emma offered. She thought it was a strange question to ask.

"I think they're a way for us to understand our own world," Mary Margaret said. "In a new way." She shook her head. "Regina is sometimes hard on Henry, but his problems go so much deeper than that. He's like so many adopted children—angry, confused. Wondering why anyone could have ever—" She stopped herself, realized who she was talking to. Emma had felt herself tearing up and was glad Mary Margaret hadn't said it out loud. It was the chink in her armor, talking about parents.

"It's okay," Emma said quickly. "It's old news."

"I don't mean to judge," Mary Margaret said. "I apologize. I think I gave Henry the book just to give him what no one around here seems to have. A new feeling. The feeling of hope."

She sounded sad—strong and sad at the same time. Emma realized that Mary Margaret was talking about herself.

"You know where he is, don't you?" Emma said.

Mary Margaret cocked her head and sighed. "Well," she said. "I can't say for sure. But you might want to try his castle."

. . .

SHE DID.

Henry's "castle" was a bit of a dump.

That's what Emma thought, anyway, as she pulled up to the playground near the edge of town. It was beside the ocean and it overlooked the breakwater. From her VW, Emma could see Henry sitting on the second floor of a shoddy wooden structure with a single spired roof. He was cross-legged, staring down. She reached for his book.

"You can't keep running away, kid," Emma said to him, once she'd trudged up to the rickety structure. "People will worry."

"No they won't," he said. "They don't care."

"I got your book," she said. "You left it in my car."

He took it and said, "This is supposed to be the start of the final battle. The whole big thing."

"At some point you gotta grow up and move past this stuff, Henry," she tried. "Stories are great. But eventually you have to look at the real world." She didn't like how much she sounded like Regina, but it was true—it wasn't good to believe in things that weren't true. It left you vulnerable. That was pretty much the only life lesson she had to offer, and she lived by it.

"You don't have to be mean."

"Kid, that's not—"

"But it's okay, I know why you gave me away."

Emma felt her throat tightening. He was looking at her now, a sweet smile on his face. God, Emma thought. This kid knows how to get me.

"You wanted to give me the best chance I could have," he said. "I know you did it for me."

She couldn't keep the tears from welling in her eyes. She wanted to pick him up and hug him, hold him to her chest. She'd given him away once, and now here she was, doing it all over again . . . and somehow, it didn't hurt any less this time around.

She managed to say, "How—how do you know that, Henry?"

"Because it's exactly why Snow White gave you up," he said, proud of himself for his logic.

Emma looked at the book in his lap. Stories to help us understand our world. Mary Margaret did have a point about that.

"We have to get you home, Henry," she said. "I'm not in that book. There's not gonna be a final battle. But I am real. And I do want you in my life. Somehow."

"Don't make me go back there."

"Where?" she said. "To your home? Where people care about you? I never had that. They found me on the side of a highway. That's where my parents left me. I was in the foster system when I was your age. The closest I ever came to having what you have is three months here, three months there. And then I got sent back. You have something stable, something good. You're safe, Henry. You're wanted."

"They didn't leave you on the side of the highway, though," Henry insisted. "That's just where you came through. In the wardrobe."

Emma had no idea what wardrobe he was talking about, but she could see he wasn't going to be able to give up his fantasy. Not yet. Maybe soon, maybe in a few years. Maybe when he found out about girls. But she was tired of trying to talk him into a reality. "Come on, kid," she said, holding out her hand. "Let's get you home."

• • •

"STAY WITH ME."

Snow White had found him on the floor, bleeding, barely conscious. He'd been run through, and he lay still now, quietly staring at the ceiling, his breath shallow, his eyes glassy. Snow held her beloved's hand, weeping. She was now too weak to move—she had used all of her energy to get to him. The Queen's soldiers had invaded the castle, searching the wardrobe and the rest of the workshop, ignoring her as she tended to her dying husband. But he had succeeded. Baby Emma was safe. The wardrobe had gone through to the other side. She kissed him on the cheek. "Stay with me, my love," she whispered.

"Oh, how truly lovely."

Snow White shuddered at the sound of the voice. She'd heard it her whole life; she'd heard it grow colder and colder over the years. She'd heard hope and happiness seep out of it day by day. She'd heard it at the wedding.

Snow looked up at the Queen, who was looking disdainfully at one of her own knights.

"The child?" she said. "Give her to me."

"Gone," the knight said gruffly. "Disappeared."

"Disappeared to where?" the Queen demanded.

"She's safe," said Snow. "And that means you'll lose, eventually. You will always lose. It's because of what you are. Good will always win."

"Spare me," said the Queen. "Good does not always win. In fact, good almost always loses, my pretty young thing. You're brainwashed by this ridiculous world, do you know that? No, of course you don't. Try a week in a different realm. Try having a monster for a parent. That'll teach you to grow up fast."

She was looking at the doorway. The green-and-purple mist Snow White had seen from the window had finally reached them here in the castle—it billowed in around them as though the room were flooding with pure hatred. The mist, somehow, was the curse. The Queen smiled, opened her arms. Snow White, eyes wide, held on to Charming as the castle began to tremble. She felt dizzy, but then realized that the room itself was spinning . . . cracking open. Strange objects showed themselves in the cracks in the sky, a wild wind howled through the room. Snow White heard what she thought was screaming. "Where . . ." she said. "Where are we going?" she yelled.

"To that other world, my dear," laughed the Queen, eyes insane, arms now up over her head. "A place where the only happy ending is my own."

· · ·

FOR THE SECOND TIME in twenty-four hours, Emma watched Regina run from the doorstep of her home, relieved to see her son. She gathered him up at the door of the car and hugged him for a long moment. Henry abided it, but did not hug back. Again Emma was reminded that whatever thorny edge Regina had about her, she did care for Henry.

After a moment, he disengaged from his mother's embrace and ran into the house.

Regina watched him go, and Emma saw the slamming door seem to cause Regina a moment of physical pain.

Regina turned back to Emma. "Thank you."

"My pleasure."

"He seems to have taken quite a shine to you."

"You know something crazy?" Emma said. "Yesterday was my birthday, and when I blew out the candle, my wish was that I wouldn't have to spend my birthday alone. And right when I blew it out, he showed up." She hadn't really considered the coincidence.

Regina watched her coolly. "I hope there's no misunderstanding here."

"What do you mean?"

"This is not an invitation back into his life. You made your choice. Ten years ago. It's hard enough to be a single mother. It's even harder to compete with a stranger filling his head with stories about Twinkies and fun times and whatever comes into her head."

"I don't—"

"And in the last decade while you've been doing God knows what, I've been here, changing every diaper, nursing every sickness, doing the difficult work. You may have given birth to him but he's my son."

Emma couldn't compete with that and she didn't want to even try. "I wasn't—"

"No, you don't get to talk," Regina said, her voice becoming angrier. She took a step forward. "You don't get to do anything. Do you remember what a closed adoption is? Do you remember that that's what you asked for? You? You have no legal right to Henry. You're going to be held to that. I suggest that you get into your car and leave this town forever. Immediately. If you don't, I will destroy you if it's the last thing I do."

Emma was stunned. She stared back at Regina, who'd worked herself up into a rage with the speech. And again Emma had that same feeling: The more Regina wanted her out, the more she wanted to stay.

Her heart pounding, Emma nearly turned to go. But she thought of one more thing she wanted to ask.

"Do you love him?" she said.

Regina looked surprised, then angry.

"Of course I love him," she spat.

And she turned and went back inside.

. . .

EMMA WAS NOT SURE what came over her as she drove down Main Street. She decided not to think too much about it. She had a bad habit of doing that. Instead, when she saw the sign for Granny's B&B, a sudden certainty overcame her: She knew she couldn't leave Henry. Not again.

She stopped the car.

Inside the B&B, Emma came upon a silver-haired woman in the midst of a heated argument with a young, black-haired girl. "It's my house, and they're my rules. You cannot stay out all night."

"I should have moved to Boston," the girl said dismissively.

"I'm so sorry that my heart attack prevented you from sleeping your way along the Eastern Seaboard!" yelled the woman, and just as she did, Emma cleared her throat, and she spun. She gave Emma a sweet smile. Emma asked for a room. The girl stared at her impassively.

"Of course, of course!" said the older woman, going to the counter. "We have a lovely room available."

"Great," said Emma.

"And what's your name, dear?" the woman asked, writing in a ledger.

"Emma," she said. "Emma Swan."

"Emma," came a man's voice. "What a lovely, lovely name."

Emma turned to see a strange, silken-haired, suited man standing behind her.

He held a cane and watched her curiously, then strolled up to the register, eyeing the old woman.

"Thanks," said Emma.

"Everything is in order," said the woman, and Emma could see that she was visibly intimidated by the man, whoever he was. "It's all here." She held an envelope toward him.

"Yes, of course it is," said the man, taking it. "I trust you completely." Emma saw the bulge of cash peeking out of the top of the envelope.

The man smiled again at Emma. "Lovely to meet you, Ms. Swan. Perhaps we'll be seeing one another."

He nodded and strolled out of the room.

"Who was that guy?" Emma asked, once he was gone.

"That was Mr. Gold," said the girl conspiratorially. "He owns this place."

"The B and B?"

"No," said the old woman. "The whole town."

Emma raised her eyebrows. "Huh," she said.

"Here's a key for you." She handed Emma a large metal key, almost comical in its artful flourishes. Nothing in this town was normal, it turned out. "How long will you be staying?"

"Just a week," Emma said, looking at the key. "Just one week." That was what she needed to make sure Henry was okay. She had to. What else made any kind of sense? She had to know about her son. She had to stay near him now that she'd found him. What else could a person do?

"A week!" cried the woman. "So wonderful. Welcome to Storybrooke."

Emma took the key.

Outside, the second hand on the clock tower began to move.

CHAPTER 2

THE THING YOU
LOVE MOST

MMA WOKE THAT FIRST MORNING AND briefly wondered what the hell she was doing in this damned town.

But she knew. She knew why she was here.

She was in the bathroom when she heard a knock on the door. When she opened it, she was surprised to find Regina Mills smiling at her.

"Ah, good morning!" Regina said. "I thought I'd stop by and offer you a gift." She held up the apples and walked into the small room, not waiting to be invited. Emma watched her warily. "I'm sure you'll enjoy them on your drive home," she added. "It's too bad you didn't make it out of town last night, after all." Looking around the room with mild disdain, Regina set the apples down on the countertop.

"I've decided to stay," said Emma, looking at the apples. "But thank you."

"Are you sure that's such a good idea?" Regina asked brightly, apparently not surprised. "Henry has been dealing with a number of emotional problems. I think this will just confuse him more, don't you?"

"The fact that you've now threatened me two times in the last twelve hours," Emma said finally, "makes me want to stay more."

"What?" Regina said. "You take apples as a threat? I wouldn't—"

"I can read between the lines," Emma said. "I think I'll stay until I get a sense for Henry's situation here. I want to make sure he's okay."

"I see," said Regina. "You're worried that I am in fact evil, are you? You've been reading his book as well. I can promise you that he's just fine. And that his problems are being taken care of. He doesn't need you."

"What does that mean?"

"It means he's in therapy," Regina said. "It means that he will soon learn that reality makes more sense than fantasy. As I keep telling him. It means that only one of us knows what's best for Henry."

"I'm starting to think you're right about that."

The audacity of this woman was unbelievable—Emma could not imagine making the choice to enter so boldly into a stranger's private space and speak so disdainfully, especially to someone who might be around for some time. Regina smiled a crisp smile and took a step toward Emma.

"This has been nice," Regina said. "But it's time for you to leave this town."

"Or what?" Emma said, arms still crossed.

Regina took another step toward her. Their faces a mere foot apart, Regina said coolly, "Do not underestimate me, Ms. Swan. You have no idea what I'm capable of."

Emma paused and considered that.

"Well, then," she said finally. "You're just gonna have to show me, aren't you?"

Regina's eyes closed to the thinnest of slits. "So be it."

Ten minutes later, in great need of coffee, Emma made her way to the diner. She also needed to think; she needed to figure out why Regina was so bent on getting her out of town. This place—there was something just off about this whole place. What was it?

She felt the strangeness all the more when she saw her own face staring back at her on the cover of the town daily, the *Storybrooke Daily Mirror*.

It was an old mug shot. She picked up a copy of the paper and sat down in a booth.

Seriously? she thought. One day to put this together?

Whoever had written the article—Sidney Glass was his name—had managed to dig up a lot about her life in a very short period of time. He knew that Henry had been born in Phoenix; he knew where she'd lived since then. He knew about her trouble with the law. Not quite everything, but plenty. Emma shuddered. This was exactly why she didn't like small towns.

"Here you go."

Emma looked up. The same girl from the inn, the one who'd been arguing with her grandmother, stood beside her table, smiling. She had a cup of hot cocoa and set it on the table.

Emma looked at her name tag: Ruby.

"Thanks, Ruby, but I didn't order this," Emma said.

"I know," said Ruby. She smiled, cocked her head. Emma was impressed by the brightness of her lipstick's red; it was almost incandescent. "You have an admirer."

Emma turned to look across the room and saw Sheriff Graham seated at a booth. He was sipping coffee and reading the paper as well.

She got up and stormed over to him, carrying the cocoa.

"Ah. You decided to stay, did you?" he said pleasantly.

Emma just stared.

"Would you like to join me?" Graham said. He motioned for her to sit.

"Look, dude. The cocoa is a nice gesture. And it's impressive that you were able to guess that I like cinnamon on my chocolate—not many people do—but I'm not here to flirt. So thanks but no thanks, Sheriff." She slammed the cocoa down on his table.

"I didn't send that," he said. He shrugged, looking at her innocently.

"I did," came a voice.

It was Henry. He was in the next booth, down so low that she hadn't been able to see him. "I like cinnamon, too," he added. "Hi. I'm glad you stayed."

"Henry, what are you doing here?" Emma asked. "Don't you have school?"

"Yeah, I'm going right now," Henry said. "Will you walk me there?"

Emma sighed and gave an apologetic look to Graham. He smiled kindly in return and went back to the paper. There was something about the sheriff that she liked. Sure, he was under Regina's thumb, but he seemed to be his own person. He was also somewhat handsome. Somewhat.

She nodded her good-bye.

Henry led Emma out of the diner.

"I seriously can't believe you stayed!" Henry said, once they were outside. "This is gonna work." He was excited. Emma smiled.

"Your mom would have preferred it if I'd left, I think," she said. "It's very unlike me to have stayed."

"That's because she's the Evil Queen."

Emma frowned. He did seem to have a rich inner life, but she couldn't help but think of what Regina had said back in her room. He was seeing a shrink, for God's sake. What if there was something really wrong with him? Was it the right thing to just go along with it? She didn't know. She would have to talk to Archie.

"Explain it to me," Emma said, deciding that she would rather talk to him about something he was enthusiastic about than scold him for making things up.

"What? The curse?"

"Yeah," she said. "What's it all about?"

"Okay, yeah," Henry said, getting excited as he talked more about it. "So you and me have to break it. That's our job. And step one of the operation is 'identification.'" He looked up at her knowingly. "The whole operation is called Operation Cobra."

Emma listened dutifully as Henry explained the curse. All the people of Storybrooke—"Everyone!"—came from another land. Fairy Tale Land. They had been happy there, and they lived with different identities. And then, in order to punish Snow White and Prince Charming for wronging her, the Evil Queen decided to put a curse on the whole land. A curse that meant nobody could be happy. This curse transported everyone who lived in Fairy Tale Land to this place, their world, on

Earth, which was a land without magic. No one could leave, time did not move, and no one was aware of what had happened. They all had amnesia, and they'd all been stuck here for twenty-eight years, living the same days over and over again. Except for Henry, who got it, and that was only because of the book, and because he hadn't been born in Fairy Tale Land.

"The Evil Queen had to get the curse from her old frenemy, Maleficent," Henry explained. "She went to her castle and they had this huge magic battle, and the Queen stole the curse from Maleficent's scepter. It was a crazy battle!" Emma nodded. "But to make the curse work right," Henry said, "the Queen had to use the heart of whoever she held most dear in the world."

"Whoa," Emma said. "Intense."

"I know!" said Henry. "And guess whose heart she ended up taking to make the whole spell work? You're never gonna guess."

"I can't imagine who an Evil Queen would hold dear."

"Her father's heart. She killed her father to make the curse!"

"Now that," Emma said, "is some serious Oedipal anger."

"The best part," Henry said, "is who you are."

"I'm from Fairy Tale Land?" Emma said. "Who knew?"

Henry ignored this and explained to her that she was the daughter of Snow White and Prince Charming.

Emma found this to be hilarious.

Not only that, Henry said, but she was the only person who could break the curse. It was all in the stories. She was the little baby born right before the curse came down.

He spun his backpack around and removed a set of pages— Emma saw that he must have ripped them out of his book. He showed her an illustration of the baby wrapped in a blanket, with the word "Emma" embroidered on the front.

"That's your smoking gun?" Emma said, looking at the illustration. "There are other Emmas in the world, you know." Emma took the pages from him and looked through them, searching for an author name or a copyright date. But there was nothing—no date, no author. Maybe in the book itself. It was anyone's guess where the thing came from. Either way, though, quite a coincidence that the baby had that blanket. It reminded her of the one she had had with her when she was found, the one she carried through all the foster homes. She still had it somewhere, packed away in a box back in Boston. It wasn't the type of memento she liked to pull out, though. Most of the memories that came along with it were painful.

"I think you should read all of the pages," Henry said. "This part is your story. I know you're not going to believe me until you do." He nodded to himself, then said, "You can't let her see these pages, though. You can't. That's why I ripped them out. It would be . . . very bad."

Emma looked at the book.

"Really?" she said, looking at a picture of the Queen. It did look a little like Regina; she could see how Henry could have convinced himself of all this.

Sort of.

"Really bad," he said. "Really really really bad."

Emma and Henry soon reached the school. Before he left, he looked up and smiled and said, "Thanks for believing me about the curse. I knew that you would." It almost killed her, he was so much in earnest. No problem kid, I didn't believe you at all!

"I didn't say that I did, kid," she said, thinking that it

would probably be best to be honest, but a tempered honest. "I just listened." That was totally true.

Still, Henry continued to smile, then turned and ran off toward class. Emma watched him go, still unsure how to handle his "interesting" relationship to reality. This "Operation Cobra" game seemed to give him endless joy, and some instinct told her it was never a bad thing for your child to feel joy. That was a mother's job, wasn't it? But a part of her thought that she was behaving recklessly, like the grandmother who steps in and gives the grandkid sweets until he's sick. An outsider who is playing the game for short-term gains, not long-term goals.

"It's good to see him smiling."

Emma, startled, saw that Mary Margaret had approached.

"Oh. I guess it is," she said. "I didn't do that, though. Magic did."

"Does Regina know that you're still here?"

"Yes. She charmed me this morning with an angry speech. Really, really pleasant. How did that woman ever get elected to public office? She has no social skills."

"It seems like she's always been mayor," said Mary Margaret.

Emma looked at her and cocked an eyebrow.

"What do you mean?"

"I think everyone is too scared of her to run against her," continued Mary Margaret. "And I'm afraid I only made things worse for Henry by giving him that book."

"Where did you get that book?" Emma asked.

"Hm," said Mary Margaret. "I'm not totally sure. Here at the school, I think?"

"And who does he think you are, by the way?" Emma asked.

"Me? It's silly." She smiled and looked down. "He actually thinks I'm—that I'm Snow White."

"Wow, Snow White," Emma said and nodded, impressed. "Not bad."

"And who are you?"

Emma looked at her, and didn't want to say it once she realized what it implied about their relationship. Emma was surprised at how eagerly some part of her imagination entertained the idea, tried to dock with it, albeit for just a few seconds. It was just the kind of thing she used to do when she was a kid, a game she played by herself. Making Up Mom was what she called it, even though she never told anybody what it was she was doing for all those hours, hiding in closets or tucked in a ball beneath a tree. She spent that time envisioning what her mother was like—who she was, where she was, why she'd been forced to give Emma up for adoption. The fantasizing had eventually cohered, over a couple of years, into one blurry image in her mind that was almost a memory. The woman was smiling and coming toward her with her arms out, saying, "Emma, Emma," in a sweet, tender voice. It was silly. Made up. It was all stupid. She'd realized that when she was eleven or twelve, and had quit playing the game then. Forever.

"Me? Oh, I'm not in the book."

"That's right," said Mary Margaret. "You're from someplace else."

Emma smiled. "But I do have to go see Jiminy Cricket."

Mary Margaret frowned.

"His doctor. Archie," explained Emma. "Know where I can find him?"

She did, and Emma walked through town to Archie's offices,

wondering if it was wise for her to get involved in Henry's therapy, but unable to stop herself either way. Most likely he wouldn't be able to tell her anything. But then again, she was Henry's mother. . . .

Strange how easily she'd settled into thinking of herself as Henry's mother, and she thought again of the moment with Mary Margaret, the leap of believing. In Henry's case, it was true, she was his mother, but still, the concept was the same, wasn't it? You don't know something, then you find it out, and *blam!* You start to rethink everything. She had to be careful. There were soft spots in her psyche, ways in which she was vulnerable in this place. For so many years she'd developed armor, and now, in just a couple of days, the chinks were showing up. If enough of them did, eventually someone would exploit them.

At the door, Archie smiled and said hello, invited her into his small office. As she strolled in, Emma told him that she needed to talk about Henry.

"Oh, no, no, ethically I really can't—"

"I know, I know. I get it. Doctor-patient privilege. I just want to know one thing. Maybe you can bend the rules."

Archie relaxed, crossed his arms. "What is it?"

"What causes it?" Emma asked.

That simple question had been on her mind all morning. "Why is he confused about what's real? Is he . . . crazy? Or is it just his imagination? I guess I need to know if he's sick, or diseased, or just . . . I don't know. What is the actual diagnosis?"

Archie looked pained by the question, especially by her use of the word "crazy." He adjusted his glasses nervously, shook his head some more, and walked her over to his desk. "Please don't talk like that to him—please don't tell him you think he's crazy, that would be terrible." He motioned for her to sit down; he sat as well. "These stories are his language. Think of it that way. This is how he communicates with the world right now. He's been through so much. This is him communicating, Ms. Swan. That's a good thing."

"He's dealing with his problems."

"That's right."

"What are his problems, then?" The logical follow-up.

Archie seemed to realize where she was going. He pursed his lips, tilted his head.

"It's Regina, isn't it? She's making him unhappy?"

"No, no, that's an overstatement, far too reductive," said Archie. "Of course not. She's a complicated woman and a stern mother, but she's a good mother, too." He nodded as he said this, Emma noted. He appeared to believe it. "What is your relationship like with your mother? Do you see my point?"

Another arrow to the heart.

"You obviously haven't read the morning's newspaper," Emma said.

"What do you mean?"

"I'm adopted, too," she said. "I don't know my mother."

"Oh," Archie said quietly, as though this made sense to him. He nodded to himself, touched his chin. "I see. Well. You understand the point. Relationships with mothers are always complicated." He smiled. "Fathers, too."

"Something tells me things are even more complicated when it comes to Regina."

"She tries, but she pushes too hard," Archie continued. Apparently struggling with something else now, he sighed, then opened a file cabinet. "You should take his file, go over it. You'll see."

Emma frowned, skeptical. The doctor was acting strange; something was off. "Why would you do that?"

"Because he cares about you," Archie said, handing her the file. "And I care about him."

Emma considered that. Something felt wrong about it, sure, but she wanted the file. Whatever Archie was up to, she was sure she'd be able to handle it. She reached out and took the file.

"Simple math, right, Doc?"

"Exactly," he said, adjusting his glasses again. She got up, and he stood to see her out.

. . .

IT DID NOT TAKE LONG for her to realize that her instincts were right about the good doctor. It was only a few hours later that the sheriff was "mysteriously" at her door, looking at her grimly. "I'm sorry, Ms. Swan," Graham said, showing her his cuffs. "But you're under arrest."

Emma couldn't believe what she was hearing. She was at the door of her room, having just showered and changed. The sheriff looked at her with sympathy in his eyes. She had opened the door expecting Granny carrying a load of fresh linens. Instead, Graham had informed her that she'd been accused of arguing with Archie and stealing Henry's file from his office.

"He gave it to me," she told the sheriff, handing over the documents. "This is ridiculous. You realize Regina set this up, don't you? She's somehow forcing him to say that."

"I'm going to have to cuff you," Graham said. "Sorry."

"Fine," said Emma. "Arrest me again. Have a problem? Arrest Emma!" She spun and locked her wrists behind her back. "Some police force."

At the police station, as he was taking her mug shot, she asked Graham about Regina: "This whole town is afraid of her. You know it, I know it. Why don't we do something about it? What else does she have her hands in?"

"She's the mayor," Graham said. "She has her hands in everything."

"Everything?" Emma asked, raising an eyebrow.

"Hey, easy," he said, and escorted her over to the cell. "You've been here for two days. She's been here for decades. Maybe you don't know everything, okay?"

"I know what I stole and didn't steal," Emma said. "Archie is lying."

Again, Graham said nothing. But Emma could have sworn she saw something in his eyes.

. . .

SHE SAT IN THE CELL, fuming, before she heard a familiar voice and stood.

"Hey! You have to let her out!"

It was Henry. He came into the room ahead of Mary Margaret Blanchard. Graham, surprised, looked up from his desk.

"Henry, what are you doing here?" he said. He turned to Henry's teacher, confused. "Miss Blanchard?"

"We're here to bail her out," Henry said. Then, after looking at Emma, he smiled and said, "Well, *she* is. I don't have any money."

"Why would you do that?" Emma asked.

Mary Margaret looked sheepish and began digging in her purse. "I don't know," she said. "I trust you."

The sheriff seemed a bit surprised by this turn of events, but he took it in stride.

As Mary Margaret and Graham attended to the paperwork, Henry sidled over to the cell.

"Good job," he whispered to her.

She bent down and whispered back: "Good job with what?"

"With getting arrested. It was the plan. I get it." Henry nodded. "Intel. Operation Cobra, right?"

"Sure, kid," she whispered back. "Something like that."

"Okay, then," Graham said from across the room, holding up a piece of paper. Mary Margaret smiled, nodded. "Looks like everything's in order."

Emma stood to her full height. "Good," she said. "Let me outta here." She looked at Henry. "I've got something to do."

. . .

SHE WENT DIRECTLY to the hardware store.

Emma was good at finding people, yes. And she had a knack for telling when someone was lying. Both qualities had helped her in her life hunting down bail-jumpers, but there was a third quality—the underbelly, the dark link between the first two, she sometimes thought—that made her really good at what she did. Push her far enough, and she could find chinks in armor, too. She knew how to hit people right where it hurt. If she wanted, she could find those chinks, and when she did, she wasn't afraid to start shooting.

She chose a chain saw with a two-stroke engine, asked a clerk to take it out of the box and gas it up, and paid with her credit card. "Doin' a little yard work?" asked the woman behind the counter.

"No," Emma said. "Not at all."

Who in the hell did that woman think she was? Take

something precious from me, she thought, and I will return the favor. The thought moved in a circle; Emma's rage kept her from going much further than that as she strode down Main Street. She hit the choke and yanked the rip cord as she strode into the back garden, eyeing Regina's apple tree. Apples meant something to this woman—she knew it. At the trunk, she hesitated, then decided not to take the whole thing down. A major limb would suffice. A wound, but not a mortal wound. This was only the beginning, and she wasn't quite ready to use the nuclear option.

The Solo cut through the branch with relative ease, and the limb emitted a satisfying *CRRAAACCKK* just before it fell from the tree. Emma smiled, stepped back. She didn't need to look up at the window—she had sensed Regina there, watching it happen.

After a moment of silence, with the smell of gasoline and oil in the air, the wounded tree not complaining at all, Regina burst outside.

"What are you doing?" she screamed, striding toward Emma, who raised the chain saw like a weapon. It wasn't running, and it was not as though she would cut Regina in half. She wasn't quite to that point, yet.

"Picking apples," she said coolly.

"You're out of your mind."

Emma took a step forward and met her in front of the broken tree. "No. You are if you think your shoddy frame job is gonna scare me off. You'll have to do better than that, lady. Come at me again, and I'll be back for the rest of this pile of bark and worms. Because, sister? You know what? You have no idea what I'm capable of."

She turned and walked away, leaving Regina beside the branch, speechless.

Over her shoulder, Emma said: "Your move."

. . .

A FEW HOURS LATER, having finally cooled down with a walk in the woods, Emma returned to Granny's B&B with new resolve. She didn't know how, but she was going to find a way to be a part of Henry's life. She wasn't going anywhere.

Granny, seeming rather uncomfortable, stopped her in the hallway.

"I'm sorry, dear," she said. "But we have a no-felon policy here. I'm going to have to ask you to leave."

"What?" Emma said. "The newspaper report? From this morning?"

Granny nodded sadly.

Emma, no longer surprised by any of it, produced the key to her room. "And let me guess," she said. "It was a call from the mayor's office that reminded you of your own policy."

"We try to keep things safe for our travelers," Granny said, taking the key. "That's all."

Well, I've lived in a car before, Emma thought. She packed up her few things and took them out to the VW.

"What the . . . ," Emma said, squinting as she approached with her bag. There was a boot on the front wheel. Regina again. Did the woman ever take a break?

Just as she had the thought, Emma's cell phone rang. She didn't recognize the number.

She did, however, recognize the voice.

It was Regina. She wanted to make a deal.

EMMA LEFT HER CAR and walked the half mile to the mayor's office. Emma and Regina greeted each other tensely, and Regina motioned for Emma to sit. She brought over a drink—not cider this time—and had one for herself.

"Thank you for coming," Regina said. "I'd like this to be civil. I think we can make it work."

"Make what work?" Emma said.

"All of it," Regina said. "You. Here. I get the sense that you're more determined than ever to stay in town. And I'm not blind. I know that standing in my son's way will only make him want something even more than he already does."

Emma relaxed—a little—and sank back into her chair. She took a breath. "Okay," she said. "I'm listening."

"I accept that you're here to take my son from me."

There it was. Emma thought for a moment, then said: "That's not what I'm doing here."

"Then why are you here?" Regina asked.

She wasn't entirely sure herself; she'd been grappling with the same question all day.

"I'm worried about Henry, frankly," she said finally. "He thinks everyone in this town is a fairy tale character. That's not a great sign."

Regina nodded. "And you don't, I take it?"

"Of course I don't. I don't think my mother is Snow White and I don't think you're the Evil Queen. Henry is having a hard time distinguishing between fantasy and reality. All of it is crazy."

Emma frowned, seeing Regina's grin. Her eyes had ticked to the right, and Emma spun to look at the office's door. Henry, a look of sadness on his face, stood watching.

"You think I'm crazy?" he said, his eyes welling up. Emma's heart shot up to her throat.

"Henry, no, I—"

But it was too late, and he ran away. Before Emma could even stand, he had disappeared from view.

Furious, she turned to Regina. "You did this on purpose. You knew he'd be here."

"Of course I knew he'd be here," said Regina coolly. "He's my son. He's here at five o'clock precisely, every Thursday. Mothers keep track of their children."

Emma, her pulse racing, felt the anger mixing with sadness and regret. She had lost—she had hurt Henry. It didn't matter how it had happened. She was a fool to have come here.

"You have no soul," she said to Regina. It was all she could think to say before hurrying off after Henry.

• • •

HE WAS IN THERAPY, at Archie Hopper's office. Emma saw them through the window as she hurried up to the building. The quick glance told her all she needed to know. Henry, inside, sat in his chair, hunched and deflated, and it broke her heart. She couldn't stand to see him sad, and it brought her joy to see him happy. Perhaps that was the simple compass that could guide her.

She burst into the office without knocking, and both Henry and Archie looked up in surprise.

"I need to talk to you," Emma said.

Archie stood. "Miss Swan, this is highly irregular," he said, hand out. She glared at him, and he withered a bit. He began fidgeting with his glasses. "I'm sorry about the file. She told me—"

"It's okay, Archie," she said. "I'm not worried about that right now." She turned to Henry. "I need you to know that I stayed for you," she said. "I'm here because of you. I don't think you're crazy. I think this town is crazy and this curse is crazy, but that doesn't mean I think you're crazy."

Henry seemed skeptical at the start of this speech, but his posture improved as she went on.

Encouraged, Emma pulled the wad of papers from her pocket and said, "I read the pages. You were right—they are dangerous. And there's only one way to keep her from knowing my story." She walked over to the fire and cast the papers in. "She can't ever read it." They all watched the pages burn. "Now we have the advantage."

Henry smiled. "Brilliant!" he cried.

Emma looked at Archie, expecting an admonishing look, but she could see that he was pleased at how happy this had made Henry.

"I knew you were here to help me!" Henry cried.

"That's right, kid," Emma said. "That is why I'm here. Not even a curse can stop that."

CHAPTER 3

SNOW FALLS

T WAS ON THE HIGH ROAD BEYOND MIDAS'S castle, about a year before their wedding, where Prince Charming and Snow White first met.

The terms, initially, were not amicable.

Snow White had been living as a fugitive when she dropped from the tree onto the carriage escorting Charming and his bride-to-be through the forest. Of course at the time, Snow White didn't know who he was, what their future held, or the curious way he'd arrived at this betrothal—to her they were only wealthy people down below, their carriage only a target to be ransacked. Her aim was the same as with the others she'd robbed while on the run: to make some money and escape unscathed. To live to fight again. To avoid the Queen and her soldiers, to find a way to clear her name.

Stretched across a horizontal branch, she watched from above as the carriage trundled up, then stopped. The man—quite arrogantly, she thought—got out, strode down the path, and investigated the fallen tree that had stopped them. The tree was there because Snow had cut it down in the night and placed it there. A simple and elegant plan. She was amazed how often it worked.

She dropped from the tree onto the carriage. In a matter of moments—she'd grown quite good at this—she snatched a purse from within, barely noticing the regal, sleepy-looking blonde who sat twirling her hair. The purse was all she cared about, and as she darted away she noted its heft. There would be something valuable within. She'd made it to one of their horses before the woman even started to scream.

Thirty seconds later, the wind in her face, Snow White galloped away atop a sturdy brown stallion, thinking already of the Troll Bridge. She was surprised when she heard a cry behind her. She turned and saw the arrogant man in pursuit.

She rolled her eyes.

They always think they can catch me, she thought.

The man, however, surprised her with his riding ability; when she looked over her shoulder again, he was only two horse-lengths away. She kicked her stallion once more, but it was too late—she felt the man's heavy hands on her shoulders, as the two of them careened off of their horses and crashed into the ground.

They rolled together. Snow made herself compact for the impact, but she heard the man grunt and knew he'd lost his breath. When their rolling finally stopped, he was on top of her, but his breath was ragged. He squinted at her face, and Snow assumed he was only now figuring out that she was a woman. She disdained the surprise in his eyes.

(Even though she had to admit, it was a pretty nice set of eyes.)

She used this strange little moment—the two of them locked in each other's gaze—to hit him in the chin with a rock.

He fell back, stunned. She was galloping away again when she heard his words trail behind her: "I will find you! I will always find you!"

. . .

MARY MARGARET BLANCHARD walked alone down Main Street, counting the cracks in the sidewalk, hands in the pockets of her skirt. She'd just had a date with Dr. Whale. A terrible, terrible date.

She sighed, kicked at a stone, looked up at the clock tower. When was the last time she'd been out with somebody she liked? She didn't know. He'd been superior, which was perhaps to have been expected—he was, after all, a doctor. But he'd also been uninterested in a way that made Mary Margaret feel a familiar old sadness. Was she boring to other people? She had so much trouble just connecting. It was as though she'd been going out on dates with the wrong men her entire life. She—

Her reverie was interrupted by what she saw across the street: Emma Swan, Henry's birth mother, sat in the front seat of her yellow VW Bug, poring through a newspaper.

Mary Margaret smiled, crossed the street, and tapped on the window.

"You decided to stay in town for Henry," Mary Margaret said. "Didn't you?" She admired it. She couldn't imagine what it would be like, but she admired it.

"Either way, I decided to stay," Emma said, stretching her legs. "What I can't believe is that there are no places to rent in this town." She held up the newspaper. "And no jobs. What gives?"

"I'm not sure," Mary Margaret said. "People like things to stay the same around here, I suppose."

"What're you doing out?"

Mary Margaret crossed her arms. "I was on an unsuccessful date, thank you very much."

Emma nodded. "One of those," she said. "I know them well."

"No one ever said true love was easy, right?" Mary Margaret said. Emma nodded again, and Mary Margaret thought she saw something in her eyes—something about true love, maybe, that hurt her—and she suddenly felt terrible. Why was she always talking herself into corners?

"Well," Emma said. "Have a good night. I'll just go back to my office."

"You know you could stay at my place," Mary Margaret said suddenly. It surprised her, but as the offer hung in the air between the two women, she decided that it felt right, somehow. That it would work. That they'd get along just fine.

She offered a follow-up smile and added: "I mean just until you get your feet on the ground."

"That is, um, very nice of you," Emma said, "but I gotta say, I'm not really the roommate type. No offense. You know? But that's nice of you, really. I appreciate it."

"Of course," said Mary Margaret. She took one step back. "Of course. Whatever works."

They separated, and Mary Margaret went home, trying to distance herself from the feeling of being rejected two times in one night. Tomorrow she would volunteer at the hospital. The people there, at least, would be happy to have her around.

What had possibly compelled her to make that offer to a perfect stranger? She didn't know. Not for the life of her.

. . .

"I FOUND YOUR FATHER."

Sitting next to Henry on his castle's top platform, her legs dangling down, Emma looked over at him.

"Excuse me?" she said.

It was Saturday, but Regina was busy all day, which meant that Emma and Henry could spend some time together. She'd met him out here before, and this seemed best, really. No reason to involve Regina, no reason to make it messy.

"I seriously doubt that, kid," Emma said.

Because she had tried, once, to find him. To find both of them. She hadn't gotten very far, as the circumstances of her own abandonment as a baby were a tad murky. There was nothing. Zilch. There wasn't a chance in hell this kid knew anything she didn't know.

"No, I did," Henry insisted. "He's here, he's in town." He twisted and picked up his book. Emma glanced up at the sky quickly, realizing what he meant. It just kept going and going.

"Look," Henry said, flipping to a page that showed a man—a handsome man, strong-jawed, eyes closed, bleeding from the chin—lying in the grass. "It's Prince Charming. After Snow White hits him and gets away."

"What kind of twisted version of Snow White are you reading here, kid?" Emma asked, taking the book. She flipped back a few pages and let her eyes wander across the text.

"It's complicated," Henry said, "but the point is that he's here, and he's Miss Blanchard's true love, and she doesn't even know that he's here. I saw him. In the hospital. He's been in a coma for years."

Emma flipped back to the picture. "This guy?" she said, pointing.

"His name is John Doe," Henry said.

"So they don't know who he is."

"That's right, but I know," he said. "And now you know. And we have to get him to wake up so he remembers who Ms. Blanchard is."

Emma was settling into her strategy of going along with what Henry said. The next question came pretty naturally: "How are we supposed to do that?"

"I thought of that already," Henry said. "All we have to do is get her to read this story to him."

"What story is it?"

"The story of them falling in love," Henry said. "It's important."

Emma said nothing, just looked out at the water.

"What?" Henry said. "Don't you think that it is?"

"I do, actually," Emma said. "Believe it or not. I completely do."

Henry smiled his beaming, irresistible smile. "So you'll help."

"Sure," she said. "But we're doing it my way. Not your way. My way. Got it?"

. . .

"LET ME GET THIS STRAIGHT," Mary Margaret said, eyeing Emma skeptically. "You want me to read the same children's stories I gave to Henry to John Doe? Who's been in a coma for years? At the hospital?"

"That's right."

"And you want me to do this because Henry thinks the story will wake him up, because he is Prince Charming, and I am Snow White, and we are soul mates, and true love can conquer the curse?"

"Yup," Emma said, nodding and biting into her celery one more time. "That's pretty much it."

"That's nuts."

Emma cocked her head. "A little," she said. "But not that nuts."

They were at Mary Margaret's apartment, both of them sitting on the couch. Mary Margaret was glad when Emma knocked on the door, and initially she'd thought it was about the offer to be roommates, but Emma—who was always a straight shooter, it seemed—launched right into the plan about the anonymous man at the hospital. It was all ridiculous. But Mary Margaret studied the strange woman, thinking about the plan's implications, what it would mean. She was right. Maybe not so nuts.

"And what you didn't say," Mary Margaret said, "was that he won't wake up, Henry will see that, and it will be a gentle way of showing him that he might be wrong about this curse of his."

Emma smiled a quick smile, bit again into her celery.

"Something like that," she said.

And so Mary Margaret agreed. Why? There were many reasons. She liked Emma Swan; she liked the plan to help Henry; she liked the simple elegance of the solution. She liked, even, the opportunity to read to a patient—a handsome patient—in front of Dr. Whale. Yes, that part was silly, but if she was being honest, she'd have to admit that she had noticed John Doe several times, had walked past him and felt that quiet glimmer of familiarity rustle somewhere down in her mind. On her way into the hospital, book under her arm, she wondered if she liked John Doe because he was always there, always so consistent, always so reliable. No, he didn't talk back, and no, he had no idea who she was, but he always stayed the same. He was like her. He was alone, and he was stuck here in Storybrooke.

It was incredible to her how little life seemed to change in the town. She had been here for so long, but each year, the children seemed to be the same, her mixed feelings about Storybrooke seemed to be the same, and her loneliness—some murky part of herself that simply did not believe that she was meant to be a homebody, to know nearly no one, to spend her nights alone, drinking tea—well, it never changed. Was Storybrooke stagnant or safe? It was both. Little things like this— visits to the hospital—were as much about occupying her time as they were about the work itself.

She sat herself down beside his bed, made herself comfortable, and opened the book.

She looked at the words, looked back up at John Doe.

"I know this is odd," she said. "I'm doing this for a friend. Try to bear with me." She glanced through the broad glass windows and saw Dr. Whale on the far side of the floor, doing his rounds, head stuck in a chart. She looked back at John Doe and raised her eyebrows. "Sorry if it gets boring."

She read. She read the story Emma had told her to read, and slowly fell into it herself. She read about Snow White on the lam, no better than a forest bandit; read about her first encounter with the Prince, and the second encounter, and the smoldering feelings between the two, who had so much more in common than they even knew. Mary Margaret hadn't read the whole book before giving it to Henry, and at one point she paused, looked up, and said, "Maybe this isn't completely for children? What do you think?" To her it seemed suited to both.

She saw the word again: "bandit." Someone on the run, someone who broke rules, someone who lived bravely, lived in a way that didn't fit into societal norms. She was most definitely not a bandit, no. She was good, careful, kind, cautious, law-abiding. She didn't make trouble. She wasn't like Emma Swan. She wanted to be, but she didn't know how.

I may not be a bandit, she thought. But I have a bandit's heart.

She was still caught up in the emotion of the story at the very end, when her eyes moved toward the final paragraph, her curiosity piqued by the tale. Prince Charming and Snow White were coming together, even though they'd been fighting all along. She read: "... stared into each other's eyes; they didn't need words to express what they felt in their hearts. For it was here, in the shadow of the Troll Bridge, that their love was born. Where they knew, no matter how they were separated, they would always fin—"

Mary Margaret stopped, her voice stuck in her throat.

Impossible.

But she had felt it.

Slowly, knowing what she would see, she let her eyes move from the book to her left hand, resting on its edge. Her heart, already beating fast, began to pound.

John Doe's hand was on her hand.

Not just on her hand. Squeezing it.

She stood, covered her mouth, shucked his hand from hers. After one last glance at his still-closed eyes, she went to find Dr. Whale.

. . .

SNOW WHITE TOOK ONE LAST GLANCE at her belongings, knowing that she'd probably forgotten something important but too harried to worry about it now. Her tree-trunk home was not far from where she'd robbed the arrogant (handsome) fool and knocked him over with a rock, and she now felt that it might be prudent to vacate the area. But there was something about that man. . . .

She looked down at her most precious belonging: a tiny crystal vial containing a minuscule amount of very potent fairy dust. She had learned to fight with weapons over the last few months, but this was a weapon of a higher order. Magic. With this dust, she would be able to fell even the most dangerous of enemies. Her plan, of course, was to use the dust against the Evil Queen. She didn't know how she would get the opportunity, or when it would come, but when it did, she would be ready.

She put the vial around her neck, strapped her gold to her waistband, and turned from her tree. She took one step then and saw the ground beneath her feet begin to move.

Move up, actually. A net, covered in leaves. Before she could even react, she was hanging twenty feet off the ground, bundled up, trapped.

"Ah. Hello there," came a voice—a voice she recognized—and a grim expression came across her brow.

It was him, the arrogant man. There he was, hands on his hips, looking very proud of himself.

"I told you I would find you."

"Please," said Snow White, reaching for her dagger. She drew it and was about to start cutting.

"Ah ah ah ah," said the Prince, seeing this. "Quite a fall. Be careful. You're bound to break your neck. I will lower you down very gently."

They stared at each other.

"For a price," he added.

"And is this the only way you can catch a woman? By catching her in a net?"

"It's my preferred method of catching thieves, actually," he said. "I have various methods for catching women."

"Well, aren't you a real Prince Charming?" Snow White said.

He grinned at this. "I do have a real name."

"I don't care," she said. "You're Charming. Cut me down, Charming."

He stopped smiling. "I will. As soon as you return my property."

"It's long gone."

"Then we'll have to recover it. I imagine it hasn't gotten too far away. That pouch contained a wedding ring very dear to me. It was given to me by my mother, in fact."

"Oh, of course," said Snow White, rolling her eyes. "That nag in the carriage! Ha! Of course you would be marrying somebody like that. Let me guess. She's a princess. The marriage is all very important."

"You're incredibly rude for someone trapped in a net," said Charming. "Are you aware of that?"

"Why would I help you?" Snow White said. "Why would I possibly help you? What will you do, Charming? Torture me if I don't?"

"No," he said, and now Snow White could hear in his voice that he'd stopped playing her game. "Someone else probably will, though."

She studied him through the holes in the net. He looked back up, unblinking.

"What do you mean?"

"I mean that I know you're Snow White," he said, "and if you don't lead me to those jewels, I'll turn you over to the

Queen's men." He pulled a wanted poster from within his vest and held it up. The likeness was uncanny. She doubted it would make much sense to protest. "It's your choice. Help me or I turn you in. I have a feeling the Queen's not so charming as I am."

. . .

SHE AGREED to lead the Prince to where she'd sold the jewels, and he immediately lowered her, telling her that he trusted that she wouldn't run, that he would only find her again, it made no difference. As much as she would have liked to hit him in the face with a rock (again), it made more sense to recover the ring.

For three hours they walked and said little to each other, and all the while, Snow White fumed as she picked her way through the forest. Behind her, he strolled casually; there was something about his swagger that she detested. Near noon he called for a rest, and she leaned against a tree, looking off to the west.

"And what is that?" he asked.

She realized she was toying with the charm she wore around her neck. "It's none of your concern," she said, pulling her hand away from the glass.

"Now it is," he said, and with a quick snatching motion, he grabbed the delicate thing and pulled it from her neck.

"Be careful!" she cried. "It's a weapon. It's fairy dust. It transforms any enemy into something easily squashable."

The Prince, amused, raised an eyebrow and studied the small glass vial. "Is that so?" he said. "And why haven't you used it on me, then?"

"I'm saving it for someone who matters," said Snow White.

"Like the Queen?"

"It's none of your business."

"Maybe not," said Charming. "But tell me, what exactly did you do to her to incur that wrath? It's quite impressive."

"She hates herself and so she hates everyone else, too, especially me apparently. I've done nothing to her."

The Prince studied her, and she looked back, aware of the fire in her own eyes and doing nothing to hide it.

He shrugged. "Okay then," he said. "Teach me to pry." He held out the vial.

"What?" said Snow. "You're just ... giving it back?" He wasn't playing by the rules of master and prisoner.

"Yes," he said, shrugging again. "Of course. It sounds like you'll be needing it."

. . .

HENRY AND EMMA sat together at the diner, waiting for Mary Margaret to arrive and tell them about reading the story to John Doe the night before.

"I don't want you to get your hopes up," Emma said, sipping her hot chocolate. "We—"

They both looked up as Mary Margaret, looking more excited than Emma had ever seen her, burst into the diner and beelined for their table.

"He woke up," she said, sliding into the booth.

Emma didn't even want to guess what kind of smile was on Henry's face. This was not the plan. "Excuse me?" she said.

"He grabbed my hand. Right at the end of the story."

"He's remembering," Henry said. He nodded to himself, as if this made perfect sense, and stood. "Let's go to the hospital," he said. "Come on!" He ran toward the door.

Emma tilted her head and looked at Mary Margaret. "What are you doing?" she said.

"He really did grab my hand," Mary Margaret insisted, sounding more like Henry now than Emma cared to consider. "We made—there was some kind of connection."

"Not the kind that has to do with Snow Whites and Prince Charmings, though?"

"No, no," Mary Margaret said. "No. Just a connection."

"Well then I guess we better go see for ourselves," she said.

. . .

SHERIFF GRAHAM MET THEM all at the door, hands up in a way that made Emma think something more had happened. "What is it?" she said, stopping short.

"It's nothing for you to be concerned with," Graham said, looking over his shoulder. "I assume you're here because of what happened last night? Between John Doe and Miss Blanchard?" Graham nodded curtly at Mary Margaret, and Emma was reminded that all of these people had relationships. She had no idea what theirs was.

"What's wrong?" Mary Margaret said. "Is he okay?"

"It's not that he's not okay," Graham said, turning and leading them onto the floor. "It's that he's gone."

"Gone?" Emma said. "How is that possible?"

They approached Dr. Whale, who was shaking his head, studying a chart. "We're not exactly sure," Graham said.

"It's not possible," Dr. Whale said. "Scientifically, at least," he added.

"And yet he's not here," Emma said. "Did someone take him?"

"I don't know." Dr. Whale went silent, looking over their shoulders. Emma heard the clicking of heels. She tensed up and turned in time to see Regina stalking toward them. "What are they doing here?" she demanded. "What kind of operation are you running here, Sheriff? Is this or is this not a crime scene?"

"What did you do?" Henry asked Regina.

Her face softened just a bit as she looked down at him, bent, and touched him on the shoulder. "Nothing, Henry. I'm here to find out what happened to him."

"Why would the mayor get involved with a missing person?" Emma asked.

Regina straightened up. "Because I'm his emergency contact."

"You know him?" Mary Margaret asked. "How?"

"I don't know him, I found him," Regina said. "Years ago. On the side of the road."

"But hold on," Mary Margaret said. "If he's out there, somewhere, wherever he is, can he— You can't just wake up from a coma and be okay," she looked at Dr. Whale, "can you?"

"He's been on feeding tubes for years, his legs are atrophied, and if he's conscious, he's disoriented and panicked. So no. He's not okay. He needs to be back here immediately. I don't want to speculate on what could happen to him."

"Then find him," Regina said, taking Henry's hand. "This is not a place for you," she said to him. "Let's go. I don't want you hanging out with that woman."

Protesting with his eyes, Henry looked at Emma knowingly before being dragged away. She knew what was in his head. Go find him, he was saying to her.

· · ·

AN HOUR MORE into their walk, Snow slowed her pace, then stopped the Prince with a hand on his arm. "Okay," she said, peering toward the bridge. "We're here. We gotta be careful."

"Careful of trolls?" he said. "Are you joking?"

"Have you ever met a troll?"

The Prince looked back at her.

"So we gotta be careful," she repeated, and then led him out to the old stone bridge.

She hated trolls, but they weren't the worst business partners. They always had gold and always seemed willing to buy her stolen goods. Her heart beating a little faster than before, Snow steadied herself, took a breath, and together she and Charming walked out to the middle of the bridge.

Seeing her looking at him, he smiled at her.

She found herself a bit disarmed by it, actually.

"What?" she said.

"What now?" he said, going to the edge, looking down. "Do we make troll noises?"

"No," she said, reaching for her purse. "We knock on their door."

She stepped across the mossy stone and set a half-dozen gold coins on the ledge of the bridge. "Step back," she said, and the Prince obeyed.

They heard the scrabbling first. She had seen the trolls climbing the great support structure of the bridge, and she didn't care to see it again. They were like spiders, only uglier. They lived down below, in what she imagined was squalor. She shivered, imagining it. God forbid she ever found herself down in such a place.

Charming, a querulous look on his face as they listened, said, "So are they—"

The leader of the trolls was the first to burst up over the side. Lean, shambling, coated in moss and dirt, he pulled himself over the edge and straightened up, all eight feet of him. Snow touched Charming's hand, which he'd moved to the hilt of his sword, and shook her head. He looked at her, and let it drop.

"Not very charismatic, are they?" Charming muttered.

"Who in God's name is this?" boomed the head troll, pointing at Charming. He slowly craned his neck and looked at her. "And why are you back? Our business is done."

"I'm here to make a new trade," she said evenly. "I want to buy back one item. The ring."

The lead troll frowned, grunted, looked toward one of his compatriots, who produced a small burlap sack, dug around, and pulled out a ring. He held it up, then dropped it back in the bag.

The head troll looked back at Snow White. "I won't do business with him here," he said again. "I asked you once, I'll ask again. WHO IS HE?" These last words exploded out of him, out of some pit of anger and torment. Snow didn't let anything show on her face, but she was scared. Very scared.

"He's no one," she said. "Let's do the deal. How about I give you all your money back and you just give me the ring. You can keep everything else."

He cocked his head, thought it through. Finally, after a long and skeptical look at Charming, he turned to one of his companions and nodded. The other troll again pulled out the sack full of jewels.

"Thank you," said Charming, and Snow thought: No, do not thank him. But Charming didn't catch her look of warning, and continued with his ridiculous manners: "We appreciate your help."

The head troll held up a hand, looking at Charming, telling the other troll to wait.

"Look at those hands," sneered the head troll, pointing at Charming's clean fingernails. He grinned devilishly. "Look at that well-fed posterior. This one is a royal." The head troll snarled this last word, and Snow knew that the deal would not be going through—not with any civility, at least. All five trolls pulled their daggers.

"So what?" said Charming, defiance in his voice.

Snow hung her head. "Never admit that," she said to him.

"Take him down," the head troll commanded, and the others moved in around Charming, who pushed Snow away and raised his sword.

He did not get a chance to use it, though—he was swarmed and brought down by the fast-moving, catlike trolls, whose movements were impossibly smooth, and twice as fast as their lumbering frames suggested they'd be capable of.

Snow watched helplessly as they tore open the sack Charming was carrying, containing all of Snow's possessions. The dust the Prince had taken from her fell to the ground, and soon, one of the trolls had found the wanted poster in Charming's vest. The head troll unrolled it, took a long look, and shook his head, looking back at her.

"Snow White," he said. "We've been doing business with Snow White all along." He laughed. "Quite the reward!" he said. And then, to his cronies: "Take her as well."

Two trolls scrambled toward her, and as they did, Snow glimpsed Charming shaking free of the others. She ducked at the last moment, and both trolls missed her. As she scrabbled forward and gathered up their possessions, as well as the jewels, she saw Charming tossing one of the trolls into two more—

impressive, she thought—and she knew that they both had a clear path to run. "Come on!" she cried to him, and she turned to run. She heard his steps behind her.

And then she heard him go down.

She turned back and saw it then: Another troll had climbed up and grabbed Charming's ankle as he ran, and now all of them were piled onto him. If she left, she'd be free, and she'd have everything. But he'd be dead.

She didn't think for long.

Snow dropped the satchel and opened the vial of dust all in one quick motion, then pivoted and headed back toward the fight. The head troll saw her coming and smiled a disgusting smile. "Royal blood," he said, "is the sweetest blood."

As a response, Snow tossed a handful of dust in his face. He turned into a snail, then fell through a crack in the bridge.

The other trolls came for her, and one by one, she threw dust at them, turning each and every one into a snail. By the time she was through, Charming lay alone on the bridge, looking at her in awe, and a number of impotent snails were sliming their way around on the wood. Her vial was empty.

"You saved me," Charming said, getting to his feet. "Thank you."

"It was the honorable thing to do," Snow said.

He looked at her empty vial. "Now you don't have your weapon," he said.

"I'll think of another way," she said, "to kill who I want to kill. I couldn't go and let Prince Charming die."

"I have a name, you know," he said. "It's James."

"Well, James," she said. "Nice to meet you."

She was almost embarrassed by the way he was looking at

her now, and she felt herself starting to blush. She turned. "Come on," she said. "Let's get out of here before more of them show up."

He nodded. They walked together, side by side. Snow heard a satisfying crunch when Charming stepped, firmly and deliberately, onto one of the snails.

. . .

EMMA, GRAHAM, AND MARY MARGARET stalked the woods for hours in the hope of finding the lost man, each of them swinging the beam of a flashlight back and forth across the trunks of trees and the thick, prickly bushes. Graham was a good tracker, and he'd managed to follow John Doe's trail for a decent distance before he lost it. Mary Margaret, Emma noted, seemed oddly emotional about it all. Emma wondered what was going through her head. Most likely, she was thinking she was responsible in some way. God help her if she thinks he's her Prince Charming, Emma thought.

They spiraled off where the trail ended, but the three reconnoitered after thirty minutes of little success. Emma had been about to suggest they wait until morning to resume the search, when they heard a rustling in the direction of the hospital.

"Who's there?" Graham said curtly, decisively, in the direction of the noise.

Without responding, Henry appeared in the clearing, trademark smile on his face.

"Good lord, kid," Emma said, going toward him. "Your mother's gonna kill me if she knows you're out here."

"Have you found him?" Henry asked, looking from Emma to Sheriff Graham.

"Sorry, Henry," Graham said. "Not yet. And Emma is right—we need to get you home."

"I can help, though," Henry said. "I know where he's going."

"Where?" Mary Margaret said. "How could you know?"

"I know because I know the story already," Henry said. "Come on."

He ran off before Emma could snag him by the back of his shirt, and after an awkward moment of dumbly looking at one another, the other three ran after him, calling his name.

Fast for a little half-pint, Emma thought, dodging left and right to avoid barely visible tree trunks. She was running too fast to hold her light steady, and she caught only occasional glimpses of Henry's big, bouncing backpack. "Kid!" she yelled. "Come on! Where're you going?" But Henry never slowed.

He led them through the forest until she and Graham emerged, panting, in the clearing at the shores of a river Emma had not yet seen. Henry stopped and turned, waiting for them to gather—Mary Margaret had fallen behind, and finally emerged as well. "It's the bridge," Henry said, pointing into the darkness.

Emma looked to where he was pointing. The road that led out of Storybrooke crossed the river here, spanning it with a white and rusted bridge.

When she looked back at Henry, ready to ask him what the hell he was talking about, he was already looking around near the tree line. "He's gotta be here somewhere."

"Oh my god," Mary Margaret said, hand over her mouth. She pointed toward the river. "There," she said "He's there. I see him."

John Doe was there indeed. Facedown in the river, not moving, his hospital gown billowing up in a cloud around him.

Graham got to him first, wading into the river. He had John Doe upright in a flash and dragged him to the shore, then pulled his walkie-talkie from his belt and called for an ambulance. As he spoke, Mary Margaret knelt, put a hand on John Doe's chest, and slowly leaned over his face.

"Come back to us," she said to him.

Emma—uncomfortable, fairly certain that the man was dead—watched grimly from above as Mary Margaret administered mouth-to-mouth. Emma didn't know what to make of it—any of it. She didn't have it in her to tell Mary Margaret what was obvious. Holding John Doe's wrist and waiting for a pulse, Graham probably was thinking the same thing. And was she crazy, or was Mary Margaret kissing John Doe?

Before long, Henry was standing beside Emma, watching as well. She had the urge to cover his eyes.

"He'll be all right," Henry said knowingly. "Don't worry. She has to kiss him to wake him up. It makes total sense. It's not gross."

"Let's hope he wakes up, kid," she said, putting a hand on his shoulder. "I don't care whether it makes sense or not."

Emma could hear the sirens in the distance now; Graham, watching sadly, seemed to be on the cusp of stopping Mary Margaret. He looked up at Emma, and she shrugged.

And then John Doe gasped.

Emma could feel Henry's excitement at the sound, and she took a few steps toward them, Henry following behind. "She woke him up!" he said. Emma didn't know what had happened. She turned her light on John Doe's face and was shocked to see that his eyes were open, and he was looking up at Mary Margaret.

"Thank you," he managed. He wiped his face, wet from the river, and looked around confusedly.

"My name is Mary Margaret. Do you know who you are?"

He stared at her, apparently trying to decide. "No," he said eventually. "I—I don't."

. . .

MINUTES LATER the ambulance arrived, and Dr. Whale and the paramedics loaded John Doe into it. Emma watched Mary Margaret, who looked on with concern. In another minute the ambulance had pulled away.

She's got it bad, Emma thought, looking at Mary Margaret, who'd now begun to futz with her necklace. "We should go to the hospital and check on him," the teacher said to no one.

Emma walked up. "Yeah," she said, nodding. "We should. Come on. Let's go."

They quietly trudged up the grade and wound up to the bridge. Emma grinned a bit when she saw the sign attached to the bridge. It said TOLL BRIDGE in simple black lettering. But someone had seen fit to scribble a little R between the T and the O.

. . .

CHARMING AND SNOW ran miles through the forest before stopping for breath, keeping a brisk pace as they put distance between themselves and the trolls. Snow was a better runner than Charming, she soon realized, and she slowed her pace (slightly).

After an hour, the run became a walk. They were safe. There was no reason to stay together, Snow reckoned.

And yet they walked, saying nothing.

They walked some more.

A little more.

Finally, after another hour had gone by, they reached the road and came to a fork. It was time to part.

Charming looked down at his boots and said, "Well. That was interesting."

"It was, I agree," said Snow. "You stepped on one of them when we ran off." She looked at him mischievously. "Surely not on purpose?"

"Oh, no," said Charming, looking up. "That was on purpose. Very satisfying squish."

She laughed. They both twisted a bit, faced each other.

"I suppose we should make our exchange," Charming said. "We're heading in different directions."

"You're right," she said. Her eyes lingered on his for an extra moment, and then she reached into her vest and removed the small sack of jewels. He in turn removed the pouch of gold coins. He held it up, dropped it into her other hand, and turned his palm up. Snow emptied the sack of jewels into his hand. They both looked down as he sifted through them and found the ring.

"I know, I know," he said, looking at her eyes. "Not your kind of jewelry."

"Who knows?" she said, plucking it up. "Only one way to find out, right?" She smiled and slipped it onto her ring finger. The fit was perfect; she lifted her hand and splayed her fingers.

"You're right," she said. "Not for me."

He nodded, put the rest of the jewels back in the sack, and took her hand into his. As he pulled the ring from her finger, he said, "If you need more, you can have the rest of the jewels."

"That's not necessary," Snow said. "We both got what we needed today. I think."

"Yes, maybe so," said Charming. An awkward moment passed; Snow resisted the urge to say something silly, to relieve them from the moment. She didn't want to.

"Good luck to you," he said. Then: "If you ever need anything . . ."

". . . you'll find me?" she offered, a crooked smile appearing on her face.

"Yes," he said. "Always."

"You know it might sound crazy," she said, "but I believe you."

He nodded and took a step backward. "Perhaps we'll have to wait and find out," he said. He nodded again and looked at the trail he was headed down. He twisted back to her. "Good-bye, Snow White," he said. "It was a pleasure doing business with you."

"Good-bye, Prince Charming," she said, and turned, walking away down the path. She didn't turn back, as she didn't want him to see that her cheeks had gone so scarlet.

.   .   .

THEY HAD TO WALK all the way back to Storybrooke's small hospital, and by the time they arrived, Emma noted, a number of new vehicles were parked out front. She looked disdainfully at Regina's Mercedes, then up to the ambulance parked atop the emergency stripes near the door.

Inside, a number of nurses, as well as Dr. Whale, stood around John Doe's bed, examining him. Emma noticed another woman beside him, someone who did not look like a medical professional. She was blond, tall, regal-looking. On her face was caring concern. She spoke to John Doe slowly, like she was explaining something, and he looked at her.

Just as they got to his bed, Regina saw them and came to intercept. "I'm not sure what you think you're doing in this town, Nancy Drew," Regina said to Emma, "but I'm getting tired of the disruptions you've begun to cause." She glanced at Mary Margaret and said, "There seem to be a whole lot more . . . conflicts in Storybrooke since you've been here, Ms. Swan. I don't think it's a coincidence."

"Maybe it's not," Emma said. "Maybe you're right."

Regina glared back, trying to figure out what Emma might have meant. Emma herself didn't know, but she liked the reaction she'd gotten.

"Who is . . . that woman?" Mary Margaret said faintly, ignoring this stare down, ignoring Regina's anger. She was instead looking at the blond-haired woman beside John Doe, who was now stroking his hair.

"Her name is Kathryn," Regina said. "John Doe's wife. And John Doe's name is David. David Nolan."

"Is this them?" Kathryn asked, looking over, relieved smile still on her face. "Are you the people who found him? Thank you. Thank you so much." She left David's side and crossed the room. She took Mary Margaret's hands in her hands and said, "I don't know how to thank you."

"I don't understand," Mary Margaret said. "How could you not have known he was here? Before?"

A pall came over Kathryn's face; she slowly released Mary Margaret's hands and looked at the group. "We—we separated. A few years ago. It was under . . . terrible circumstances, a huge fight. And he stormed out and told me he was leaving town, moving to Boston, that the marriage was over. And all this time I've just assumed he was there, that he . . . moved on." She looked back at him; he was preoccupied with Dr. Whale. "All this time he's been right here," she concluded.

"You never once tried to find him?" Emma said skeptically. She didn't like it. She didn't like the woman's delivery and she didn't like the smarmy look on Regina's face.

"Of course I did," said Kathryn, turning back. "But no one knew where he was. There's only so long you can search for someone who doesn't want to be found in the first place." She looked at Regina and smiled warmly. "But the mayor put the pieces together and called this evening. It's unbelievable. This is—it's like we're starting over. We get a second chance."

"That's so lovely," Mary Margaret said, smiling at the woman. Emma doubted she was the only one in the room who could see through the false sentiment.

Kathryn went back to David at the bed.

"Come on, Henry," Regina said. "Time to go home."

As he passed by Mary Margaret, Henry looked up at her. He didn't try hard to lower his voice when he said, "Don't believe any of it. He woke up because of you. The story. True love. It's your destiny to be together."

"Henry," Regina said. But Henry darted from the room. Regina, shaking her head, followed after him.

"Excuse me," Emma said to her back. "Madam Mayor."

Regina turned.

"A word before you go?"

Regina sighed, nodded her consent. The two left the room together. Henry was already out in the parking lot when Regina stopped walking and the two women turned to face each other.

"Isn't love sweet?" Regina asked. "I'm so happy that such a tragic story had a happy ending. That never happens."

"None of this particular story makes any sense," Emma said flatly. "Let's not play games."

"What is it that you think, then?" Regina asked, eyes alight, looking amused. "I'm using evil magic on that woman? Forcing her to lie?"

"No, but I think you're manufacturing something. I don't know why. But it stinks, whatever it is."

"You do know, Ms. Swan," Regina said, strolling back in her direction, "that bad things happen. Even in small towns like Storybrooke."

"Storybrooke's just like everywhere else," Emma said. "Full of good people, with a few rotten ones thrown into the mix."

"I'm surprised you're not happier to see two people reunited," said Regina. "There is no curse in the world worse than being alone. Am I right?" Regina smiled and looked over her shoulder toward the parking lot. "I'm lucky to have Henry," she said. "It would be terrible to have no one at all."

. . .

MARY MARGARET SAT ALONE at her own kitchen table, one hand half-clasping a glass of water, the other resting in her lap. As her macaroni and cheese sat cooling in front of her, she thought through all that had happened since John Doe (his name is David, she reminded herself) had reached out to touch her hand.

She sipped her water, sighed, ran her fingers through her hair.

She swirled a few pieces of macaroni in the orange sauce, set the fork back down, twirled the ring on her middle finger.

When the knock on the door came, she knew that it couldn't be him, that right now, he was home with his wife, relearning his own history. She had seen their embrace. And besides, why would she be hoping a stranger was at her door? No one wanted that.

She was convincing herself that she wasn't hoping it would be him when she opened the door and saw Emma looking back.

The two women looked at each other. Mary Margaret found herself smiling then, just a bit.

"Hello, Emma," she said.

"Hey."

"What can I— Is everything all right?"

"Everything's fine," Emma said. "The mystery man is awake and the Evil Queen is asleep in her tower. We're good."

Mary Margaret laughed a little and opened the door a bit more. "Do you want to come in?" she said. "I have some dinner I could share."

"I was actually wondering if that offer still stood," Emma said. "About the room."

"Oh," Mary Margaret said, legitimately surprised. She'd managed to forget all about it in the excitement of the day, but she was glad Emma had not. "Absolutely. Come in."

Emma nodded and walked into the room. She took a look around, obviously pleased. Mary Margaret felt better. She didn't want to think much about why.

"Nice place you got here," Emma said. She rested her hand on the counter. "Much nicer than the back seat of a car."

"That is true," Mary Margaret said, and the two women laughed. "But I'm glad that you're here," she said. "Really, Emma. Welcome."

CHAPTER 4

THE PRICE OF GOLD

HE NEXT MORNING, EMMA WALKED WITH Henry from his house to the bus stop, unconcerned whether Regina would see.

He was happy to see her, abuzz about John Doe and Operation Cobra, and Emma listened to his patter happily. Regina was not going to push her around. Not anymore.

After Henry waved good-bye and the bus pulled away, Emma had to stop short when the town's sole police cruiser pulled into a driveway and blocked her way on the sidewalk.

Graham popped out and nodded good morning.

"You almost ran me over," said Emma. "Hi."

"Had to get your attention," he said.

"Are you going to arrest me again?" Emma said. "Lemme guess. Trumped up jaywalking charges."

He smiled and hung his head, which Emma took to be his way of acknowledging how unfair she'd been treated here so far. She knew Graham was sympathetic to her, even though he and Regina seemed to have a complicated relationship. There was something between the sheriff and the mayor, maybe something romantic. She couldn't tell, but she felt it. And it made sense. Late hours, working together, neither of them attached . . . She didn't yet know how it fit into the equation of Storybrooke, but it certainly mattered.

"I want to offer you a job, actually," Graham said. "I need a deputy. I know that you're good. I think we'd work well together."

"Something tells me your boss wouldn't like that," Emma said. She was surprised by the offer. Flattered as well. She wouldn't mind working a few late hours with Graham, either, now that she thought about it.

She said no. He asked her to think about it. She said she would, and he drove off, apparently pleased that he'd gotten that out of her.

The next surprise came at the diner twenty minutes later, when Regina slipped into her booth, smiled her devious smile, and said, "Good morning, Ms. Swan. Have a nice walk with my son?"

"Of course you already know about that."

"It's really not what I'm here to talk about. I don't mind. I understand the urge; he's a lovely child."

"What is it," said Emma flatly, "that you'd like to discuss?"

"Roots, Ms. Swan. The problem of roots."

"Roots?"

"That's right," Regina said. "You don't have any. You drift, you don't stay in the same place for long. Phoenix, Nashville, Tallahassee, Boston . . . and here you are now. With no lease, staying with Miss Blanchard. How long will it be before you leave again? Do you see what I mean? I'm happy that Henry is happy, but I'm making this appeal to you. If you're being honest, don't you think this will all eventually hurt Henry more than help him?"

Emma stared, feeling the cold recognition of a fear she'd had herself.

Regina saw it and drove in the knife: "You will leave eventually. People don't change. Why not spare your son's feelings and rip the Band-Aid off clean?"

The mayor stood and walked away. Emma was so flustered by the comment that she stood as well, trying to think of something to say in response. But no words came. All she managed to do was knock over her hot cocoa and spill it all over her sweater.

Ruby saw this happen, took pity, and sent her back to the diner's laundry room to clean up. "My friend's back there," she said, passing by with an order. "She's nice. Talk to her, will you? She's going through something." Ruby zipped away.

Sure thing, Emma thought. Happy to help. She shrugged and headed to the back room.

Ruby's friend was indeed back there, trying (and failing) to wash a set of white sheets, crying as she did it. Emma gave her some advice based on her very limited knowledge of laundry: Try some bleach, lady. But at the hint of a connection, the girl—Ashley was her name—glommed on to her like a lost puppy dog and soon was telling Emma her whole sad story. Ruby had sure been right: She was going through something. Nineteen years old, very pregnant, all alone in the world, no plan, no way to make money. Where have I heard this story before? Emma thought, listening to the young woman's worries.

"I don't know, I don't know," Ashley said. "I just—I just feel like giving up sometimes."

"You're nineteen now," Emma said. "I was eighteen."

Ashley looked up, realizing what Emma was saying.

"It gets easier," Emma lied. "But listen. This is the important thing. You are the one who decides. You get to choose. And if you choose that you can do it, you're gonna make it."

Ashley wiped her face, let this sink in.

Emma added: "Life is there to be taken. You have to take it. It doesn't seem like it could be that simple, but it is."

This seemed to strike a chord with Ashley. Some of the clouds that had been darkening her face lifted. Emma had surprised herself a little with the speech, but it was how she'd made it this far. Be bold, be strong—there's no other way.

It would be a few hours before she found out just how literally Ashley took her advice.

. . .

IT WAS SATURDAY, and Mary Margaret and Emma were together in the apartment. Emma's few possessions had been delivered from her apartment in Boston. She was going through her clothes as Mary Margaret made scrambled eggs. Life was starting to feel a little more normal.

"That's it? That's everything you've got?" Mary Margaret asked, sizing up the box.

"I'm not a hoarder. I don't keep things."

"Makes it easy to move, right?" Mary Margaret said.

Before she could get too upset at Mary Margaret's innocent comment, the doorbell rang.

Mary Margaret answered, and gasped a bit when she saw who it was.

Mr. Gold, a bandage on his head, darkened their doorway.

"Hello there, Miss Blanchard," he said politely. "I'm looking for Ms. Swan."

Emma walked up behind Mary Margaret. She remembered him from Granny's on her first night in town. Creepy dude.

"Yeah?" was all Emma said.

"Ah, Ms. Swan, hello," he said. "Perhaps you recall meeting? I am Mr. Gold, a local . . . businessman."

"I remember."

He nodded curtly and continued: "I've heard through the grapevine that you're quite good at tracking people down. And as I have a need to track somebody down, I thought to stop over and offer you some work."

Both she and Mary Margaret looked at him for a long while. Mary Margaret then made an excuse and retreated into the apartment. Emma, cautious but intrigued, shrugged and invited him in.

"Her name is Ashley Boyd," he said as they both sat in the living room, "and she's stolen from me."

"Why not use the police?"

"Because this is a delicate matter. I don't want her to get into any trouble. I just need what she stole to be returned."

"What did she steal?"

"I don't think it's important for you to know that," he said. "Find her, you'll find it."

Emma didn't know what to think, but it wouldn't hurt to earn a little money. She hadn't made a dime since she'd been there.

"She broke into my shop last night, muttering something about taking control, choosing to take control of one's life, some such nonsense." He shrugged, touched the bandage on his head, and as he did so Emma tried to conceal the glimmer of surprise in her eye. Good grief, she thought, it's Ashley from the diner.

"Okay," Emma found herself saying. "Okay. I'll find her."

Mr. Gold, apparently delighted, stood and thanked her. At the door, he was nearly run over by Henry, who came bounding in, a big smile on his face. "I have until—" Henry was exclaiming, but he stopped in his tracks when he saw Mr. Gold looking down at him.

"Hello, young man," said Mr. Gold. "Ms. Swan and I were just discussing a business matter. I was just leaving."

Henry looked terrified. And Emma knew why; she remembered from the book: Henry thought Gold was Rumplestiltskin.

"Hello, sir," Henry said quietly, then entered the apartment, head down.

Once Gold was gone, Emma sat down with Henry and told him that he couldn't keep showing up in secret, even though she did want to see him. She explained that Regina would find a way to use it against them. Henry assured her it was okay—that he had until five o'clock and that his mother would never know. Emma didn't like it one bit. Before she could insist that he leave, though, Henry started asking questions about why Mr. Gold had been there.

"He asked me to find someone," she said. "A girl. It's just a job."

"What girl?"

"I doubt you'd know her, kid," she said, regretting saying anything at all.

Henry sat down on the couch, removing his backpack. He dug around and took out his book, started flipping through the pages. "Is she pregnant?"

Emma turned, eyes wide. "How did you know that?"

. . .

EMMA'S PLAN WAS SIMPLE. She never made a complicated plan unless she needed a complicated plan, and in her experience, whenever she was trying to find somebody, it was simplest to start with friends. Emma didn't know much about Ashley, but she knew she had one friend in Storybrooke. Ruby.

She and Henry went right to the diner. When she saw that Ruby had a moment free, Emma pulled her over to the back entrance and asked her if she had any guesses about where Ashley might have gone.

"I don't. No," Ruby said, shaking her head. "Excuse me." She pushed on the back door and propped it open. "I'm waiting for them to drop off my car, sorry."

"You don't think the boyfriend could be involved?"

"He would have to be involved to be involved," Ruby said. "He hasn't talked to her in at least six months. He's such an ass."

"She mentioned he hadn't . . . done the right thing," Emma said. "When he found out she was pregnant."

"He dumped her," Ruby said disdainfully, chewing her gum loudly. She looked like she was about to say something else, but just then a tow truck trundled into the back parking lot, pulling a cherry-red Camaro. The truck stopped, and the driver got out, waved to Ruby (who waved back quite flirtatiously, Emma noticed, and added a hip-twisting curtsy for good measure), and started lowering the vehicle. Nice car for a waitress, Emma thought.

"And where's Ashley's family?"

"She doesn't really have one," Ruby said. "Horrible step-mother somewhere. I think stepsisters. I don't know. She doesn't talk to them."

Henry tugged conspiratorially on Emma's jacket, and nodded up at her when she looked down. She shook her head and gave him a "not now, kid" look.

"You know, maybe you should go ask Sean," Ruby said. "Maybe he knows something. He lives with his dad." She took Emma's hand, pulled it up, then took the pen from behind her ear. "I'll write down the address."

. . .

A BURLY MAN in his fifties opened the door when Emma rang the bell of the two-story midcentury on Randolph. The father, she assumed. She asked for Sean, and the man introduced himself as Mitchell Herman, asked her what she wanted. The way he said his own name, the way he shook her hand, the way he crossed his arms afterward—Emma could feel it when she wasn't going to like somebody. Pushy fat rich men were not exactly her type.

Emma was glad she'd left Henry in the car as she explained that Ashley was missing and that she'd been hired to find her. She told him few other details, but Mitchell took what she gave him and ran: "Of course she disappeared, of course she bailed on the agreement. Can't trust her to be a good mother, can't trust her to do the right thing. She let herself get pregnant in the first place, didn't she?"

Oh, Emma thought. I really don't like you.

"Who's at the door, Dad?" Emma heard, and behind Mitchell, she saw Sean emerge from a back room and come down the hall. He was so young—just a baby, not even twenty. Just like Ashley. Emma couldn't believe that her own son would one day turn into a similarly gangly, bright-eyed creature. She couldn't believe that she used to be like Ashley. . . .

"Is everything all right?" Sean asked.

"No, Sean, everything isn't all right," Emma said, her voice suddenly stern. "Ashley is missing. If you know anything, you need to tell me where she is or go to the police. Right now. And I mean anything."

Sean became extremely agitated when he heard this information, and he tried to push past his father, who held him back and blocked the doorway. "What do you mean, disappeared?" Sean said. "Where is she? What about the baby?"

"No," Mitchell said. He turned to his son. "Get inside, we'll talk in a minute."

"I get it," Emma said. "You're the reason. Right? The reason he broke it off in the first place?"

Mitchell looked at her like an idiot. "I had everything set up for that girl. She was set. She agreed. It was all very civil. All she had to do was follow through."

"What do you mean you 'had everything set up' for Ashley?"

"I mean exactly that," he said. "I made an arrangement."

"For the baby. You sold the baby. And who's the buyer?"

Mitchell Herman looked honestly confused now, and Emma backtracked through the conversation, wondering what she'd missed.

And then she realized.

"Gold," she said. "Of course."

"Yes, of course, Gold," he said. "Isn't that who hired you? To bring him the baby? I thought you worked for him."

Emma closed her eyes; she should have guessed it all the way back at the diner, when she was talking to Ruby . . . Ruby, who had known as well. Known everything, and had sent her here to buy Ashley time. The possession of Gold's that Ashley had taken was . . . herself. Damn it, Emma thought, turning and running back to the VW.

Inside, she cranked the engine. "We gotta find this girl, Henry," Emma said, reversing out of the driveway. "She panicked and she needs our help. She's running."

"There's only one road that leads out of town," Henry said, "but—"

"Don't talk to me about a curse right now, kid," Emma said. "This is real. She's running and she's too far along to run."

Ten minutes later, feeling like she was playing the lead in a bad nightmare, Emma rounded a bend on the road outside of town and saw the bright red of the Camaro's backside sticking up out of the ditch. She crashed, Emma thought, as she hit the brakes then got out to run to Ruby's car. Ashley wasn't behind the wheel, which was a relief, actually. Emma looked up, scanned the woods. She heard the moaning almost right away.

She and Henry found her ten feet past the tree line, sitting on the ground, holding her belly. When she saw them, she looked up, eyes filled with terror. "The baby!" she cried. "The baby is coming right now!"

. . .

EMMA AND HENRY sat together in the ER's waiting room as Ashley delivered down the hall. Emma, nervously staring at her shoes, didn't notice when Henry looked up from his book and studied her. She wrung her hands and fidgeted, busy imagining what Ashley was going through. Imagining and remembering. She couldn't believe how close Ashley had come to disaster. A girl like that alone in the woods . . .

"You're the only one," Henry said.

Emma looked up.

"What did you say?"

"You're the only one who can leave Storybrooke," he said.

"All of us are stuck here. You can go if you want. You know that, right?"

"What do you mean?"

"The rules of the magic. That's how the curse works. People who are already here can never leave because bad things happen whenever they try to get out of town. You're not stuck, though. You're special. You don't come from here. So you can go. It's fine, I get it."

She felt the urge to reach out, pull him to her, cradle his head against her chest. To protect him from the things that didn't make sense. She steadied herself by reaching down and taking hold of the arm of her chair.

"Anyone can go, kid," she said. "There's no curse." She saw the doctor coming toward them down the hall. "And besides," she added, standing, "I'm not going anywhere. There's too many lost people around here."

The smile on the doctor's face told Emma everything she needed to know, even before she heard the details: six pounds even, baby girl and mother healthy and happy both.

"Thank you," Emma said, the tension easing out of her shoulders. She took the doctor's hand and shook it. "Thank you so much," she said. Henry had to be home by five o'clock if she was going to avoid another plumage-puffing session with Regina, and so she told him to gather his things, then crossed the room toward the bathroom. Out of the corner of her eye, through the front window, she saw Mr. Gold approaching the hospital, cane swinging happily. He came in, looked around.

She went to him, took him by the arm, and walked him over to the vending machines.

"You should have told me," she said. "About the baby. She's

not a piece of merchandise and this whole thing stinks to high hell."

"Ah!" Gold said, delighted. "It's a girl, then?"

"She's keeping her. You don't get to choose. She chooses."

"But she already chose, Ms. Swan," Gold said. "Months ago. We have a contract."

"Then go home and tear it up," Emma said, "because it means nothing. Not anymore."

They stared each other down for another moment. The tension broke when Mr. Gold bowed his head, an admiring twinkle in his eyes. "Very well, Ms. Swan. I'll let her off the hook. But no debt goes unpaid. You'll have to give me something in return."

"How about a bag of dirty laundry?" she said. "I've got one back at the apartment."

"You owe me a favor. One favor," he said, holding up a finger. "Simple. You like simple, don't you?"

She didn't like it, but she'd do it.

"Okay," Emma said. She held out a hand. "Deal."

Together, Emma and Henry drove across town—drove past the diner, where Emma glimpsed Ruby flirting with Billy, the kid with the tow truck. Emma had Henry home by 4:45, time to spare, and she was back at Mary Margaret's ten minutes later, unsure of what to make of the day. What she did know: She wasn't going anywhere. She called up Sheriff Graham and told him if the offer still stood, she'd take him up on the job.

"Protect and serve," Emma said, looking at the clock tower. "I'm kinda good at that."

"You certainly seem to be," Graham said. "I'll see you Monday morning, Emma."

THE SHEPHERD

MMA WAS FINALLY SETTLING INTO STORY-brooke. She always liked the feeling of a new town, especially in the early days, when life itself seemed new again and the past hadn't yet found her. It never lasted. But the honeymoon period was enlivening, electric. It was her favorite feeling.

That Storybrooke was different, a place literally populated by her past in the form of her son, made Emma very aware that she had entered a new chapter of her life now, and that the next steps wouldn't be the same as before. This scared her. She had only ever had to take care of herself.

But for now, she felt okay. Something that had always been out of whack seemed to have corrected itself in her heart.

Graham showed her the ropes of simple police work, joking (or was it flirting?) with her as he made her aware of all the nooks and crannies of Storybrooke, telling her about the long-standing feuds between various residents.

But she still didn't know what to think of Henry's belief in the curse. He talked about it nonstop, and she was still playing along. Whenever he began to discuss it—to tell her, for example, that the reason Marco and Archie were close friends was that Marco was Geppetto, and Archie ("Jiminy!") had always been his friend, conscience, and companion—she nodded agreeably and thought: What are you doing, Swan?

Mary Margaret was another story, and a story that was a little more recognizable. She'd fallen for David Nolan, a married man she didn't even know. Not good. Not good for a whole slew of reasons. She talked about him too much and spent more time at the hospital than she should. He encouraged her visits and asked her to stay late on many occasions. He had even told her that he felt a special connection with her, that he felt like he knew her more than he knew his wife. She'd come home that evening and abruptly told Emma she'd resigned from the volunteer staff, that she "couldn't go there anymore," which made Emma think that her friend was self-aware enough to make the wise choice. But Emma had seen love and felt love, and she knew what it could do to a person. Her new roommate, who at first had seemed so even-keeled, was coming apart at the seams.

Emma didn't press too hard, hoping it would fade. Not just for Mary Margaret's sake, but for Henry's as well. To him, as he told her again and again, it made complete sense that the two were drawn to each other. It was only a matter of time before the natural order was restored. Prince Charming and Snow White together, their daughter Emma grown and present, the grandson Henry smiling up at all of them, the whole family stable and solid and united.

When Emma thought about it like this—in terms of the perfect family tree Henry had constructed for himself—his fantasy life went from seeming innocent to seeming dangerous. Something that could end up hurting him far worse than he'd already been hurt.

EMMA TOOK HENRY to David's "Welcome Home" party, and on the way, Henry—who had noticed when Mary Margaret muttered to Emma, "I can't go, I shouldn't go"—explained to his mother how Prince Charming had ended up betrothed to the woman Abigail. Not that Emma asked.

"He didn't really love her!" Henry told Emma. "That's the thing. He got stuck in this huge thing with King Midas, her father, and he had to agree to marry her even though he believed in true love."

"He had to agree?" Emma asked. "Why?"

"Because he was a fake Prince Charming anyway." Henry nodded to himself, as though all of this made perfect sense.

"What's a fake Prince Charming?"

"Okay. I'll explain it. It's not that complicated," Henry said. "A long time before Snow and Charming met, this other king, King George, couldn't get an heir and called up Rumplestiltskin and was like, 'Hey, Rumplestiltskin, I need a baby, can you bring me one?'"

Emma smiled at her son's retelling of the tale.

"Rumplestiltskin trafficked in babies?"

"Yes," said Henry. "For a price."

"Good to know."

"And so Rumplestiltskin took one boy from this family of shepherds and made a deal and gave the baby to King George, and that was who grew up to be Prince Charming."

Emma tried her best to listen as Henry told a convoluted tale of twins, false identities, and dragon slaying, but her mind drifted to Mary Margaret, and to the very real David Nolan, who was clearly having a difficult time readjusting to his married life with Kathryn. The whole story was strange, and Emma still suspected that Regina had fabricated something here, although she didn't know what, or why she would do such a thing.

When they arrived at the party, David drifted over to them.

When he came up and smiled, Emma could tell that he was uncomfortable here, surrounded by his old "friends," who he didn't recognize. He knew Emma because she'd been there at the hospital and she'd helped to find him.

He greeted her and Henry and took their coats. Kathryn came and said hello, but she dashed off toward the kitchen right away.

"You look like a lost man," Emma said. "Come on. Hide over here with us. We don't bite."

David smiled, obviously relieved, and the three of them went to the corner of the room. "Thanks," he said. "It's a little overwhelming."

"I can't even imagine," Emma said.

He seemed to grow nervous then, and Emma tried to give him a "spit it out" look.

"And I'm sorry, I know that—I know that you live with Mary Margaret. I was wondering if you knew when she would be here."

Ah, Emma thought.

Emma crossed her arms, smiled a curt smile. "Yeah. She can't come" was all she said. "I'm sorry."

David continued to watch her, looking for a signal as to what that might mean. Emma felt no need to elaborate.

"She was busy, huh?" David said.

"No, she's not!" Henry said, smiling. "She's at home, hanging birdhouses. You should go talk to her. Because of your eternal love."

"Henry," Emma said, putting a hand on his shoulder. "It's

his party, he can't go anywhere." She turned to David. "Besides," she said, "she's not feeling well. It's really for the best."

"Yes," David said. "Probably for the best."

. . .

MARY MARGARET was standing at the top of a stepladder when she heard someone say her name.

Startled, she nearly fell from the ladder, but she caught herself by reaching for the tree trunk in front of her. She twisted to see him.

"Oh, David," she said, feeling a sudden and inexplicable sadness, looking into his eyes. Seeing his face was like looking directly into an unsolvable problem. "You shouldn't have come."

"There was no one at the party I wanted to see," he said.

She climbed down the ladder and crossed the yard.

"You're married," she said, once she'd gotten to him. "We can't do this. It's—it doesn't make any sense." She nearly laughed at this last word, but he didn't seem to find it funny. But it was the truth. More than anything, she just didn't understand any of it. Including her own feelings.

"That doesn't matter," he said, taking her hands. She resisted, but he held them. "Look, listen to me. I know, I get it. I was in a coma, I had this whole other life, but you— There's just something, Mary Margaret. We both feel it. I don't know what kind of person I used to be, but I know who I am right now. I'm a person who trusts his heart. And my heart's telling me that my authentic life, that my real life, is somehow over here. Not back there."

Tears welled up in her eyes, and she felt herself smiling a worried little smile.

Then she pulled her hands away.

"I think it's simpler, David," she said. "I think it's just that I happened to save you. That's all. The feeling will go away."

She turned and retreated to her back door.

· · ·

EMMA CAME HOME to find Mary Margaret abusing the kitchen with a scrub pad and pulled her away to calm down, talk it through, and have a drink. Mary Margaret obliged and told her about David's visit to the yard. She admitted that she'd been tempted, that she felt something as well.

"He's married," Emma cautioned. "His life is a mess. It's not the right time, Mary Margaret. You can't get involved."

"I know that," she said quietly. "So I told him to go."

"That's good," Emma said. "It might not feel good now, but that's good. I think you know deep down that something isn't right, that your conscience doesn't like it. Trust that. Trust yourself."

· · ·

MARY MARGARET did not sleep well and dreamt of the toll bridge, where they'd found David, dreamt of him facedown in the water. Over and over again, she saw him rolling upright, saw herself placing her lips on his lips. When she awoke, it was light and she heard birds cheeping outside. She felt unrested and considered calling in sick. Instead she pulled herself from her bed, got dressed, and went to the diner.

She soon wished she hadn't. She ran into Dr. Whale at the door.

He really was an unlikable man—she'd always thought it. Handsome enough, sure, but obviously smug. And smarmy, too. The kind of person you wouldn't want your daughter dating.

His eyes lit up and locked with hers before she could brush by him and go to a table. He touched her arm, which she pulled away. "Mary Margaret," he said, sounding contrite. "I've been wanting to talk to you. I hope your resignation from the volunteer staff didn't have anything to do with our date."

His narcissism came close to making her laugh, but she kept a straight face.

"It's very boorish of me not to have called you, I know," he said. "I apologize. If you'd ever like to go out again, you have my number." He left the diner, oblivious to her very different interpretation of the night in question.

She couldn't quite laugh it off, though. When she was alone in a booth with her hot chocolate, Mary Margaret's mood sank down a few more notches as she wondered what life in this town really held for her. How had she gotten to where she was? It was as if her whole history weren't quite real, even though she was always the first to take responsibility for her actions, for her choices. . . .

"Hello, Ms. Blanchard."

Mary Margaret looked up and was surprised to see Regina standing at her table.

"May I join you for a moment?" Regina asked. "This really won't take very long." She slid in across from Mary Margaret. "It's about my friend. Kathryn."

Regina let this sink in.

Mary Margaret, for her part, tried not to reveal anything. But she knew what was coming, and quietly braced herself.

"I didn't know Mrs. Nolan was your friend," she said.

"I don't know what you're trying to do, but it's never wise to put 'home wrecker' on your résumé, Mary Margaret," Regina said. "Especially in a small town. Things can get very uncomfortable, very quickly."

Eyes wide, Mary Margaret could think of nothing to say.

"Don't play dumb with me, Miss Blanchard," Regina said. "David left his wife last night. You wouldn't know anything about that, would you?"

"No," she said. "I wouldn't."

And she thought: He left her?

"I'm sure you wouldn't," Regina said. "Kathryn is devastated. You and I both know he is a confused man who hasn't yet remembered who he is. Why don't you do everyone a favor, go back to your mousy little existence, and give a healing couple the space they deserve?"

Not waiting for a response, Regina slid from the booth, straightened her power suit, and strode out of the diner, heels clicking the whole way.

. . .

BUT THERE WAS NO SIGN of him. Peace and quiet. Nothing happened. Mary Margaret began to believe it was all finally fading, and that life would move forward, back to normal.

Then on a Wednesday morning, halfway through the day, she looked through the window beside her classroom's door.

David was outside her classroom, peering in at her, waving for her to come outside.

Her students were all reading silently, and she sighed, stood from her desk, and walked out of the room.

"What are you doing here?" she whispered, not bothering to conceal her anger. "You can't just come here."

"I can't stop thinking about you," he said. "I left Kathryn. I didn't choose her. I think we should be together." He spoke directly, deliberately. Mary Margaret was taken aback by his frankness. How had so much happened in so short a time?

"This is crazy," she said. "You have to go."

"Is it crazy?" he asked. "Don't you feel it as well? Answer me that."

Mary Margaret could only look back at him.

"Listen," he said. "You don't have to decide anything right now. Just meet me tonight. Near the bridge where you found me. If you think this can work, meet me there at nine o'clock. I'll be waiting." David smiled. "If you meet me, we'll just go from there."

Mary Margaret said, "Go."

"Meet me tonight."

"I can't."

"Just think about it," David said. "Just think. That's all I ask."

. . .

AGAINST HER BETTER JUDGMENT, she did think about it. She thought about it that whole day, during class, and she thought about it as she walked from the school to the police station. She asked Emma for her advice, and Emma surprised her by telling her she should go to meet David. It was one thing for him to show up outside of her house; it was another thing entirely to leave Kathryn. That made all the difference, apparently. Emma said he had made a choice; he was committed. Maybe it was time for her to make a choice as well.

"None of it feels based on anything," Mary Margaret said.

"Yeah, but love never makes sense," Emma responded. "It's never based on something. Not on something you can see right away, at least."

"What, then?"

"Don't you think," Emma said, "that hearts can kind of see truth? A little better than eyes?"

"I'm surprised to hear you say that," said Mary Margaret.

"Who said there wasn't a romantic in me?" Emma said. "Somewhere. Deep down."

"Not me."

Mary Margaret was surprised by her friend's advice, but in her heart she knew that she wanted to go, she wanted to choose David. She didn't understand how they'd gotten here quite as fast as they had, but she didn't care.

. . .

THE MAYOR had a meeting that night, and Henry took the opportunity to sneak out and come to Emma and Mary Margaret's apartment.

At the door, Emma took one look at him and said, "You can't keep doing this."

"She's out," he said. "She won't be home until like ten!"

Emma begrudgingly let him in, knowing that she was close to helpless against him when he got that excited about things. It was only eight o'clock, after all, and Mary Margaret had come in, changed her clothes, spilled her guts, and hurried out an hour ago.

"So," Emma said, sitting down across from Henry at the table. "What should we do?"

"You didn't let me tell you the end of the story," Henry said. "About Prince Charming."

"That's right, I didn't."

"I know you think it's stupid, but it's important," Henry said. "I saw the way he looked when he was asking about her. And it's natural!"

"Why is that?" Emma said.

"Because of the ring," Henry said.

"Explain."

"After Charming agreed to stay as Prince Charming, he had to go and say good-bye to his mother for the last time. She knew he was being forced to marry Abigail, and that he believed in true love, so it was his mom who gave him that ring. When she gave it to him, she told him that love always would follow the ring."

"Cute," Emma said. "He and Snow White fell in love trying to get the ring back."

"Right!" Henry exclaimed. "So it turned out that love did always follow it."

"Kind of," Emma said. "I guess so." She did always like that about fairy tales, the way prophecies would end up coming true, but in a way no one ever expected.

"It's a nice story," Emma said.

"It's not a story."

"Fine," Emma said. "It's a nice story about something that's not a story."

"I think next time you see Mary Margaret," Henry said, "you should look at what she wears around her neck. Before you think you're so smart."

"Why is that?"

"Because she has it," Henry said. "That's the ring."

Emma realized she knew what he was talking about—she'd seen the ring on a chain around Mary Margaret's neck. She hadn't thought much about it and had never asked her what it was. She'd always just assumed it was a family heirloom.

"So just to get this straight," Emma said. "Your teacher, who is Snow White, who is also my mother, who has fallen in love with a man with amnesia, who is Prince Charming, is right now wearing a ring around her neck that was, for a time, in the possession of a gang of greedy bridge trolls and which was, before that, stolen by her from Prince Charming, who was on his way to give it to King Midas's daughter, Abigail."

"Who is actually Kathryn," Henry added.

"Got it," Emma said. "All cleared up."

Henry nodded. "Yup. All cleared up."

. . .

MARY MARGARET went to the toll bridge knowing she was going to get hurt. Despite the fact that she'd believed David when he told her about his feelings, the man was flaky somehow, he was . . . he didn't know who he was. Not literally, not metaphorically, not any way. Why was she letting herself fall into this?

Because a part of you believes, came an answer from somewhere within herself.

She was early to the bridge, and she went down beside the water to listen to it trickle, to wait. The moon was big and bright. Her hand went to her necklace, and she twisted the ring between two fingers as she wondered what life might look like with him. Would the town hate her for taking David away from a married woman? Did it matter? She didn't know. Love was worth quite a lot, though. She knew that much.

She waited alone for what felt like a long time. The pleasure of the fantasy was now starting to shift into anxiety. He was late, and this brought reality into sharp relief. Another side of her—the skeptic—began to tick off all the problems with this situation, starting off with what was glaringly obvious: She didn't know him. She did not know this man and was acting like she loved him. How much, she wondered, could loneliness make you believe in something you'd invented, just to make it hurt a little less?

"Mary Margaret."

She turned and smiled, saw him.

"You came," he said, moving toward her. He stopped when he reached her, and held her arms as she tried to embrace him.

"Of course I did," she said, looking worried. "But you sound . . . disappointed."

"It's not that," he said, still out of breath. "It's that I . . . I remember."

Mary Margaret looked into his eyes, considering this, then took a step back.

"Your old life, you mean," she said flatly.

"Everything," he said. "I—I got lost on the way, and I went into Mr. Gold's shop, and I saw this . . . this windmill for sale there. And I had this whole flood of memories about Kathryn, about getting the house together. I— It's in there, Mary Margaret. A lot of things are in there. And I'm remembering."

"And you remember that you love Kathryn."

He stared at her.

She didn't say anything—she had no interest in letting him off the hook.

"I don't know," he said. "I just don't know. But I remember her now, and I feel like I have to honor those memories. It's the right thing to do."

"The right thing to do, David," she said, her voice quivering, "was to not lead me on in the first place."

"I know that," he said. "I'm so sorry."

"I understand," she said. "You've made your choice."

Her eyes were dry. She felt more angry than hurt. Angry at

herself for not knowing better. This was all just a result of her loneliness, and the feeling she'd always had that she deserved more—so strong it sometimes felt like she'd even had more, somewhere, at some time, and was being tortured by the illusion of a life in which she had very little.

"I don't know," he said.

An arrow pierced her heart. Hearing him work out his feelings so violently, so sloppily, so cavalierly . . .

She turned.

"I guess it's just not meant to be after all. You should go," she said, her back to him.

"Mary Margaret."

She said nothing, walked away.

She didn't cry until she was alone.

. . .

EMMA DIDN'T KNOW the details, what had happened between David and Mary Margaret, that Mary Margaret had headed for the bar, that she'd had more to drink than she'd had in the last six months combined, and that Dr. Whale was talking into her ear. As Emma patrolled the town, though, she sensed a new tension in the air. Storybrooke didn't seem so sleepy anymore. Affairs! Intrigue! She kind of liked this new Storybrooke. If she were to ask Henry, he would probably say that it was her presence pulling apart the status quo. She still—

"What in the . . . ?" Emma said out loud.

She stopped the car.

Case in point.

She was on the corner of Mifflin and Main and could swear—swear—she'd just seen someone jumping out of the second-story window of Regina's mansion.

She killed the engine, grabbed her nightstick, and crept toward the gap in Regina's hedge, which she knew would be the spot someone tried to get out through. She took a quick breath and heard footsteps, raised the stick, and slashed downward when she saw the dark figure.

The stick connected, and the figure went to the ground.

After a groan, she heard a familiar voice say, "Ow."

"Graham?" she said, kneeling and putting a hand on his back. "What the hell are you doing here?"

Realizing the answer to her own question, she helped him up, brushed him off.

"Ah. I get it. Well, sorry. You okay?" she asked.

"The mayor needed me to—"

"—sleep with her?"

They stared at each other, and then Graham tried to explain.

Emma, a little grossed out by him, didn't want to hear it.

Just like that, her attitude toward intrigue changed.

THE HEART IS A
LONELY HUNTER

OU DO REALIZE," MARY MARGARET SAID, eating her cereal, "that those were mine. Right?"

Emma looked across the kitchen at the shattered vase and pile of dripping flowers in the corner. She'd come out and seen them and had lost control. A little.

She couldn't stand the idea of Graham continuing with his quest to get her into bed, especially now that she knew about Regina. She'd seen the flowers, assumed they were from him, and had thrown them across the room. Sometimes she was definitive.

Sometimes he was, too. Last night, Emma had gone to Granny's Diner for a nightcap, only to find Sheriff Graham there, completely hammered and completely belligerent. Things had been very strange between them in the few days that had passed since she'd caught him outside of Regina's, and in a way, this was to be expected. He couldn't handle the idea of someone knowing his secrets, which was true of all the men she'd tracked.

Sudden disdain. That was what she had thought, at least,

when Graham drunkenly tossed a dart in her direction and nearly hit her. Things got stranger, though, after she left Granny's Diner and he followed her out to the street.

"Stranger" was one way to say it. She left the diner and he grabbed his jacket and followed her out. Outside, the air was crisp.

"Let me talk to you," he said on the sidewalk.

She didn't stop, but she did slow.

"About what?" she said eventually.

Graham hurried to catch up. "I'm sorry. Let me apologize. Let me—let me explain, Emma. Everything."

"Explain what? You're sleeping with the mayor, who I don't particularly like, who is trying to keep me from my son, and who is, incidentally, our boss. There's nothing to explain. I don't want your apology. Go home."

"But I don't *feel* anything with her. I don't—you don't understand."

Emma stopped walking and turned to face him. "I've been in bad relationships, Graham," she said. "Big deal. Get out of it and get over yourself. It's not my problem."

"I am trying to explain this to you," he said. "Because I do feel something. With *you*."

This caught Emma off guard.

He leaned forward and kissed her before she could react.

For Emma, it was a foreign feeling to be caught off guard in this way, and she honestly hadn't expected him to do something so brazen. For a fleeting moment before the anger came, she allowed herself to feel what it might be like to be with Graham. Not for long. But it was a nice moment. The kind of feeling she hadn't felt for a long time.

She couldn't show him that, though.

"What the hell are you doing?" Emma demanded, pulling away. There was a faraway look in Graham's eyes.

"Did you just see that?" he said quickly, looking around.

"Did I see you kiss me without my consent?" Emma said angrily. "Yes. I was here."

"No. Did you see that wolf?"

"Don't cross lines like that with me again," Emma warned, stepping back, not interested in any more of his games. "It's not okay. You're drunk, and that was a little too close to assault for my comfort. Go home, get over this."

"I'm sorry," he said. "I just want to feel something. I can't—"

"Fine," Emma said. "Feel something. That's good. But whatever it is, you're not gonna feel it with me."

That was last night. She hadn't stopped thinking about the kiss since then.

"Yours?" Emma said, looking at Mary Margaret. "I thought they were from Graham."

"Um, no," Mary Margaret said. "They were from Dr. Whale."

"Oh," Emma said, going to the cabinet for the dustpan. "Oh."

As Emma cleaned up, Mary Margaret told her about her one-night stand with Dr. Whale. It gave Emma a kind of gleeful satisfaction to imagine her friend indulging in such things, harmless as they were. It was the opposite of her experience with Graham. Mary Margaret needed some more risk in her life, and besides, she needed to get past David. This was good. Emma told her so.

"Maybe," Mary Margaret said. "I guess so. But do you know what's also good?"

"What."

"Admitting that you have feelings about somebody," Mary Margaret said. "For example. You admitting you have some feelings for Graham."

Emma screwed up her face. "What are you talking about?"

"It's obvious, Emma," Mary Margaret said, smiling mischievously. "Everyone can tell. You don't have to be smashing vases for it to be obvious."

"The guy gets under my skin, that's all," Emma said, knowing she wasn't quite telling the truth. "Can't I be irritable without people gossiping?"

"Emma," she said. "Come on."

"What?"

"The wall," Mary Margaret said. "This wall you have up around your heart." She shook her head, shrugged. "You think it protects you. And it probably does. But there's a cost to that."

Emma was surprised at the plume of sadness that expanded in her chest as she listened to her friend's words. A wall. A shield. She didn't want to risk saying anything, for fear of sounding choked up. So instead she waited, privately admiring Mary Margaret's emotional intuition, privately resenting it as well.

"It makes it hard to love," Mary Margaret said, "when you're defended so well."

. . .

WHEN HER FATHER DIED, there was a haze. Snow White would not have been able to describe it that way immediately after it happened, and besides, there was nobody with whom she could talk to about her feelings. One day he was okay; the next, he was gone. The haze came, and she dwelled alone within it through the funeral. Pain. That was what made the haze. That was what created the fog that rolled down through her soul. Snow White couldn't see through it and wasn't herself within it. She was a lost girl alone in the world. She was blind.

The haze never fully cleared, of course. She had never felt

loss like this, and her whole self seemed to have come undone. She could not find clarity; peace seemed to have left her, and peace no longer even seemed possible. It never does after the death of a parent.

She also felt guilty, as though she might have saved him, even though she didn't know what she could have done. Again, it was all very hazy.

She was quickly shuttled away from the castle by Regina and sent to one of the country estates. She slept fitfully on the first night there, dreaming of her father as a younger man. Her father, the man who'd showed her the world. The man who'd taught her to know reason, and kindness, and compassion. But in the dream, she kept losing him down on the beach; she would show him seashells, and whenever she would find one, she would turn, holding it up, but he would not be there.

She hardly slept.

The next morning, a knight—one of Regina's guards?—awaited her in the gardens. He offered to escort her on a walk through the forest.

Snow White looked at him. He wore a helmet, and she couldn't see his face, but she felt uneasy, and couldn't place his voice.

She nodded at the man, and he nodded back. "M'lady?" he said.

"I keep a brisk pace," she said, consenting. A walk would do her good. "Please try to keep up."

He nodded again, and they set out toward the woods.

They walked in silence for some time. She had seen that the man was uncomfortable in the heavy armor.

The forest was calm. Her thoughts went again to her father—this time, to the man whom she had watched fall in love with

Regina, all those years ago. He was still kind and still compassionate then, but Snow—young as she was—had seen how loneliness had worked away at his spirit. Even the wisest man could become . . . something else. After heartbreak, anything was possible.

When they were far from the castle, Snow White began to speak.

"When I was a little girl," she said, "the summer palace was my favorite place. The mountains surrounding it were like a cradle. They always made me feel safe. I look forward to returning there, I do." She paused in her speech but continued to stroll. "But I wonder now whether that feeling of safety didn't come from my father, not the palace itself."

The strange knight studied her through the slit in his helmet. She stopped walking and turned to face him, studying him right back.

"Go on," she said. "You can take it off."

The man did as he was told and pulled the helmet from his head.

She studied him. He was handsome, gaunt, and sternlooking. A ragged beard covered his jaw. He said nothing.

"Much cooler this way, isn't it?" she said.

He nodded, tucked the helmet under his arm.

"And you are not a royal knight, are you?" she asked.

"How would you know that?"

"Because without fail, whenever I mention my father, I receive condolences from a knight. But you are someone else, aren't you?" she asked. "You are who she chose. To take me. To get me out of the way." She took a deep breath, readying herself.

"You have good instincts," he said, dropping the helmet. He reached for his sword.

"And you have too much armor," she said.

Before he could react, she coiled up and exploded toward him, both arms out. She caught him in the stomach, enough to send him stumbling backward. Not used to his center of gravity being so high, the stumble turned into a crash. She had a good hundred-yard head start before he was on his feet again, chasing her.

. . .

"YOU KNOW THAT I'M A GOOD PERSON, don't you, Mary Margaret?" Graham was at the school. Class was over. He and Mary Margaret stood outside of her classroom, the trickle of remaining students whispering through the halls. She was looking at him with tender concern in her eyes. Apparently, he'd been a mess since this "incident" with Emma last night. Mary Margaret couldn't tell what was going on with these two, but she wanted to help. Somehow.

"Of course, Graham," she said. "Of course. And you—are you okay? You're covered in sweat and white as a sheet. Have you not been sleeping?" She felt his cheek. "You're burning up. What have you been doing all night?"

"I've just been having this sense that you and I used to know one another," he said. "In some kind of—in some kind of other life. I don't know. It sounds crazy." He shook his head, looked down the hallway. "I'm sorry for coming here. I don't know what I'm trying to accomplish."

"Why do you think that?"

"Last night," he said, "when I kissed Emma, I saw this whole vision. Of . . . of something. Another world. And you were there, and we knew each other. Somehow. I was—I was attacking you. With a knife. I think? I don't know. I don't know why I would be doing that."

"You sound like Henry, actually," she said.

"Henry?"

"He thinks that we're all characters from his storybook," she said. "And that we just can't remember."

"What kind of storybook?" Graham asked.

"Fairy tales," Mary Margaret shrugged. "Snow White and the dwarves, that kind of stuff." She rolled her eyes.

"Yes, I know," he said. "That boy. How insane."

. . .

EMMA SWAN WAS SITTING with her feet up on the sheriff's desk when Regina stormed into the office. Emma glanced at her and didn't move.

"So wonderful to see you, Regina," she said.

"Wonderful," Regina said with disdain. "Doing your civic duty, then?"

"I'm on break, lady," Emma said, scowling at her. "What do you want?"

"I want to make things clear," Regina said. "To you. About Graham. Stay the hell away from him."

Emma absorbed this, wondering what Regina must have thought was true. Had word gotten out about the kiss? Maybe. Or maybe Graham had said something to her.

"He's my boss," she said finally. "And so I can't. If you're talking about what happened last night," she added, "that was unsolicited. So I don't know what to tell you other than telling you I'm not interested. You can have him."

"You've been disruptive since you got to this town, Ms. Swan," Regina said. "If I were you, I'd be very careful that you don't paint yourself as the town slut."

Okay then, Emma thought.

"Do me a favor, Regina," Emma said flatly. "Get the hell out of my office. And don't ever talk to me that way again."

Regina seemed satisfied that she'd hit a nerve. She smiled and left without another word.

Emma watched her go, locked the door, and did some paperwork for a few minutes, letting the irritation cool down. She was used to Regina barging in on her and saying incendiary things—that was apparently part of the job—but this time it was a little different. This time it was about her romantic life, not her son. Emma could see that Regina's anger had a new edge to it this time around.

But it wasn't just that. *She* felt something, too. Maybe Mary Margaret was right. Maybe she did have some kind of wall up. One so seamless that she didn't even know it was there, much less see over it. Did she have feelings for Graham?

She was shaken from her reverie a few minutes later by the sound of her son calling her name.

"Emma! Emma!" cried Henry, running into the station, his backpack flopping behind him.

"Whoa, whoa, whoa, kid," she said, standing. "Calm down. What's wrong?"

Henry, panting, pulled the backpack from his back and dumped it on the floor. "It's Graham," he said. "I think he's starting to remember!"

"Remember what, kid?" she asked. "Sit down. Catch your breath."

She got him some water, and Henry eventually sat down at her desk and gathered himself. Graham had been to see him, he told her. Been to see him to ask about the storybook and ask about the fairy tales.

"And what did you tell him?" Emma asked.

Henry looked down.

"Henry?"

"I told him what I thought had to be true," Henry said. "I told him that he was the Huntsman, and that those flashes he saw when he kissed you were flashes of him remembering that time."

"He *told* you about *that*?"

Henry shrugged. "Yeah," he said. "But I heard about it anyway."

Small towns, Emma thought. That solved the mystery of how Regina knew.

She didn't like the idea of Graham, who was obviously not himself, running around town having visions of anything, and she certainly didn't like the idea of him going to a child and *believing* what the child had to say about the intersection of fantasy and reality. Graham was potentially in the midst of a psychotic break, she realized. She had to find him.

"Where did you send him?" she asked.

"I didn't send him anywhere," Henry said. "I told him about how the Queen trapped him into a bargain and that she ordered him to go kill Snow White."

Emma furrowed her brow. In Henry's universe, the Queen was Regina and Snow White was Mary Margaret.

"And why did she do that?"

"Because the Queen killed Snow White's father, and she knew that she had to get rid of Snow White as well. But she couldn't do it herself because she couldn't risk being found out. So she went looking around the countryside and found the Huntsman."

"Okay."

"That's where the wolf thing comes from," Henry said. "He loved them, and he had one as his friend. And Regina knew that, and she promised to protect the wolves if he helped her kill Snow White."

"And so what happened?"

"He dressed up as one of Snow White's guards," Henry said, "and almost killed her, but she ran away. While he was chasing her, he realized he didn't want to do it."

"How good of him," Emma said, leaning back in her chair. She looked over at his backpack. "You really know these stories cold, kid, don't you? You don't even need the book."

"I know them all," he said. She didn't like the way he said it.

"So where did he go when you were done?" she asked.

"I don't know," Henry said. "He got really upset when I told him that the Queen stole his heart when she found out that he—"

"So you don't know where he is?" she said.

"All he said," Henry replied, "was that he had to find that wolf. Before it was too late."

A wolf.

Sure.

Emma had seen one of those things. Once.

. . .

SHE WAS FASTER than he expected her to be—men were always underestimating her. She knew that she would not be able to outrun him forever, but she had enough time to do what she needed to do. After a few minutes of tearing through the woods, Snow White found a tree to hide behind, crouched low, and began composing the letter to the Queen. So long as she could say what she wanted to say, she could accept her death. So long as the message got through.

Within minutes he had found her. She had already completed the note.

She hardly looked up when he came around the corner.

Panting, he took her in, saw what she was doing, and shook his head. "You're running for your life and you stop to write a letter?" he asked. "I will never understand people. Royals or otherwise." He raised the dagger.

"You would have caught me eventually," she said, setting aside her quill and beginning to fold; the man paused. "This was a better use of my time." She looked up and held the letter toward him. "Please deliver this to the Queen after you've killed me."

"What does it say?"

"You can read it if you like," she said. "It's not a trick," she added, seeing the skepticism on his face. "Read it first, then you can kill me. I'm ready."

Cautiously, he reached out with his free hand and took the letter. While he read her words, Snow White watched as he slowly let the dagger fall to his side.

And then, a surprise: She saw a tear in his eye. She watched as it trickled down his cheek.

Snow White said nothing.

The man stuffed the letter into his tunic.

"Take this," he said, holding out a reed. "It will work as a whistle. Blow into it when you need help. Help will come."

"You're letting me . . . ?"

"Yes, go," he said, straightening up. "I'll buy you as much time as I can."

"But why?"

"Run," he said. "Don't ask another question. Just run, girl."

. . .

GRAHAM WAS RUNNING AWAY from Regina's house when Emma spotted him. She drove past him, back toward his truck, and parked, waiting for him. Soon he trotted up.

"Hey, Sheriff," she said. "You look stressed. Can I have a second?"

He glanced up and saw her standing in front of his car, arms crossed.

"Not now, Emma," he said, continuing. "I'm busy. You should be at the station."

"I'm trying to help."

"You're not."

"Hey, stop," she said, coming toward him. She put a hand on his arm and told him that he needed some rest, that it was no good to listen to a ten-year-old. Graham, frustrated, told her that Henry was the only one who seemed to make any sense. He tried to tell her about the wolf—to tell her that it somehow fit, that he couldn't feel anymore; he hadn't felt much in a long time.

"I have no heart," he said. "I can't say it any other way."

"You do," Emma said, shaking her head at him. How had he descended into *this* much of a tailspin after one awkward interaction on the street? Sure, he'd crossed a line, but it was just one bad moment. They could fix it. She didn't understand what had happened to him.

"Graham, come on," she said, stepping close. She took his hand and put it on his own chest, held it there. "Feel."

He closed his eyes, breathed in.

"That's just the curse," he said. "It's not real."

"No," Emma said. "It's not. That's you. That's your heart. You're fine."

Looking over Emma's shoulder, Graham said, "Am I?"

She frowned at this, twisted, and turned to look. She gasped.

The wolf. The wolf was there, standing on the sidewalk not ten feet from them.

"I've seen that wolf before," Emma said.

Her first evening here. In the middle of the road, when she had tried to leave Storybrooke. Graham had made fun of her. And now here he was, chasing it.

What in the hell is happening? Emma thought.

"That makes two of us," Graham said. "Come on."

. . .

THEY FOLLOWED THE WOLF into the woods. Graham retold Emma the story he'd heard from Henry—that in the other world, the Queen had taken his heart—and he said that it had occurred to him that the wolf was taking them back to his heart. "This wolf was my companion at one point," he insisted. "I think it's trying to show me where to find it."

"You *have* it, Graham," Emma said.

He shook his head. "No. And I have to get my heart back, Emma," he said. "I have to."

"Do I need to again point out how insane you sound?"

"Not necessary," Graham said, distracted. "Look."

They were at the edge of the cemetery, and the wolf had trotted up to a large crypt and stopped, nosing at the door, looking back at them. Emma had to admit—it looked a whole lot like the wolf she'd seen the first time she'd tried to leave Storybrooke.

"In there," Graham said. "My heart is in there."

He rushed to the crypt. Emma followed him in.

The inside of the crypt was relatively clean, considering, and Graham started to feel along the walls and the floor of the small stone room, clearly intent on finding a secret panel, something. Anything. Emma just watched, unsure what to do. Could she find a way to snap him back to reality? Or was this something bigger, something that would require . . . a hospital?

His brief search revealed nothing.

He looked around again. Then let his eyes rest on the coffin itself.

"No. You are not digging up some grave, Graham," Emma said. "Stop for a second. Think about this. The law aside, you're not well. You're—"

"What are you two doing here?"

Emma and Graham both turned, startled at a third voice.

Regina, holding flowers, stood outside of the crypt, a few feet away, a look of legitimate shock on her face.

"Police work," Emma said, stepping out into the grass. "What are you doing here?"

"Putting flowers on my father's grave," she said, "like I do every week."

Bullshit, Emma thought, looking at Regina with great skepticism. It was her father's grave? It was nothing if not suspicious. That word didn't even do it justice.

"We're looking for something," Graham said to Regina.

"You don't look well at all, dear," Regina said, her face softening now that she'd seen Graham. "Let's take you home."

"No."

Regina, tense, looked back and forth between them. Eventually she raised her chin and nodded. "I see. You and she."

"It has nothing to do with that," Graham said firmly. "It's about you. I don't love you and I don't want to be with you. Not anymore, Regina. It doesn't feel right." He shook his head and looked down, frustrated. He tried again: "I don't feel anything when I'm with you. I want the chance to feel . . . something."

Regina took this in, a new rage building in her eyes. Emma saw Graham bracing himself for some standard Regina-style verbal abuse, but her eyes snapped to Emma.

"This is your fault," she said. "You can't stay away from what I love, can you?"

"They keep coming to me, Regina," Emma said. "Maybe you should ask yourself why people keep running away from you."

It felt good to say that.

"Regina, it's not—"

But Regina ignored Graham's words as she took a quick step toward Emma, dropped her flowers, and—to everyone's surprise—punched Emma square in the mouth.

Her head snapped back as a circle of pain opened up around her mouth, but she didn't fall, and she held herself steady by reaching for the coffin. She saw as Graham lunged to restrain Regina before she could strike again.

Emma stared at Regina for another moment, rubbing her jaw.

Then, without another word, she walked away. She heard the last of their conversation as she headed back to town. She wasn't going to do this now.

"Graham," Regina tried. Her voice had softened.

"Don't talk to me," Graham said. "Don't talk to me anymore. We're done. Forever."

Emma smiled.

. . .

LATER, GRAHAM DABBED hydrogen peroxide near the small cut on Emma's jaw. She protested, but she let him. She liked being close to him, she liked the care he was taking. She liked what he had said back at the crypt. For Emma, this was the beginning of a new story. A new love story, maybe, even though Emma would never have called it that.

"I don't understand any of it," Graham was saying. "The wolf, any of it. I think—I think so much of it has been Regina. You almost start to feel insane when you're in the wrong relationship."

"Tell me about it," Emma said.

"I don't know how I went so far down that road with her in the first place."

"I know why we do that," she said, thinking of all the times it had happened to her. "It's safe. And being alone is terrible. Ow!" He'd dabbed the peroxide over the open cut and it stung. He smiled apologetically, touched her hand.

"All better," Graham said.

"Getting there," Emma said, and she leaned forward and kissed him. It felt right.

It was nice, and brief. A little breach in the wall, Emma thought.

He pulled away from her after a moment. He smiled at her strangely.

"What?" Emma said. "What's wrong?"

"I remember," he said.

"You remember what?"

"The first time we kissed, I had a flash of it," Graham said. "Just a flash. That's what set it off. And now—now I can remember everything." He was getting excited. He took her hand. "She *is* the Evil Queen, Emma. She—"

Graham's legs suddenly buckled, and Emma reached for him, concerned. "You okay?" she said.

As his eyes rolled back into his head, he tried to muster a

sound, but Emma couldn't make it out. "Hey, hey, hey," she said, holding him up. "Come on, Graham. You're just dizzy, right?"

But it was worse than a dizzy spell, she soon realized, and the weight of his body forced them both down. He looked sadly at Emma. The sadness was what really scared her.

"Graham!" she cried, shaking him. "Graham!"

He groaned again and took a few labored breaths. "I love you," he said.

"Don't act like you're dying, Graham," she said, panic in her voice. "Please don't do that."

He reached up, touched Emma's face. She was crying. He was using all the strength he had to wipe away the tears.

. . .

HE WAS GONE. Gone just like that, gone with little explanation. Cardiac arrest? By the time the ambulance came, Emma knew in her heart that he'd left the world. She stayed with him on the ground, weeping over him, until the paramedics had to calmly, delicately remove her arms from his body. She watched numbly as they put him on the stretcher and carried him away. There was no need to go to the hospital. It was obvious to everyone in the room. Unlike John Doe, this one would not be waking up. There were no miracles to be had here.

PART TWO

LOST HEARTS

CHAPTER 7

DESPERATE SOULS

INCE GRAHAM'S DEATH, EMMA HAD BEEN sleepwalking through her job as acting sheriff. Storybrooke had suddenly gone quiet, giving Emma some room to mourn the loss of her friend.

The news about Graham was simple: He'd died of natural causes, a heart fibrillation that had haunted him since childhood.

Dr. Whale showed her the chart, and Emma accepted it, but a part of her suspected something was off with Graham's death. But that didn't mean she was about to start believing in a curse. It was just the type of thing people did when they were vulnerable; she'd seen it a thousand times. The truth was he was gone, and that was that.

It was a Wednesday morning when Emma arrived at the office and found a message from the service telling her that Mr. Gold had called and asked her to come by his pawnshop when it was convenient. With nothing else going on, she picked up her coffee and headed back to her cruiser.

She found Gold in his back office, applying some kind of clear liquid to a cloth. Emma assumed the horrendous odor in the room—somewhere between manure and sweat—was coming from it. As she announced herself, Gold did not look up, and instead kept applying the liquid. "Lanolin," he muttered. "That's the smell."

"Lovely," Emma said.

"It's the same reason sheep's wool repels water," he noted. "Quite amazing, really. Highly flammable, of course."

"I got a message from the service," said Emma. "What can I do for you?"

"I wanted to express my condolences about Sheriff Graham now that things have died down," said Gold, finally looking up. Emma wouldn't have called it a sympathetic look, but she could see that he was trying to be kind. "Not good for the town. But I know you two were close." Gold began cleaning up around his desk. "You'll do well as a replacement," he said.

"I'm not replacing him."

"Two weeks as acting sheriff makes you sheriff, Ms. Swan. That's what the law says."

"You don't say," Emma said. She wasn't sure what she thought of the idea. Sheriff Swan.

"I also wanted to tell you that I have some of his things here, and I wondered if you might want something." Gold stood, picked up a cardboard box on a nearby countertop, and carried it over to her. He set it down on a table and Emma saw a number of items she recognized: Graham's leather jacket, his sunglasses, his cell phone.

"I don't want any of that," Emma said flatly, staring into the box. She felt a strong aversion to having Graham's things in her possession, and the strength of the feeling surprised her. She wondered, for a moment, how Gold had come to have these items, but asking questions meant continuing to discuss Graham. She couldn't do that right now.

"No?" Gold said casually. "How about these?' He pulled two walkie-talkies from the box. "These seem to be police-issued. You don't have use for them? Couldn't your boy play with them, at least?"

Emma sighed and took the two walkie-talkies. "Fine," she said. "Thank you."

"Children grow up so fast," said Gold. "You'll want to make as many memories as you can."

Emma looked at him. He was making that same face—something between compassionate and devious.

"Don't I know it," she said.

. . .

EMMA FOUND HENRY sitting in his "castle" at the seashore. It was only thirty minutes before school and he was in a glum mood; he didn't seem all that cheered up by the walkie-talkies, and he eventually just stuffed them into his backpack. She suggested they could use them to continue their Operation Cobra work, but he only looked back out at the water when she mentioned it. What had once brought a mischievous energy to his eyes now had almost no effect.

"What's wrong?" she said, after a silence.

"I feel like we should stop Operation Cobra," Henry said. "It seemed really fun. But now Sheriff Graham is dead."

"That had nothing at all to do with you or the curse. He had a sick heart. He'd known for a long time."

Henry turned and looked at her with grave seriousness. "That's not what happened," he said. "The Queen killed him

ODETTE BEANE

because you two were falling in love and he was her slave. And she was mad."

"I know you think that, but sometimes bad things just happen for no reason."

"That's not true, either," he said, growing more agitated. "She killed him because he was good, and good always loses here. And you're good, and that means you're going to lose."

"Good doesn't always lose," Emma said. "It's just harder for good. Because good plays by more rules."

Henry seemed vaguely interested in this point, even though he still remained distracted, disconnected. "Good has to play fair," he said.

"You have to get it out of your head that Regina killed somebody," Emma said. "She didn't. That's not fair to her."

Henry smiled.

"What?" Emma said.

"You're right," he said. "We don't want to make her any angrier than she is already. Right?"

Emma cocked her head. "That's not what I meant, kid."

"I know," Henry said. "But still."

. . .

SHE DROPPED HENRY at school, then went back to the station, ready for another long day of . . . very little.

When she came in, her eyes went to Graham's desk as they always did. His badge was still there. Emma imagined herself with it, imagined changing her life in this way, settling in. She went to the desk and picked the badge up.

"You won't be needing that."

Emma turned.

Regina, arms crossed, stood in the doorway.

"The position automatically falls to me tomorrow," Emma said. "Have I misunderstood the charter?"

"It automatically falls to you if the mayor fails to appoint somebody else," Regina said, strolling into the room, looking disdainfully at the mess on Emma's desk. "I'm going to appoint someone else this afternoon."

"Who?" Emma said.

"Sidney Glass from the *Storybrooke Daily Mirror*," she said casually. "He knows the town well. He's been here for quite some time."

"A reporter?" Emma said. "He's not qualified."

"Oh, I think he'll be just fine," Regina said, smiling. "And it'll be a pleasure to have somebody here who is not actively working to undermine me."

"Graham picked me for a reason, Regina," Emma said. "I know you don't like it, but he did."

"Yes, a reason," she said. "He wanted to sleep with you."

"That's not true."

"Isn't it?" Regina said. When Emma could think of nothing to say in response, Regina continued: "Either way, it's time for us to make a clean break. You and I both know it's inappropriate for you to be employed by the town. You'll have to find some other work."

"What are you saying?" Emma asked.

"I'm saying," said Regina, taking Graham's badge from her hands, "that you're fired."

• • •

EMMA WENT STRAIGHT TO GOLD. There was something about his behavior earlier that gave her a hunch that he'd be interested in helping. He wasn't being friendly—he didn't have it in him to be friendly. Gold wanted her to be sheriff.

At his shop, Emma told him what Regina had done, and he nodded. This was all some kind of chess game to him, wasn't it?

"She's almost right," he said, pulling a document from a cabinet behind his desk. It was old and dusty. He held it up. "The town charter," he said with a grin. He laid it out on the counter. "Let me show you how she's wrong."

Regina called a press conference in her office later that morning, to announce the hiring of Sidney Glass as the town's new sheriff.

Glass, of course, was beaming for the cameras, thrilled at this promotion, always so eager to do the bidding of his beloved mayor. Emma couldn't stand that guy.

But it wasn't so simple, as Gold had pointed out. She stood and watched Regina's haughty press conference for only a minute or two before she decided to make her move.

When she strode into the office, even Regina looked surprised.

"This isn't set," Emma said. "She can't appoint him. We have to have an election. And I'm running."

"The mayor is entitled to—"

"She isn't," Emma said calmly, holding up her printout of the charter. She'd highlighted the relevant passage. "She can put a candidate forward, but there has to be an election."

"Fine, Ms. Swan," said Regina, not bothering to take the charter. "We'll go through with the formalities. And the candidate I've nominated, Mr. Sidney Glass, will then be the new sheriff." Sidney Glass, for his part, looked flummoxed by all this, but he kept up his smile for the cameras. "How's that?" Regina said.

"Perfect," said Emma.

The cameras all turned to her.

. . .

A FEW HOURS AFTER she'd rained on Regina's parade, Emma was on patrol, on foot, when she walked by the diner and saw Henry through the window. He was at a booth, alone. She smiled, seeing him there, reading what she assumed was his book of stories. But when she went inside, she realized that he was reading the newspaper, not his book.

"Studying up on current events?"

Henry looked up, and Emma could see that he was very worried.

"What is it?"

"You haven't seen it, have you?"

She sat down in the booth and pulled the paper across the table. Her old mug shot—the one Graham had taken, and she felt a twinge of sadness as the tiny memory flitted through her mind like a little bird—but the headline was new. It read: EX-JAILBIRD EMMA SWAN BIRTHED BABE BEHIND BARS.

Emma stiffened, sat upright, and picked up the paper. "How did they do this so fast?" she muttered, scanning. The article—written by Sidney Glass—included all the details of her "possession of stolen goods" incident. Which was impossible. Or should have been impossible, anyway.

"Is it true?" Henry asked quietly. "Was I born in jail?"

She looked at him over the paper and then set it down. "It is true," she said, "but it's complicated. I didn't want you to know because I didn't think that it mattered." She sighed, picked up the paper, twisted it up. "Let's chuck this. Come on. Let's go out to your castle."

"It's the same thing again," Henry said. "Evil wins because it doesn't have to play fair. You can't just throw it away. It already ruined your election."

"Nothing's ruined," she said. "We'll just have to adjust." She reached across the table, took his hand. Remembering her conversation at the pawnshop, she said, "Besides, I have a new ally. Mr. Gold."

"Him?" Henry said, his eyes alight. "He's worse than her."

"I'm not so sure about that," Emma said. "And besides, he has some good ideas."

But Henry was inconsolable, and he retreated into himself as she tried to cheer him up. In the end he crossed his arms and shook his head. "Good never wins," he said again. "It just doesn't." He took a breath and looked up at her. "It's like with Rumplestiltskin and his son."

Emma squinted. "Rumplestiltskin? The Gold guy? He didn't have a son."

Henry rolled his eyes. "His son is only like the most important thing in his life."

"Is he?" Emma said, remembering what Archie had told her weeks ago: It's his language. "I didn't know that."

"He was this huge coward, before he got magic. He was like the laughingstock of his whole village. Except his son, Baelfire, really loved him and didn't care."

Henry then told Emma the story of how Rumplestiltskin first gained power, after his hubris led him to be tricked by a wizard named Zoso, locked in a curse that had tormented him for decades. Zoso tricked Rumplestiltskin into taking the curse onto himself. It gave him powerful magic, but it interfered with his ability to feel, his ability to be human. And it made his son, Bae, fear him instead of love him.

"That's sort of horrible," Emma said, wondering what Henry might be trying to communicate with this particular story. She wondered if it had something to do with her new role as sheriff.

"You're right," Henry said. "And the worst part is, it's just another story where good loses. Zoso is the bad guy and he wins."

"Seems sort of like Rumplestiltskin is the bad guy, though," Emma said.

"Yeah," Henry said. "I know. But he didn't used to be."

. . .

EMMA FUMED FOR THE REST of the afternoon and decided, after she'd closed up the office, that she had to say something to Regina.

She'd seen the paper all over town and knew everyone was reading it. And her anger wasn't about the election or the smear campaign, not really. It was that Henry now knew something she hadn't wanted him to know, and no one—not Regina, not Sidney Glass, not anyone—had the right to tell her secrets.

She went to Town Hall. The light was on in Regina's upstairs office, where she'd been earlier in the day, and Emma stormed in without knocking.

Regina, startled, gasped when she looked up from her paperwork.

"Those were juvie records," Emma said. "You had no right. I know you want Sidney to win, but you had no right."

"It's far easier to win public elections when you haven't been to jail, Ms. Swan. I think the people deserve to know who they're getting for a sheriff, don't you? It's about Henry also. He should know the truth, too. Shouldn't he?" Emma said nothing. Regina, already bored with the conversation, returned to her paperwork. "Besides, you can discuss this during the debate and clear up any inaccuracies. How does that sound?"

"What debate?"

Regina stood and put a few folders into her briefcase. "The debate. It's tomorrow." She smiled curtly, straightened her suit, and strode past Emma and out of the office.

Emma followed. "Nice to know that," she said.

"You and Sidney can bicker for as long as you want," Regina said. "The truth will come out eventually, it always does. Maybe the town will even get to hear about who you're in bed with for this campaign. That would be interesting." They were at the back stairwell now. Regina opened the door, and the two women went down the steps. When they came to the first-floor landing, Regina stopped and said, "Don't you think they should know about you and Gold?" She reached for the door.

"I'm not in bed with anyone," Emma said. "I'm fighting fire with—"

Regina cried out before she could finish.

A wall of flame had greeted Regina as she pulled open the door, sending her backward into Emma, then to the ground. She fell hard against the stairs they'd just come down, and Emma, holding the railing for balance and holding her other arm up to protect her face from the heat, looked down and saw that Regina was holding her ankle. We're both gonna burn up in here, Emma thought, but she put the thought out of her mind and knelt down beside Regina. "Come on," she said.

"I can't walk," Regina said, eyeing the flames behind Emma. "The whole building is on fire." She locked eyes with Emma. "You have to—you have to get me out of here."

Emma, not one to hesitate, got up, and burst into the burning lobby of Town Hall, found a fire extinguisher, and started blowing frosted foam around herself and the doorway to the stairs, creating a pathway that would lead them both to safety.

She went back for Regina then, and she swore, before picking her up into her arms, that Regina seemed surprised that she'd returned. What does she think, I would leave her? Emma wondered, hoisting her rival into her arms. She carried her carefully through the burning lobby, sticking close to the path she'd sprayed.

Emma kicked open the door and saw police cars, fire trucks, and reporters clustered together in the circular driveway, all of them wide-eyed at the image before them: The sheriff, coated in soot and sweat, carrying the mayor out of a burning building.

The cameras all began to flash and snap.

"Put me down," Regina said. "Put me down."

EMTs rushed to them as Emma gently lowered Regina to the ground, panting as she did so. "You're complaining about how I saved your life?"

"I seriously doubt you saved my life," Regina said, pushing an oxygen mask away, scowling. "Where is Sidney?" she cried. Then, to Emma: "I doubt there was much danger."

Emma shook her head, stood, and stepped back as the authorities tended to their mayor.

There was no winning with this woman.

• • •

EMMA TALKED with the firefighters for some time after they'd hauled Regina away to the hospital and put out the fire. Something didn't feel right about any of it. A coincidental fire? When the two of them were there? And after she spent a few minutes snooping around in the debris, she knew exactly why it didn't feel right. When she found the rag, she headed straight for Gold's pawnshop.

"You started it," she said to him, slamming the rag down on his desk. "I can smell your lanolin."

Gold looked up, a careful smile on his face. "I have been here all night," he said. "I did no such thing." He glanced at the rag. "I admit there's a chemical smell. But there are a lot of chemical smells. Chemicals burn, often."

"I don't want to win like this," Emma said. "Is this what it means to have an alliance with you? Breaking the rules? It's not who I am."

"Who you are," said Gold, "is somebody who will be a real sheriff for this town, not a shill. That makes you better." Emma had nothing to say to this, and so Gold continued: "Are you ready for the debate tomorrow?"

"I haven't thought about it."

"Sidney Glass is slippery, I'm sure he will be ready. I'd advise you to come prepared."

. . .

THE PICTURE OF EMMA carrying Regina from the burning building was on the cover of the *Storybrooke Daily Mirror* the next morning, and all day, the town was abuzz with the news. Emma didn't mind the positivity and the confidence, but Gold's role in the whole thing gnawed at her all day, even as her friends—Ruby, Granny, Mary Margaret, Henry, Archie, and others—went about the business of last-minute stumping. Emma reconnected with Mary Margaret about thirty minutes before the debate, and the two of them walked to the library together.

"You're going to win," Mary Margaret said. "I can feel it. And with the picture?"

It was one positive comment too many, and Emma broke down and told Mary Margaret her suspicions about Gold's participation in the fire. Mary Margaret listened to the story, then was quiet for a long moment. As they approached the library, they joined together with the assembling crowds. It seemed as though all of Storybrooke was there to hear the debate.

"What kind of message would it send to Henry?" Emma said, the two of them climbing the stairs. "To win like that?"

"Would he ever know?"

"But that would mean lying to him," Emma said.

"But telling the truth might lead to you losing."

"I guess that's just a risk I'll have to take."

Mary Margaret nodded at this. "There it is, then," she said. "There it is."

. . .

WHEN IT CAME TIME for Emma to speak, she still wasn't sure what she was going to say. Sidney had given boilerplate answers and taken the safe route with all of Archie's questions. The audience seemed to respond positively. Based only on the energy of the applause, Emma knew, as she walked out onto the stage, that she could ride the "hero" wave all the way to the win.

But it didn't take much time out in front of the audience— the entire town, really—before she heard Mary Margaret's simple words: There it is. Sometimes things weren't all that complicated. We just make them complicated in order to hide from them.

"I'm sorry, I'm sorry," Emma said, partway through an answer she was giving about her thoughts on the local noise ordinance. She looked down at the first row and saw Henry, bright-eyed, smiling up at her. "I have to back up. I have to say something about the recent fire."

The crowd went still. Emma didn't know if she was about to make a big mistake, but she knew she had to do it.

"Mr. Gold started that fire," she said, and the gasps were audible. "And he started that fire," she continued, "because he was trying to help me win this election. Make me into a hero." She took a breath, waited for the whispers and shocked chatter to quiet. "I know, I know," she said. "And I'm sorry." She looked at Regina, who sat beside Henry, arms crossed, a mixture of surprise and smug satisfaction on her face. "Regina," Emma said, "I didn't know about it, but I can't condone it, and I can't benefit from it. You could have been hurt. What's most important is to tell the truth about what happened."

She could see, at the back of the room, Mr. Gold stand, an impassive look on his face. He turned and walked toward the exit.

"This will probably cost me the election," Emma said. "But I don't want to win with a lie."

. . .

AFTERWARD, Emma and Henry went to Granny's Diner. Sweets for Henry. A stiff drink for Emma. She hadn't felt this low in some time.

Henry seemed okay with the outcome. After taking his last bite of pie, he wiped his mouth, reached into his backpack, and pulled out Graham's old walkie-talkies. He gave one to her.

"What's this for?" Emma said.

"I thought about it some more," Henry said. "I think Operation Cobra should be back on. You stood up to Mr. Gold. You're a hero."

"You think?" Whatever the outcome, she was glad to hear him say it.

"I told you that he turned bad after he got his powers," Henry said. "And after that, the one person he loved was afraid of him. So what if that same thing had happened to you?"

"What do you mean?"

"What if you got your power by being bad, like he did? That would mean that whatever you did, it would always be scary. Maybe you would win, but we would all start to be afraid of you."

"So you're revising your ideas about good and evil, then?"

"A little bit," Henry said, smiling. "I guess I didn't know you could win in the right way. Lots of these stories don't have examples of that."

"Aw. You're melting my heart, kid."

"I would rather be good like you and lose, than be bad and win."

It was the first time Emma had felt good about anything in days.

The good feeling was ruined a few moments later when Emma looked up and saw Regina at the door, Sidney following close behind. Here they come to gloat, she thought. Just what I need.

"Victory party is in back," she said.

Sidney didn't respond; he didn't look particularly joyful.

Emma looked to Regina. "Congratulations," Regina said flatly.

"What are you talking about?" Henry said.

"It was a close vote, but people seem to have responded to a candidate who can stand up to Mr. Gold." She shook her head. "Imagine that."

"You're kidding me."

"She doesn't kid," said Sidney, sitting down beside Emma and Henry.

"You didn't pick a very good friend in Mr. Gold, Ms. Swan. But he does make a superlative enemy. Enjoy that."

Emma couldn't help but smile just a little.

She was sheriff.

Sheriff of Storybrooke, Maine.

Everyone who helped out with her brief campaign began to trickle in to celebrate, all of them telling Emma that she'd done the right thing. As Emma smiled and accepted their congratulations, she couldn't help but think: *I'm a lot of things, but I'm not a liar.* She was glad her son knew that, too.

· · ·

MR. GOLD was already at the station waiting for Emma when she arrived. She had walked over from Granny's, a little tipsy, intent on taking care of some paperwork before the start of her first official day. When she arrived, she saw it right away: Graham's leather jacket, hanging on the hook beside his desk.

"I thought you might want it after all," came a voice, and Emma jumped. Her hand went to her sidearm and she almost drew the weapon.

Gold was standing in the corner, grinning, resting on his cane.

"How did you get in here?"

"The doors were unlocked," he said, strolling over. "Anyhow, I wanted to congratulate you on your victory. Very well done, Ms. Swan. Your performance tonight was commendable."

"If you're angry with me for throwing you under the bus, I'm not going to apologize," she said. "I didn't ask for the fire."

"No, you didn't," he said. "And you didn't ask for the opportunity to stand up to me. But you got both. And you used them well."

Emma frowned. "What do you mean by that?"

"I mean you needed something big to win," he said. "And I gave you something big."

Chilled by the look in Gold's eyes, Emma considered his words. She could see what he was implying: that he had planned for more than just the fire. He had planned for her telling the truth, too. And she had done exactly what he'd hoped she would do.

"Why— I don't understand," Emma said. "Why would you want me to be sheriff that badly?"

"Oh, I don't know," said Gold, crossing the room, heading for the door. "You never know. You do owe me a favor, remember. Perhaps I just wanted you to be in a position to grant a good one. When the time comes for you to clear the books."

"Clear the books," Emma repeated, still processing the extent of Gold's deviousness. Never trust him again, she thought. Never.

"We'll find a way," he said, opening the door. "Don't worry." He nodded once more. "Congratulations, Ms. Swan."

Emma went to her desk, a little weak in the knees. She looked at her picture of Henry.

She didn't know what to think.

CHAPTER 8

7:15 a.m.

FTER SHE AND THE PRINCE WENT THEIR separate ways, Snow White penetrated deeper into the forest, continuing to survive off the land as she concealed herself from the Queen's minions, adding more rugged coats of dirt and toughness to her royal exterior, becoming a stronger and more self-sufficient woman. A bandit. Someone alone, but unafraid.

From time to time, her old friend Red Riding Hood would journey out to the woods to bring supplies to the small hunter's cabin Snow White had occupied. And—though she did not like to admit it—to bring her news of Charming's marriage plans.

She loved him. Somehow, out on that troll bridge, she had fallen in love with him, and it had taken her months to realize it. "What news do you have for me, then?" she asked Red one afternoon, when the two women met in a pasture, miles and miles from the kingdom, not far from the hidden hunting cabin.

"The wedding is happening in two days," said Red with sympathy. "He will marry Midas's daughter. He has agreed."

Snow White felt her hope fade a little more. He was with

someone else—it was a simple truth. She was stuck in a fantasy, some silly story that did not resemble reality. It was the kind of thing a child might do. She disliked credulous people on principle, and now she was showing herself to be one of them.

"I only wish," she said, "I could get him out of my head. It's like a madness."

"I have heard of a man," said Red, "who is capable of even the unholiest of requests."

Snow White was surprised. Could magic truly accomplish such a feat?

"What is this man called?" she said.

"Rumplestiltskin," said Red. "Have you heard the name?"

"No," said Snow White. "I haven't. And what a funny name it is."

. . .

IT WAS SATURDAY MORNING, and the town was abuzz. There was a storm coming to Storybrooke, and Mary Margaret wanted to be ready. She also wanted to avoid the diner at all costs, as she had been going there too often. So had David.

She had developed a sort of hidden, totally deniable plan to "bump into" him at the diner every morning. At first, Mary Margaret had liked seeing him, as it was the only time she ever had with him, but she knew that it was unhealthy, dangerous, and stupid. Emma thought so, too. She'd caught Mary Margaret the day before, figured it out, and told her it was a bad idea.

"You're going to get yourself hurt," Emma said. "You're playing with fire."

"You're right," Mary Margaret said. "You're right."

So instead of the diner, she went to the drugstore soon after she woke up and stocked up on batteries, bottled water, and a few other essentials. She hated storms and she always had. She couldn't remember why—something to do with the way clouds swirled in the sky and the world seemed different and changing. She didn't like the chaos.

She was thinking these thoughts when she came to the end of an aisle and ran smack-dab into Kathryn.

The two collided with such force that they both dropped everything they were carrying.

"I'm so sorry, I'm so sorry," Mary Margaret said, going to her knees to pick up her own items and help Kathryn with hers. It was mortifying enough to see the woman, let alone talk to her, let alone run into her.

Judging by the nervousness plastered all over Kathryn's face, she was feeling something similar.

"It's okay," Kathryn said. "It's fine."

She gathered her batteries, and Kathryn handed her the water. Mary Margaret reached for one more item, a small white box, and handed it to Kathryn, ready to apologize once more. Then she realized what she was holding.

It was a pregnancy test.

"Thank you," Kathryn said, taking the box and offering one more tense and apologetic smile.

. . .

WALKING HOME, Mary Margaret found herself fighting back tears. She dropped off her things and went out to the woods near the edge of town. She wanted to walk and clear her head.

She parked and headed off down the trail, still rattled by what she'd seen at the store. Why, though? She still hardly knew David, and had no understanding of why she'd fallen in love with him—love or whatever it is, she thought. A more reasonable point of view would be to note that Kathryn was pregnant, feel a quick pang of envy, and move on, happy for both her and David. But when she'd seen the box, she'd felt devastated. She'd felt like her heart had been ripped out of her chest and shown to her. None of it made any sense. And even if—

Mary Margaret stopped.

In the brush, just beside the trail, was a dove.

The dove looked hurt, or sick—she couldn't tell. It seemed to be caught up in a netting or a mesh screen, its feet tangled and trapped. It was upright and awake, but it was quivering, terrified, and struggling to move, raising its wings as though readying itself to take off, only to lower them again.

She knelt down.

"What's wrong, girl?" she said. "What did you get bound up in?"

The dove simply cooed.

Mary Margaret picked it up. She had to take it to the animal shelter. That David worked there was irrelevant.

That said, she was fairly sure he worked on Saturdays.

She took the stunned and wounded bird back to her car and drove directly to the shelter, intent on helping it rejoin its flock. When she saw David, the sting of the pregnancy test was still on her mind and she asked for the head of the shelter, a veterinarian named Thatcher.

With David and Mary Margaret watching, Dr. Thatcher cut the webbing from the bird's feet, examined the wings, and determined that there were no broken bones. "There is some bad news, unfortunately," he told Mary Margaret. "This is a North Atlantic dove. Migratory species, very unique among American doves. They form strong, monogamous bonds, meaning—"

"Meaning she has to get back to her flock or she'll be alone. Forever."

"That's right," said Dr. Thatcher. "That's not to say she wouldn't be happy here, on her own, but with the storm coming, the window of time is closing for her to get back to where she belongs."

"So I need to find her flock," Mary Margaret said, "and release her as it flies by. I need to get her back out to where I found her."

"It might work," said Dr. Thatcher, getting a small cage from the closet. He brought it to the table and set it beside the bird. "I wouldn't keep you from trying. It's probably the happiest ending, anyhow." He smiled and scrubbed his hands. "Good luck," he said as he was walking out the door. "If you don't find the flock, feel free to bring her back here."

"Listen," David said. "With this storm coming, I'm not so sure you should be—"

"Don't look after me," she said. "I don't need your help."

David watched her, a little hurt. "Did I do something?" he said. "I don't understand what—"

"You didn't do anything, David," Mary Margaret said, gathering up the cage. "Nothing at all."

She walked out the door.

. . .

IT WAS A MISTY NIGHT on the lake when Snow White met Rumplestiltskin. After Red had told her of the mysterious wizard, she hadn't been able to shake the idea of a spell that could free her of her love—or at least her thoughts—for a man who was not available to her. She sent word through the birds of the forest and Rumplestiltskin obliged her with a meeting.

Snow had just tied off when she turned and saw him sitting across from her in her own rowboat. She jumped, sucked in her breath.

"You really are the fairest, aren't you?" he said, a wry and terrifying grin on his shadowed face.

Snow White wondered what could compel a man to do such terrible things in exchange for magic.

She leaned toward him, tilted her head. She was afraid but fascinated.

"Looking at something?" Rumplestiltskin said.

"I am in need of a cure," she said finally. "For love."

Rumplestiltskin began to laugh. "Love!" he cried. "Such a fancy and beautiful thing. So wonderful, so painful. Am I right?"

"I would like to not be in love anymore," she said. "Can you make a spell?"

"I cannot," he said. "Love is too powerful to eradicate, unfortunately. What I can do, however, is create a spell that makes you forget your beloved. Perhaps not quite the same, I know. But it can do the job."

Snow White considered this. What was the difference? To not remember love or to not be in love? To her it was the same.

"Yes," she said. "I want that."

"Very well," said Rumplestiltskin, who produced a slender vial and dipped it into the river. When he withdrew the full vial, he passed a skeletal hand over the water, and a white glow came from the liquid. He smiled.

"That's all?" she said.

He reached forward and plucked a hair from her head,

causing her to reel back and yelp. The boat knocked against the dock.

"Not quite yet," he said, amused by her surprise. "Not all loves are the same. I have to make it slightly more . . . personal." He dropped the hair into the potion and put a cork in the top. "There," he said, handing it to her. "Drink this and you will forget your true love, and all of the stories of the two of you."

Forget our stories? Snow White thought, wondering if the pain of forgetting them would be worse than the pain of not having Charming.

"Don't doubt yourself now, dearie," said Rumplestiltskin. "Love makes us sick. It haunts our dreams and destroys our days. It starts wars and ends lives. Love has killed more than any disease. The cure? This is a gift."

"And what's the price?"

"The price?" he said, as though he hadn't yet thought of it. Snow White was skeptical. But Rumplestiltskin merely grinned again and held up a few more of her hairs, which had come from his original pluck. "These will do just fine," he said.

"What do you want of my hair?"

"What do you need of it now that I have it?" he asked in response.

Snow White couldn't think of why she'd need it back, and decided she didn't care. The price seemed very low.

· · ·

SNOW WHITE JOURNEYED BACK to her corner of the forest. She rowed her boat upstream through the night, then hiked on foot throughout the morning, stopping once to eat. She avoided looking at the vial in her tunic pocket, as she did not want to see it. It was one thing to fantasize about a potion and another thing entirely to have the potion. Did she really want to forget him? Even if he did get married? Was it not a part of her, either way, to have loved him and to have known of that love? Who would she be if she didn't remember? Someone else completely?

The debate raged in her mind all morning and into the afternoon. She would go an hour having decided not to drink the potion, but then a pang of sadness would come as she imagined the wedding, and the scales would tilt again, and she'd become determined to swallow it right then and there. Back and forth she went, unsure what to do, until she reached a familiar glen, looked up, and realized she was home—back, at least, to her cabin, where she'd been staying. Seeing the modest little structure, she was filled with sadness again, knowing she would spend the night alone, and the next night alone, and the next night after that. She didn't want to face a life like this with the weight of regret, too. She took the vial from her pocket, pulled the cork, raised it to her lips—

In the sky, directly above, she saw a lone dove circling, descending toward her.

Frozen, she watched as it circled down and landed at her feet.

There was a scroll attached to its feet, in a tiny cylindrical satchel. She quickly opened it and read it, and as the words moved through her mind, her heart billowed with both joy and hope.

The note read:

Dearest Snow,

I've not heard from you since our meeting and can only assume you've found the happiness you so desired. But

I must let you know, not a day goes by that I have not thought of you. And, alas, I am incapable of moving on until I know for certain my love is unrequited. In two days' time, I'm to be married. Come to me before then. Come to me and show me you feel the same and we can be together forever. And if you don't, I'll have my answer. But if there is any doubt in your mind, lay it to rest. I love you, Snow White.

For All Eternity,
Your Prince Charming

She looked up, eyes alight. Hastily, she put the cork back in the vial. Tucking the note back into her pocket, she turned and started back down the path she'd arrived on.

She had to get to the castle before it was too late.

. . .

MARY MARGARET was in the middle of the woods, and she didn't care whether a storm was coming. She cared about one thing: a bird.

She was determined to get the dove back to its proper place in the world. The idea of a living creature—dove, person, deer, wolf, dog, bluebird, it didn't matter—being forced into a position that wasn't right, that went against the true nature of things . . . well, it was too much for her to bear. She wanted to do what she could.

David had called fifteen minutes earlier and she had refused to pick up, knowing it would inevitably be a mixed signal of some kind.

The rain began with a trickle. Mary Margaret was not far

from the road, and she'd found an open pasture with a good view of the sky. From here she could see the flock coming by. She was hoping for a miracle, she knew that, but what else could she do? Her hope was that the flock would be stirred by the rains and would fly south, attempting to avoid the bad weather. If they did, she would catch them here.

She waited for twenty minutes as the rain became more intense. Finally, she heard thunder in the distance and knew that it wasn't safe to be where she was, not anymore. Soaked and disheartened, she picked up the cage and began the trudge back toward the road. This is insane, she thought. This is desperate and weird and insane. What are you doing?

She didn't have time to answer herself, however. Just then, lightning struck somewhere nearby, and a powerful clap of thunder made her jump. When she did, she stumbled backward and slipped in the mud. She felt the ground giving out beneath her feet and reached wildly for a thin tree, which she barely managed to grasp. Panicked, splayed out on her belly, she looked over her shoulder and slipped down the slope toward a ravine, her feet dangling below her torso. The rain was now a downpour, and she couldn't see how deep the ravine went. She was in trouble. Real trouble.

Until she saw the hand reaching toward her.

"Mary Margaret!" yelled David, leaning toward her. "I found you, thank God! Take my hand!"

She did, and he pulled her up, and together (with the dove), they ran to a nearby cabin, which David had spotted through the woods. It was locked, and no one was there, so David kicked in the door, and they spilled inside, so glad to be out of the rain. They were both soaked and shivering.

"We need to get you dry," David said. "Hold on." He began looking around for blankets, towels, and any dry clothes.

"Whose cabin is this?" she asked. "Do you think it's okay that we're here?"

"Your roommate is the sheriff, I doubt she'll care," he said. He'd found a blanket, and he brought it to her, wrapped it around her shoulders. They were close. Very close.

And then Mary Margaret pulled away.

"Don't," she said. "Please."

"I don't understand what's wrong," he said.

"What's wrong is that I still have feelings for you, David." David just looked back.

"Why do you think I'm at Granny's every morning at the same time, right when you're there? It's just to see you. I don't care about being punctual, it's not a coincidence, I . . . I just want to see you. And I don't. And I do. I can't— I don't know what to do."

David, throughout this speech, could not help but conceal the faintest of smiles. He looked dazzled, a little confused.

"What?" Mary Margaret said.

"You come at seven-fifteen every morning to see me?" he said.

"Yes," she said. "It's embarrassing. Don't gloat."

He shook his head. "I'm not gloating."

"What, then?"

"I come at seven-fifteen every morning to see you, Mary Margaret," he said. "We're doing the same thing."

They both stepped forward then, and embraced. Wordlessly, they got closer and closer, until their lips nearly touched. David's eyes were already closed when Mary Margaret suddenly pulled back. His eyes opened, a look of confusion on his face.

"How can you do this to Kathryn, David?" Mary Margaret whispered. She thought: How can I do this? This isn't me.

"What do you mean?" he said. "I've told you, I don't feel a—"

"Not that, David. I know. I know."

"Know what?"

"I know that she's pregnant."

It did not produce the reaction Mary Margaret had expected. What had she assumed? Some denial, some kind of rationalization, which she was beginning to see David was very good at coming up with. Instead, though, he looked legitimately surprised.

"What did you say?" he asked.

He doesn't know, she thought. He doesn't know she's pregnant.

. . .

EMMA TRIED TO TRACK DOWN the "stranger" all day. Someone—some man—had ridden into town on a motorcycle a few days ago, and he was making most of the townspeople nervous. He was also making Regina nervous—enough so that she'd come to Emma and asked her to investigate the man. He'd apparently approached Henry outside of Regina's house and asked him a number of questions.

For once, Emma agreed with her nemesis. Strangers in town asking odd questions of little boys was not exactly okay. Regardless of the boy. In this case, it was even worse.

No one knew his name, and as of right now, he wasn't even staying anywhere. He seemed to keep popping up down this street or that street, and on top of that, he had a very mysterious-looking box attached to the back of his motorcycle. She didn't like the way he lurked.

So far, she had only what she'd started with: He was a lightly bearded man in his midthirties and he rode a motorcycle. He had a certain cockiness about him, but whenever she got close to him, he always seemed to be heading in the other direction. On three separate occasions she'd seen him in town, and each time, when she started moving toward him or called out, something would come up. Either she'd be called away or he would hop on his motorcycle and disappear.

Instead of her finding the stranger, though, the stranger found her. She was sitting at a booth in the diner, trying to think of who he might be, when he sat down across from her.

"You," she said, looking up, coffee halfway to her lips.

"You've been following me around all day," he said. "I assume you want to talk."

"Why were you talking to Henry the other morning?" she said.

"You mean the little kid who came up to me and started asking me questions? Is that Henry?"

Emma said nothing.

"Does he usually ask that many questions? He seems quite . . . precocious," the man said.

"What were you doing outside of his house?"

"My bike broke down."

"That why you decided to go for a long walk with your mysterious box?"

He patted it. "Who said it's mysterious?"

"Okay. Then what's in it?"

"It's frustrating not knowing, isn't it?"

"Just tell me," she said.

"Why?" he asked. "Is it illegal to carry around a box in these parts?"

"No," she said. "Of course not."

He smiled at her, but her lips didn't even quiver.

"You really want to know what's inside, huh?"

"Yeah," she said. "I do."

"Well, you're gonna have to wait," he said. "You're gonna have to wait a long time. And watch me carry it around for a little while. Your imagination will make up all sorts of stories about it. Is it a severed head? Is it a magic machine? A stack of secret documents? What could possibly be inside of this box?"

"Don't get cute," she said. "You're very suspicious. I could get away with forcing you to show me."

"Or," he said, "we could do it the easy way. You could let me buy you a drink sometime and I'll tell you right now."

She looked back at him, trying to gauge how serious he was. She decided to call his bluff and said, "Okay. A drink it is."

"A drink?"

"Yup. One drink."

"Okay," he said. He reached over and opened the top and showed her what he had. A typewriter.

"Really?" she said.

"I'm a writer," he said. "This place is inspiring to me. That's why I'm here."

. . .

SNOW WHITE HURRIED to the castle and got to its gates the night before the wedding, only hours before Abigail was set to arrive. She snuck inside in the garb of a florist and made her way toward where she guessed Charming's quarters had to be, hiding from guards along the way. She came close, she truly did, before she stumbled in a dark corridor, and a young guard poked his head around the corner. His face tensed, and he lunged at her with surprising speed. He caught her easily and ignored her stories as he hauled her down to the dungeon, believing her to be a common thief.

The moment she was locked in her cell, she began looking for a way out. Could she pick the lock? Climb the wall? She didn't know, but she had to get out. She had to stop the wedding.

"Easy there, sister," came a voice. "You're stuck until they decide otherwise."

She looked over to the next cell, where a deep-voiced man lounged in the corner, his legs crossed.

He was bearded and bald. He smiled at her, gave a friendly wave hello.

"Good to meet you," he said.

"I don't need them to let me out of here," she said. "I'll find my own way out."

"Okay, fine," he said. "Have it your way. You'll find your own way out."

He watched her pace back and forth in her cell for some time, then said, "What's your name?"

"Snow White," she said. Did it really matter whether some common criminal knew?

"*The* Snow White?" he said, suddenly very interested. "As in Wanted-by-the-Queen Snow White?"

"One and the same," she said.

"Well, I'm Grumpy," he said, getting to his feet.

"I'm sorry to hear it."

"No, no," he said, waving her off. "That's my name."

"Your name is Grumpy?" she said, raising an eyebrow. "What kind of name is that?"

He shrugged. "It's a dwarf's name," he said. "What kind of name is Snow White?"

Snow White just smiled, and the two began to talk as she tried to find a weakness in the cell. An hour passed; they talked about many things as she grew more and more concerned that she was going to spend weeks down here, miss the wedding, miss her opportunity. Grumpy explained how he'd ended up in the cell, as did Snow White (vaguely, cautiously). They discussed love, and lost love, and regret.

Grumpy's eyes lit up when he spoke of a woman he'd once loved, and how he regretted letting her slip through his fingers.

"But doesn't love cause too much pain?" she said. "To be worth it?"

"It causes pain, indeed," Grumpy said. "But it's worth it. It's a good pain."

"Is there such a thing?"

"Yes," he said. "I guarantee that."

"I could forget my love if I chose," she said, and told him about the potion she'd gotten from Rumplestiltskin.

He seemed impressed by the idea, but after a moment, he shook his head. "No. It's not right," he said.

"Why not free yourself?"

"Because that wouldn't be real," he said. "Because it would always be deep down in you somewhere, eating at you. You can't pretend that what is true is not true. Regardless of what you remember. Give me the pain, and what's honest. I'll take that any day."

"Huh," Snow White said, and resumed her attempts at finding a way out of the cell a bit more frantically.

That is, until Grumpy explained to her that she'd be wise to conserve her energy.

"If you really want to get out," he said, "just relax. Give it ten minutes."

"How would that help me?" Snow White asked.

"You'll see," he said. "I got good friends."

She was exhausted, not only from her furtive search for an escape but from the days and days of travel . . . the deal with Rumplestiltskin, the flight to the castle . . . She allowed herself to sit down and close her eyes. She fell into a deep sleep almost immediately.

• • •

"HEY. SISTER!"

She woke to see Grumpy and another dwarf standing in her cell, both of them smiling at her.

"She's pretty," said the second dwarf. The one she didn't know.

She rubbed her eyes, got to her feet.

"What's going on?" she said. "Who's this? How did you open the doors?"

"This is Stealthy, my friend," Grumpy said, pointing at the other dwarf with his thumb. "He came to spring me and now we're springin' you. Come on."

She looked over their heads and saw a guard lying on the ground, apparently unconscious.

"But why would you do that for me?" she asked, hurrying out of the cell behind the two dwarfs. She stepped nimbly past the guard, wondering how the two of them had managed it.

"Because I sympathize with your story of heartbreak,

sister," said Grumpy, not looking back. "We've all been there. God I hate love. But I love it."

"Quiet, you two!" whispered Stealthy. He led them to a grate in the floor and pointed down at a ladder. "Come on. Down into the catacombs. Let's go."

She hurried down behind the two, wary of guards spotting them. Soon, though, they were below the castle, in the winding tunnels of the crypts, Stealthy out in front, guiding Snow and Grumpy with a torch.

They ran until Snow White could no longer breathe; she had no idea where they were going. But she trusted them, trusted Grumpy to come back for her. They could have left her there in the cell, sleeping, for all of eternity.

They reached an intersection, and Stealthy stopped. "You're trying to find the Prince?" he asked her, and she nodded.

"Go that way," he said, pointing down a long tunnel. "You'll see a ladder at the end. Take it up. You'll be at the tower you need." He patted his companion on the shoulder. "We're heading this way," he said. "Out of the castle. Come on!"

Grumpy smiled at her.

"Good-bye, sister," he said. "Good luck!"

The two dwarfs ran away, leaving her alone, in the dark.

"Good-bye," she said, into the darkness.

She didn't waste any more time.

. . .

THE RAIN STOPPED in the awkward moment after Mary Margaret said that Kathryn was pregnant. David looked shocked. Mary Margaret regretted her indiscretion, but there was something good, at least, in that David hadn't known, that he hadn't continued pursuing her nevertheless. He was not very aware of himself, but he wasn't a monster; she had to give him that. He was confused, too.

She picked up the birdcage. "Come on," she said. "Let's go get her back to her flock."

They walked in silence back to the same field Mary Margaret had been in before she fell. She looked warily at the ravine and the muck and mud where she'd nearly gone over. He'd found her. He'd found her and saved her. There was that. . . .

"Mary Margaret," he said. "We have to—"

"Shh. Do you hear that?" she said. They both looked up at the same time. "The flock!" she cried. "They must have waited for the storm to end! They're here!" Excited, she knelt in the wet grass and opened up the cage. She brought out the dove, stroked its head once more, and held it up so its beak was skyward.

It didn't take anything beyond that, just showing the dove. It burst from her hands and gained altitude quickly, flapping hard (and with what seemed like joy) as it rejoined its family.

Mary Margaret had a beaming smile on her face. She hadn't felt this happy in a long time.

David, watching too, stepped close and tried to put his arm around her.

"David, no," she said. "Don't. Please." She stepped away and hugged herself. "We can't. It's not right."

"How can you say no after we both just admitted it? I don't understand."

"Because you chose her even so, David," she said. "Why haven't you left her if you love me so much?"

"I don't know," he said. "Because I had a life with her, too. Because both paths seem right."

"You don't get to take both paths."

"It feels like one is real and the other isn't, whichever way I go."

"No matter what, somebody is going to get hurt," she said. "There's no way you're going to not hurt somebody, David. You're not accepting that."

He hung his head in thought, then looked up at the sky. "I can't stop thinking about you," he said flatly.

"I can't stop thinking about you, either," she said. "But we have to forget each other. We have to. There's no other way."

. . .

SNOW WHITE MOVED through the dark catacombs as quickly as she could, groping her way without a torch. In a matter of minutes she found the end of the corridor and the ladder, just as Stealthy had said she would, and was hauling herself up toward the light of another grate before she even bothered to test the rungs for rot. For all she knew the wedding was happening right now. There was no time for safety.

At the top of the ladder, she pushed aside a heavy wicker grate and climbed up into a courtyard. She bolted across the open area, intent on entering through a large door at the base of the tower she knew to hold the Prince's chambers. Before she could, though, she heard some yelling far across the open area. She turned just in time to see something heart-breaking: three hundred yards away, Grumpy and Stealthy had apparently been cornered by the castle guards. As she looked on in horror, Stealthy made a break for the castle's entrance.

He didn't make it.

An arrow, shot from high atop a guard tower, sailed down

and struck him in the chest. Grumpy's scream was loud enough to give her chills, even where she was.

Snow White did not hesitate to make her way to the scene, where Grumpy was still in danger, kneeling beside the body of his fallen friend. She pulled a torch from the wall as she ran, leaping over a pile of toppled barrels, and made her way behind the group of men who'd cornered her new friend. Just as she heard the captain of the guard order his men to kill Grumpy, she reached the first mounds of hay beside the stables. Eyes wide, she cried out to them and held the torch above the hay.

"LET HIM GO!" she demanded, once they'd turned to see her.

Silence.

"I SAID LET HIM GO," she repeated. "OR I WILL BURN THIS CASTLE TO THE GROUND."

It must have been convincing, because the captain, with the flick of a wrist, told Grumpy to leave the castle and never return. His eyes red with tears and rage, Grumpy took another look at his fallen friend, then looked up to Snow White and gave a simple, subtle nod. Thank you. He turned and ran.

"A nice gesture," said the captain of the guard, walking toward her. "But something of an empty threat, don't you think?" He raised an arm, and Snow White frowned, unsure of what he meant.

She understood when she heard the screech of another arrow coming down from the tower. She braced herself for death, only to feel the torch ripped from her hand. The arrow had knocked it away from her and the hay, carrying with it her leverage, and any hope she had of survival.

"I believe King George would like to have a word, dear

girl," said the captain of the guard. "Would you mind coming with me?"

. . .

"**YOU WILL TELL HIM** you do not love him," said King George, "and that you never did. Those are my terms. They are simple. Do you agree?"

Snow White stood before the man, defiance and courage draining out of her. They'd dragged her up the stairs to the king's private chambers, where he awaited, already dressed for the wedding. He was haughty, distant. Indifferent. She hated him. She hated everything he stood for. And she could see already that he had won.

"And if I refuse?" she said.

He shrugged, pulling on a decorative gauntlet. "Then I will kill him," he said. "It makes little difference to me."

"Your own son?" she said, incredulous. "Just for spite? And politics?"

"He's not my son," said King George cryptically, not bothering to look her in the eyes. "And besides, yes. With matters of this scale, politics trump love. Every time. I'm surprised you don't understand that, considering your pedigree."

There was nothing Snow White could do—no trick, no special gambit. She could not give the Prince a secret code, some hidden signal, because that would simply mean he would come for her, and that would mean his death. She not only had to reject him, she had to convince him to stay away. She had to hurt him.

And she did. The king "allowed" her to sneak into Charming's chambers, where the Prince prepared for his wedding. She went sadly. She slipped into his room without a noise and, concealed behind a curtain, watched him for a minute or two, her heart breaking into tiny shards as each second passed. He was moving slowly. He was looking out of the window, sighing, waiting. Waiting for her.

"Prince James," she heard herself saying.

He spun, and Snow White revealed herself.

"You came!" he cried, going to her. He tried to embrace her, and she allowed it, for a moment, but stood stiffly in his arms. Eventually he stepped back and looked at her, confused. "You got my letter, then?" he said.

"I did."

"Then you came to tell me that you love me, too," he said. "Why else would you come? What is the matter?"

"No, James," she said, not allowing herself to use her name for him. Even that was painful. "I came to do the opposite. I came to tell you that I don't love you, and that I never did. You are . . . confused."

It was as though she were again witnessing the arrow striking Stealthy in the chest, only this time she had been the one to shoot. He crumpled at her words. He took a step back, looked at her.

"I feel nothing for you," she said. "Marry Abigail. Be happy with her. Forget about me. I don't love you." All of it in a monotone.

"I don't believe you," he said, finally, failing to contain the anger and pain he was obviously feeling. "You— If you believed that, you wouldn't have come."

"It's true," she said, stepping toward the door. "Believe me, it's true. I didn't want you to waste your life thinking otherwise."

She turned and left the room.

She was out the door, and a safe distance away, before she burst into tears.

. . .

ON HER WAY BACK into the forest, Snow White traveled slowly, again caught in the same loop of vacillating about the potion. It hurt much worse now, it did. She did not think she could bear it for long, even if it was more "real" to live with the pain. Whenever she imagined that the wedding would soon happen, that it would be over, that she would never see him again—well, she cried as she walked away from the castle.

Over her own sniffling, she heard a deep voice in the trees off the path: "Hey, sister."

Startled, distracted by her thoughts, she jumped back. She watched as a number of moving forms emerged from the cover of the forest and slowly surrounded her.

It was only after a moment of panic that she realized she recognized a face. Grumpy's. The two hugged. She was relieved to see anyone she knew.

"And did you find him?" Grumpy asked her. "Did you set the record straight?"

"I found him," she said, "but I didn't say what I should have said."

"You'll be all right, won't you?" he asked, smiling warmly, putting an arm around her. "It'll be okay." When he saw that she was about to cry again, he said, "Here, here. Meet my friends. All six of 'em. Let me introduce you and get your mind off this. If we don't start laughing about something soon, we're all gonna start crying."

"I'm so sorry," she said. "Stealthy. I—I'm so wrapped up in my own—"

"It's okay, it's okay," he said. "We'll remember him and pay our respects. There's a lot of time for that. Let's say hello for now."

She smiled at them all, and they each in turn smiled back. Then Grumpy went through the names, one by one.

. . .

HE TOOK HER to the spacious hovel of the seven dwarfs—a place with friends, a place with companions. The days passed, and she tried to adjust to her new life, but each night, she would think of him, and imagine his new life. The pain got worse and worse.

And then one morning, Grumpy ran toward her room, elated with the news he had received. The wedding hadn't happened! The Prince had left the castle, presumably in search of Snow White, and had left Abigail at the altar. George had issued a bounty on his head. The kingdom was in an uproar! Prince Charming, her true love, was at that moment searching for her!

"He left!" Grumpy cried, a smile on his face as he looked at her. She was in her bed, just waking up. He went to her bedside. "The Prince has left Abigail and searches for you! Come on! You can be together!"

Snow White frowned.

"Is it not what you wanted?" Grumpy asked, confused. But then he saw the vial on her small bedside table.

Empty.

"Who?" said Snow White. "What Prince?"

Grumpy was too late.

She had drunk the potion and erased her memory.

Grumpy smiled sadly at her. "Aw, sister," he said. "You couldn't hold out anymore, could you?"

"I don't understand," she said.

"That's okay," he said, taking her hand. "That's okay."

. . .

MARY MARGARET AND DAVID HAD MANAGED to avoid each
other. Neither went to the diner. But it was only a matter of
time before their paths crossed again.

And not at 7:15, but at 7:45.

7:46, to be precise.

They ran into each other at Granny's. Eventually, the two
of them ended up standing beside each other on the sidewalk,
both holding coffee, both perfectly aware of one another. Each
had tried to alter the schedule for the other, and each had
ended up altering it in the same way.

They walked a few paces together. David said, "I'm trying
not to see you." He shook his head. "How do we stop seeing
each other?"

"Apparently, we can't," said Mary Margaret.

"That's a problem."

"You're right," she said. "It is."

They looked at each other.

"She's not pregnant," David said.

Mary Margaret absorbed this information, then seemed
ready to speak. But she didn't. Instead, she dropped her coffee.
Neither looked down.

David dropped his coffee then, too, and they leaned toward one another.

The kiss, after they'd both waited so long, was like nothing
either had ever felt before.

CHAPTER 9

SKIN DEEP

INTER HAD DESCENDED ON THE TOWN WITH a vengeance, bringing with it all manner of accidents and emergencies. Emma rarely saw Mary Margaret and only sometimes managed to get around Regina's increasing efforts to keep her away from Henry. An hour here or there, but never enough. She missed the kid, but nothing was simple in this town. Not with Regina around.

She was working all the time, though, and was part of a community now. Which was different. She was glad for it, truly, but things had changed since those first fall days, when the only reason she was in Storybrooke was to keep Henry safe. What was happening now? She was sinking into something, something both comfortable and complacent. Was this what roots felt like? Was there a difference between rooted life and imprisonment? Winter had made her sleepy with security. Time passing had made this place feel normal.

Heading toward the station after telling Mary Margaret, Ruby, and Ashley that she wouldn't be joining their Valentine's Day girls' night, she got a call from dispatch.

"What's up?" she asked.

Someone, it seemed, had just been seen breaking into Mr. Gold's house.

"I'm on it," she said, and snapped shut her phone. She dumped her coffee and jogged east on foot. It took her all of five minutes to get to Gold's home, a tall and slender mansion on the town's east side, where the wealthiest citizens lived. A neighbor had called in because the front door was wide open, and when Emma arrived, she saw that it was still true.

She drew her sidearm on her way in.

Gold's house was full of antiques and antique furniture: armoires, writing desks, fainting couches, and velvet pillows made the place feel more like a Parisian coffee parlor than a twenty-first-century home. Emma made a sweep of the house, going room to room with her weapon drawn, announcing herself before each turn.

When she came back down the stairs, she heard footsteps and felt her heart begin to pound. Someone had come in the front door and was now moving into the front parlor. Quietly, Emma crossed the kitchen, steadied herself, and turned into the room, gun out and at the ready.

"Freeze!" she heard herself saying sternly, even before she'd planted her front foot.

The figure in front of her turned and swung a weapon toward her; Emma squeezed the trigger, feeling it press back against the back of her finger. She kept herself from going all the way.

"Ms. Swan," the intruder said.

It was Mr. Gold.

Emma lowered her gun and exhaled. Gold lowered his gun as well.

"I can't imagine you're the one breaking into my house," he said.

"You got a permit for that?" Emma asked, looking at his weapon.

"Of course," he said. "Do you have one for yours?"

"Cute," she said, holstering her gun.

She pointed at a broken glass case in the corner of the room. "Looks like whoever it was was after something specific," she said. "I just got the call and came over. House is clear."

Gold, quiet for once, stood looking at the glass case.

"I see," he said finally. He swallowed once. "That will be all."

"Will it, now?" Emma said. "I'm so sorry to bother you."

"That's not what I meant," Gold said. "I apologize. It's a shock to the system when one's home is invaded." He took a breath, gave her a smile. "Although I do think I can give you a strong lead, considering what was taken. I believe the man you should speak to is named Moe. Moe French."

"Okay," Emma said. "I'll check him out." She eyed Gold suspiciously. "Any reason you're worried about him in particular?"

"I imagine there will be some paperwork," he said. "Would you like tea?"

. . .

MARY MARGARET WAS EXCITED about the idea of going out with the girls, even though it was, of course, a replacement for what she really wanted to do—spend a normal Valentine's Day on a date with the man she loved. But that wasn't possible.

On the sidewalk, though, David jogged to catch up to her. "I need to talk to you," he called.

A nervous cloud overtook her face when she realized he aimed to talk to her out in the open. Since the kiss, they'd tried hard to be more discreet. She had no interest in being known as a home wrecker. She couldn't believe he was being so brazen.

"I don't think we should—"

"I don't want you to do this girls' night thing," he said. "I just don't. That's all."

It made her furious. "Do you really think you have any right to tell me what I should do?" she said. "Considering?"

"No, I don't," he admitted. "But I still don't want you to go. Considering."

"Well, I'm sorry," she said, "but I don't have anything to do on Valentine's. I have no one to take me out. So I'm going to do something fun." She shook her head. "I'm tired, David," she said. "I'm so tired of secrecy. I don't want to keep doing this."

"I don't want this to be the situation," he said. "I feel like you're punishing me."

"Funny," she said. "That's how I feel every day. About you."

"Where is this coming from?" he said. "Just the other day we were—"

"I don't know, David," she said. "Maybe I woke up to something. Or maybe I remembered something. About respecting myself. I just can't help feeling like you'd go on like this forever if I gave you the chance."

"That's not true."

"Isn't it?"

David looked deflated by this comment, but she didn't feel bad for him. She felt bad for herself. She walked away.

· · ·

EMMA CALLED GOLD when she got back to the station, and soon he was there, an eager look in his eyes. She showed him to her desk and to the items she'd discovered at Moe French's home.

Sloppy work, really. Hilariously, or perhaps just idiotically, Moe French had even used a pillowcase to steal Gold's antiques. She'd acquired a warrant and searched his home. Standard stuff. The pillowcase, still full, was sitting on his kitchen table. No sign of French.

"It's not here," Gold said, after a moment of scanning the desk.

There were lamps and candelabras, nice pieces of china, cigarette cases, pieces of jewelry.

"These aren't your things?" Emma asked, surprised.

"They are," Gold said, irritated. "But not everything. He took something very specific. And very valuable to me." He brushed past her, heading toward the door. "I wish you knew how to do your job."

What's stuck in his craw? Emma wondered.

"It might help if you told me what it was you were looking for, Gold," Emma said, watching him storm away. Even for him, this was prickly. "I'm running in the dark here. How about a hint?"

"No matter," he said, over his shoulder. "Please find Mr. French. He'll lead you to the rest."

"Who is he to you?"

"A client."

"An enemy?"

"A client."

He stopped and turned just enough to look at her sidelong.

"If you can't find him, I'll take matters into my own hands."

"Don't do anything stupid, Gold," she said.

"Thank you for the warning," he said. "I never do."

. . .

DAYTIME BLED into the night, and darkness overtook Story-brooke. Emma, despite her best efforts, could not locate Moe French, and as she drove up and down the streets of the town, she wished that Graham were here with her to help. He'd always had a knack for finding people, hadn't he? Nothing had been quite the same without him.

Their kiss, that last kiss, still lingered.

Mary Margaret met Ruby and Ashley at the Rabbit Hole. She smiled along with the other two as Ashley told some funny stories about what a handful the baby was some days. She listened diligently as Ruby described her problems dating and complained about how difficult it was to find a good guy in Storybrooke. She wanted to tell them more about David, and to describe how frustrating it had been to be with someone in secret, but it wasn't time, and she couldn't do that to him. She loved Ruby, but she was afraid that the story would be all around town by tomorrow morning if Mary Margaret admitted to the affair.

"What about you, Mary Margaret?" Ashley said, after Ruby seemed finished with her outburst.

"What about me?"

"Your love life," Ashley said. "Anything new with Dr. Whale?"

"God no," Mary Margaret said, frowning and taking another sip of her drink. "That was a huge mistake."

"I think it's kinda fun that you guys hooked up," said Ruby. "He might be bad news, but he's hot bad news."

"I just—" Mary Margaret didn't finish the sentence, though. She couldn't believe what she was seeing. Across the room, at the bar, David was sitting down next to Archie. The two of them were chatting, but he cast a furtive glance in her direction.

"What?" Ashley said, looking where she was looking. "OMG," she said when she saw David. "What a weird match."

"I don't think they're dating," Ruby said, and the two of them laughed. "Wouldn't that be funny, though?"

"Don't you think it's weird that he's not spending Valentine's with Kathryn, though?" said Ashley. "What's he doing here?"

Mary Margaret ordered another drink. She knew, of course. He was here to check up on her.

She ignored him for the duration.

When it was time to go, Mary Margaret gathered up her things, said good-bye to the girls—who protested, but she was exhausted—and left the Rabbit Hole. David followed, just as she had guessed he would, and when the two were a few blocks away, he called out to her, and she turned.

When he caught up, Mary Margaret said, "I saw you in there. It was creepy."

"What do you mean, creepy?" he asked.

"I don't need you stalking me," she said. "It's bad enough as it is. What will people think?"

"I don't know," he said. "A part of me doesn't care."

"Well I do," she said, arms crossed. "It's a small town. And what we're doing isn't right."

David absorbed this, nodded, and reached into his jacket. He pulled out the card and handed it to her.

"I got you a Valentine's card," he said. "Here."

Mary Margaret accepted the card, against her better judgment, and opened it.

She read it, frowned, and looked at David, holding it up: "Kathryn, I woof you?"

David looked surprised. "It's the wrong one, I'm so sorry,"

he said, plucking it out of her hand. He reached into his jacket and produced the other card. "Here, here. This is the right one."

She took the second card, but did not open it.

Instead, she looked sadly at David.

"This isn't working," she said. "We both know it."

"We can make it work," he said. "Just give me time. Please, Mary Margaret."

She sighed. "You should go home to Kathryn," she said.

"I'm going to," he said. "But I thought it was important to wish you happy Valentine's Day. I did."

"Well, thanks," she said stiffly. "Happy Valentine's Day to you, too."

．　．　．

EMMA HAD HAD A STRANGE DAY. After a few hours hunting down Gold's missing property, she'd become very suspicious of his intentions. Something told her that Gold was up to something, and that Moe French was more than just a "client."

After her strange exchange with Gold in her office, she went to the diner with a stack of papers—information about Mr. Gold's many properties in and around Storybrooke—and started digging through his holdings in search of connections to French. She was deep into an incredibly boring spreadsheet about his tax records when she looked up and saw Henry smiling at her.

"What're you doing?" he asked.

"Work," she said, sipping her coffee. "Why aren't you at home?"

"My mom's busy again," he said, sliding in across from her. "And we never get to see one another anymore."

Emma looked at him. He was right—Regina had been

working hard to keep them apart. Which made it even more frustrating that, right now, she didn't have any time to give him.

"Do you want to hear about Rumplestiltskin?"

"I'm not really in the mood, kid," she said. She looked up and frowned. "Where's your book?"

"I'm just remembering this one," he said quickly.

"I don't really have—"

"But it's crazy," he said, his eyes going wide. "There was this kingdom that needed his help, and so Rumplestiltskin went, and they said that they needed him to end the Ogre War because it was so dangerous, and in return he asked for the hand of a beautiful young—"

But Emma had spotted something on one of her papers, and she held up a hand.

Gold owned a house out in the country. A cabin.

She hadn't known that.

She had a hunch. Moe French was missing; Gold was nowhere to be seen.

She decided to go check it out.

"Sorry, kid," she said. "I have to go check on something."

"Really?" he said, slightly disappointed.

"Next time—promise," she said.

She drove out to the edge of town, then turned down an old dirt road, following the dusty map that had come along with the police cruiser. There was just something . . . Something was wrong with this whole thing. It wasn't that one person was lying. Everyone was lying. There was a whole story underneath it all, and the story was missing. She could feel its absence.

She came around a bend and saw the truck.

Moe French's truck.

Her hunch had been right.

She entered the cabin with her gun drawn, and when she did, she came across a horrid scene: Gold, manic, beating French, who was bloody and unconscious.

She stopped Gold and restrained him; he seemed to give up the second he saw her face. She called an ambulance and booked him on assault charges. The EMTs rushed French to the hospital, unsure about his chances.

Emma and Gold did not discuss much on the ride back to the sheriff's office.

.   .   .

"I KNOW WHAT YOU'RE THINKING," Emma was saying. "I owe you a favor, and you're in my jail right now. And you don't want to be in my jail. Am I right?" Having finished the processing, Emma sat at her desk, eating a sandwich. Gold was in the cell, sitting quietly, listening to her make light of the situation. She was not normally so glib. Perhaps she was trying to make the best of a bad situation.

"When I need the favor, I will take the favor," he said finally.

Emma took another bite of the sandwich and watched him carefully. Before she could respond, however, the two heard the front door and both looked up. The mayor and Henry came in.

"I was wondering if you might like to spend an hour with Henry," Regina said.

Emma finished the sandwich, looked at Regina, then back to Gold. "Let me guess. So you can talk to him alone."

Regina shrugged. "Maybe," she said. "Do you want to go with Henry or not?"

Emma nodded. "I do," she said. "Actually." She looked back at Gold. "You okay with this?"

"Of course."

"Just this once, then," Emma said to Regina.

She and Henry left.

For a few minutes they didn't speak, and Emma tried to imagine what was being said between the two very strange people in the jail. They were enemies, clearly, but Emma knew there was more to their relationship than simple animosity. It went back. There were secrets.

"What is it," Emma said finally, "about those two?"

"What do you mean?"

She shook her head. "I don't know, Henry," she said. "It was a strange day."

"What did Mr. Gold do to get in there?" Henry asked.

"He attacked someone," Emma said. "I caught him hurting a man."

"What man?"

Emma looked at him and squinted. "Moe French," she said. Henry nodded sagely but said nothing.

"What?" Emma said.

"You won't believe me if I tell you," Henry said, "so why should I tell you?"

"Entertain me."

"Well," Henry said. "Do you know how I told you that Rumplestiltskin turned kind of evil when he got his power?"

"Yes."

"A little while later, after he was all alone and his son, Bae, was gone, he met a girl and fell in love with her, and he almost turned good again."

"Almost?"

"Yeah," Henry said. "He had the choice. Right after she kissed him. And he chose to stay powerful instead of being in love and being normal. Which is exactly what happened when he lost Bae, too."

"His son died?"

"No," Henry said. "He just disappeared."

They walked in silence for a few more minutes. They were at the school now, and the night was cool and still. The leaves were gone from the trees, and the wind rattled the branches. There wasn't this kind of quiet in Boston.

"Belle," said Henry.

"What?"

"That was the girl he fell in love with," Henry said. "But after he rejected her, she went back home, and her father thought she was no longer fit to marry, and so he locked her up."

"What happened to her?"

"She killed herself," Henry said. "That's what the Queen said, anyway."

Emma thought again of the sight of Gold beating Moe French. What had she heard Gold yelling? *You sent her away!*

"And let me guess," Emma said. "Moe French was the girl's father."

"Do you even have to ask?"

Emma shook her head. This kid's fantasy life was put together pretty well, she had to admit. And there was wisdom in it, and truth. He did know a lot about this town, even if he didn't know he knew.

"Love's tough," Emma said, putting a hand on his shoulder. "So are fathers."

Henry looked up at her, then nodded. "I guess so," he said. "I guess that's true."

CHAPTER 10

WHAT HAPPENED TO FREDERICK

T SEEMED LIKE EVERY TIME EMMA SWAN cleared up a problem, two more grew in its place. Her tense ongoing conflict with Regina? Détente for now, but who knew where that would lead? The case of Gold and Moe French? Sure, she'd found Gold's property, and Mr. French had stabilized in the hospital, but Gold, with a team of lawyers, had somehow snaked his way out of prosecution and had gotten away with nothing more than a slap on the wrist as punishment for beating a man within an inch of his life. She was beginning to remember why bounty hunting was so much more appealing than law enforcement itself. It was simple to find a person. It was a lot more complicated when the whole story came into play.

She still didn't understand what had happened between Gold and the florist. She was resigned to the idea that she'd never really know.

There was more. Henry, it turned out, had lost his book during the big storm. (Or, according to him, Regina had used the storm as an opportunity to steal his book.) His castle had been knocked down by the high winds, and before anyone could lift a finger to clean up the mess, Regina had sent in the bulldozers to clear away the wreckage. She'd never liked that Henry had a special place of his own, and she'd hated that it was the place where Emma and Henry talked. Had she known that Henry's book was buried in the sand? Emma didn't know. She wouldn't put it past Regina, but she also wouldn't be surprised if the storybook wasn't sitting at the bottom of a landfill right now, a casualty of circumstance.

Henry was upset without his stories, but Emma wondered whether it might not be the best thing for him. She'd promised him she would look for the book, but so far she hadn't put much effort into it. She wouldn't mind a little more honesty and a little more reality injected into their relationship.

Seeing him at the diner one afternoon, though, she couldn't keep herself from asking him to tell her one of the stories. She thought it might help him remember his book and snap him out of his funk. And so when he looked up, mildly interested, and said, "Which one?" Emma responded by saying, "I don't know. One about love."

"Have I told you how Charming got Snow White to remember him again, after she drank the potion?"

"I don't believe so. What potion again?"

"The potion that made her forget that she'd ever known him," Henry said, the pitch of his voice rising. Emma was glad to see him snap back to life a little bit, although she didn't smile, knowing it might stop him. Instead she nodded seriously.

"That's right," she said. "Rumplestiltskin made it for her."

"Right. And she took it while she was with the dwarfs, because King George told her that he would kill Charming if she got in the way of the marriage."

"Poor girl."

"I know!" Henry said.

"But Charming went looking for her anyway."

Emma listened as Henry told the rest of the story. Charming found Red Riding Hood, and with her help, he eventually found Snow White. Snow White, however, didn't remember him, and what was more, she didn't want anything to do with him, as she'd become fixated on killing the Queen. Charming tried to stop her—several times. But it wasn't until he saved her, throwing himself in front of an arrow she'd shot at the Queen, proving to Snow White that he truly did love her, that his kiss was powerful enough to break the curse, and Snow White was able to remember who he was.

"So after that," Emma asked, "she didn't want to kill the Queen anymore?"

"She still hated her," Henry said thoughtfully. "But she had love again, and that was more important."

"And then they lived happily ever after?"

"No!" Henry said. "It was only just starting. Because right when it seemed like they'd be okay, King George's henchmen caught up to them and dragged Charming away again." Emma found herself wanting to ask him more questions, but just then, Henry stood. "I gotta go to school," he said. "If I still had the book, I'd give it to you so you could read these for yourself."

Emma smiled. "I'm still looking for it," she said. "Don't give up hope. Not yet."

Henry left, and Emma sighed, sipping her coffee. She was starting to love that kid.

She was at the till, paying Ruby, when the stranger strutted into the diner, his motorcycle helmet under his arm. Not the person she wanted to see right now. She gave him a curt nod.

"Hey," he said. "Just the person I came to see."

She rolled her eyes and collected her change from Ruby, who eyed him, then smiled at Emma.

"I was hoping we might get that drink you promised me," he said. "What do you say?"

"Here's one problem," Emma said. "I don't date guys whose names I don't know. Just a little personal policy."

He nodded again and looked down. "Fair enough," he said. "It's August. August W. Booth."

"What's the W for?" she asked.

"Wayne. Is that a deal-breaker?"

"No," Emma said. "I suppose not."

"So now you don't have a reason not to go out with me," he said. "Tonight. When you're done with work. I'll meet you right outside." He pointed at the door, gave her another smile.

He didn't wait for her response, and instead walked past her, went out the door, got on his bike, and rode away.

Confident or obnoxiously cocky? Emma couldn't quite tell. She was still standing at the till, thinking it through, when she looked up and saw Mary Margaret at the counter, in the back corner, watching her with a big, curious smile.

Emma went over.

"I didn't know you were here," Emma said. "You're hiding out like a bandit."

"You were engrossed in some kind of story with Henry," she said. "I didn't want to interrupt. More important, who was that?" she asked as Emma sat down.

"That's what I'm trying to figure out," she said. "I don't know. It's nothing."

"Nothing with you means something," said Mary Margaret. "If it really were nothing, we wouldn't be talking about it."

"What are you doing way back here, anyway?" Emma asked. "If I didn't know better, I'd say you were hiding."

"Yes," Mary Margaret said, sipping her coffee. "I am avoiding."

"Avoiding what?"

She took a deep breath.

"For the last couple of weeks," she said, "David and I have been—"

"—having an affair, I know," Emma said. She nodded at Ruby, who knew the look: more coffee. This was one of her more epic diner stops in some time.

Mary Margaret was stunned. "How did you . . . ?" she began.

"It's obvious," Emma said. "I'm the sheriff and your room-mate. But I think I would have been able to tell if I were a blind shut-in, the way you've been acting."

"I didn't realize it was that obvious."

Emma shrugged. "Yeah, well," she said. "What are you gonna do?" Just then Ruby set the coffee down in front of her, and Emma smiled her thanks.

"It's not what I'm going to do," Mary Margaret said. "It's what David is going to do. He's telling Kathryn. Today."

"Everything?" said Emma, impressed. She didn't think he had it in him. She was worried for her friend, and David seemed to be a classic manipulator in the end. Apparently it didn't matter whether you were in a coma and had your brain reset; if you had it in you to be a pig about relationships, that part stuck.

"Everything," Mary Margaret said. "Absolutely everything."

"And what brought this on?"

"She told him that she wants to move to Boston," said Mary Margaret, "and that she wants to go to law school. So it seems like everything's coming to a head."

"He's made grand proclamations before," Emma said. "And now he's got you sneaking around town. Be careful, Mary Margaret."

"I know," she said. "I know. I will."

. . .

MARY MARGARET WAS BETWEEN CLASSES, walking down the hall amid a sea of students, when her cell phone rang. Most times she wouldn't pick up, but it was David.

"Hey—did, um, did you do it?" Mary Margaret asked, trying not to sound too hopeful.

"Yeah, it was bad," he said.

"I'm sorry," she replied, trying to sound sympathetic.

"No, it was—it was really bad."

"But you told the truth—so now we can pick up the pieces. We can start over from a real place," she said, feeling a tremendous weight lift from her shoulders. Despite the people around her, she stopped walking, closed her eyes, and let it sink in. Finally. Finally they could be together.

He seemed to take a strange pause before answering.

"Hey, I want to see you. Can I come by when you get done with school?"

"Of course. I'll see you then! And David? You did the right thing."

They both hung up.

When she opened her eyes, her smile became something different. First, it changed into a smile of confusion. Then the smile faded entirely.

Kathryn was walking directly toward her.

"Kathryn, I—" Mary Margaret began, but she wasn't able to finish the sentence, because Kathryn wound up and slapped her hard across the face.

Mary Margaret saw stars for a moment as she recoiled, absorbing the blow. The many students—and other teachers—in the hallway went silent, seeing the slap. Suddenly, no one was moving. Everyone was watching.

"Let's talk," Mary Margaret said. "Not here."

"I don't care about how embarrassing this conversation is for you," Kathryn said. "What you did is unforgivable. Unforgivable. If I were you, I wouldn't be able to live with myself. And the same goes for David. You two can have each other."

"Kathryn," Mary Margaret said, "neither of us meant for this to happen. It was just something that did happen. And we knew that the only thing to do was tell you now, before it—"

"Tell me? You think that's what he did? He didn't tell me. He lied to me all morning. Said that we didn't have a connection. Well you know what? He was right. We didn't. Because he was too busy having a connection with you." She snorted and shook her head. "He's always been a coward. You should know that. It's not like that's going to change with you."

But Mary Margaret was too hung up on what Kathryn had said to notice her comment about cowardice.

"He didn't—he didn't tell you?" she asked.

"No," she said. "He didn't. And if he lied to you about that, too, good. Now you know what that feels like, as well."

That was apparently all Kathryn had to say. Without another word, she turned and stalked down the hall, back in the direction she'd come.

• • •

A LITTLE LATER THAT DAY, Emma, irritated, again stood out in front of Granny's Diner—she was doomed to spend her entire life there, apparently—waiting for August to arrive.

She could not believe she had agreed to any of this. She heard the growl of his motorcycle's engine before she saw him.

He came down Main Street from the west and pulled over beside her. "Hi there," he said. "Wasn't sure you'd show up."

"I always keep my appointments," she said.

He smiled, and gave her a spare helmet. "Come on," he said. "I want to show you something."

"You gotta be kidding me."

"What?"

"Isn't this a little . . . close for a first date?" she said, looking at the bike.

"I don't mind if you don't mind," he said. "Come on. It'll be fun."

Emma shook her head, sighed. "Fine," she said. "Drive safe."

They went east, on the road that led out of town, but before they came to the sign—the sign that was by now famous because so many people seemed to have vehicle trouble right around this point—August slowed and jerked the wheel, and they tore up into the woods. Emma grabbed him tighter when he made this turn, and she said, "Are you kidding me? I'm the sheriff!"—but he ignored her.

It took only a few minutes to reach an open field. Another minute of riding and then August brought the bike to a stop and killed the engine.

They both got off, and he led her up to the hill to an old well. She'd never been out here before.

"Nice well, August," she said. "You sure know how to turn a girl on."

"You're disappointed?" he asked.

"When you said drink," Emma said, peering down into the well, "I was pretty sure you were talking about alcohol."

"Next time," he said. "This time, something more important." He went to the well and reached for the old rope, then began pulling it up. "You know this well is supposed to be special? There's a legend—it says that the water from this well is fed by an ancient underground lake, and that the lake has magical properties."

"Nice," Emma said. "You sound like my kid."

"Smart kid," he said. "The legend says drinking this water will return something to you. Something lost."

"You sure know a lot about this town," she said, "for being a stranger."

"And you know very little for being the sheriff."

"Have you been to Storybrooke before, August?" she asked curiously.

There was something about this guy. It was like everything was a game. He pulled up the bucket. She saw that he had two tin cups in his pockets, and he set them each on the edge of the well. He poured a few swallows into each.

"I know this all for one simple reason," he said. "I read the plaque."

He nodded, and Emma looked over at the plaque outlining the story. It was all right there. She grinned and shook her head.

"You really believe in magic, though?" she asked.

"I'm a writer. I keep an open mind."

"Sure, but magic?"

"I believe in water," he said. "Water is powerful. Cultures as old as time worshipped it. It runs throughout every land, connecting us to one another. What else would have mystical properties?"

"A little evidence might be nice," she said. "To support such claims."

"Evidence doesn't always lead us to truth," he said.

"Doesn't it?"

They stared at each other for a few minutes. Emma had to admit it—she felt a little electricity in the air. She didn't want to, but she did.

He handed her one cup, lifted the other, and made a toast.

"You be the skeptic, I'll be the believer," he said. "Either way, the water's good to drink."

"Cheers," Emma said.

"Cheers."

They clinked and drank.

. . .

THINGS WERE NOT SO PLEASANT in other parts of Storybrooke. School was out, and Mary Margaret was walking home, still stunned by what had happened with Kathryn. Stunned as well by what she'd learned: David had lied to her. Not only had he been too afraid to tell the truth to his wife, he'd lied to Mary Margaret as well. He'd lied to them both to protect himself. And now more damage had been done than he could possibly undo.

How had she gotten to this place? After such a short period of time? It was only a couple of months ago that everything was . . . everything was okay, at least. But then Emma arrived, and David woke up. . . . She didn't know. The world felt more awake and exciting than it ever had, but it was more danger-ous, too. She wasn't sure if she didn't prefer the illusion of calm to a more authentic version of things.

She turned a corner, onto Main, and bumped into Granny.

She smiled. "Hello, Granny," she said. "I'm so sorry. I'm lost in thought."

"That's okay, dear, I—" But Granny stopped her own apol-ogy when she saw who it was. "Oh. You."

"Excuse me?" said Mary Margaret.

"You should be ashamed of yourself," said Granny, leaning toward her. She shook her head disdainfully, and Mary Mar-garet could not believe the amount of contempt in her eyes. "What you did is unforgivable."

"But I—"

But Granny merely huffed, looked away, and continued down the road.

Head down, rubbing up against the edge of hopeless, Mary Margaret walked the rest of the way home.

. . .

SHE SAW IT FROM HER WINDOW: "TRAMP."

Someone had written it on her car, and now David was outside, trying to scrub it clean. Perfect. He knew he was re-sponsible. No, he hadn't written it, but it was his lies that made it happen. And because he knew, he was trying to clean it up. Superficially, awkwardly. And way too late.

She went out to the street.

"Who did this?" she said.

He turned, surprised, and gave her a pleading look.

"I don't know. I don't know how anyone knows."

"I'll tell you how," Mary Margaret said. "They know because

your wife came to my school and slapped me today. In front of everyone."

He took a moment to absorb this. She imagined his scheming brain doing the tabulations: How did my lies come undone?

"I'm so sorry," he said. "You shouldn't be the one who has to take the brunt of this."

"She told me, David," Mary Margaret said, arms crossed. "She told me that you never said anything. That you didn't tell her about us."

"I don't understand," David said. "Then how did she know?"

"That is exactly the wrong question to ask right now," Mary Margaret said, enraged by his audacity. "What you should be asking yourself is why you thought lying—lying to both me and to Kathryn—could ever have been the right thing to do. Do you see how much damage has been done? You can't put the genie back in the bottle, David."

"I also can't control how people will react to news," David argued.

"That's right. But you can control what you do. And you lied. That's what caused this. That's why this whole town thinks that I'm a tramp." She nodded toward the writing on her car and shook her head in frustration.

David dropped the rag into the bucket, leaned against her car, and put his head in his hands.

"I thought," he said, "that she would just leave town. I didn't want anyone to get more hurt than they needed to be."

"And now everyone is hurt," she said. "Imagine that."

"We'll make it right," he said, reaching for her. "It'll take a little time."

"Don't touch me, David," she said. "You can't fix this."

"What are you saying?" he said. "I don't understand."

"It's simple, David. It's over. We're done. You blew it."

He laughed a pathetic little laugh, and Mary Margaret's face didn't budge. She was not able to feel bad for him. Not right now.

"Do you think I'm joking?" she said. "I'm not. You get to live with this. Forever."

She left him there and stormed back into her apartment.

. . .

MAINE WAS A FROZEN PLACE in the dead of winter, and there was no colder day than this day. There hadn't been much snow this year, but it was below zero as Emma made her way home after August dropped her off at the station. She was exhausted, and she was worried for Mary Margaret. The whole town was talking about the affair, and things were going to get ugly. She'd seen it happen before—she'd been the center of the controversy, and she didn't like the memory. Not one bit.

Crossing the street, something caught her eye behind the tire of an old pickup. Something poking out from a pile of dirty leaves.

Emma frowned and knelt to investigate; she could not believe what she was seeing.

The book. Henry's book. Right there on the street.

She stood up, dusted it off, flipped through the pages. She opened to the story Henry had told her about Mr. Gold and the girl, and looked at some of the pictures.

She didn't know why, but she'd found the thing. At the very least, Henry would be happy, and that made her happy. She headed off toward the station.

She didn't have much time to feel happy about the book, though, as the emergency calls started coming in the moment she walked in the door. First from a motorist, next David, and after that, Regina.

Kathryn was missing. She was nowhere to be found.

Her car, empty, was in the ditch near the edge of town.

She was gone.

CHAPTER 11

RED-HANDED

MMA DID THE ONLY THING SHE COULD DO: She organized a manhunt. What seemed like the whole town showed up the morning after Kathryn Nolan disappeared, and they combed the woods, thirty-wide, hoping to find any sign of her. David was there, as was Mary Margaret, but they stayed far away from each other. Emma was distressed to overhear hushed muttering from so many of the citizens. Why was it that Mary Margaret was taking the brunt of the hit to her reputation, while nobody seemed to care that David—the man—had willingly participated in the same affair?

She wasn't surprised, but she didn't like it.

Both of them had made mistakes. Mary Margaret was the one who was suffering.

The manhunt turned up nothing.

Emma had gotten nowhere with the search. Until the morning that Sidney Glass, the former editor of the town newspaper and her old challenger for the badge, showed up in her office with a piece of interesting information.

Emma knew that Sidney had been fired by Regina after the

storm, but she didn't know why, and in truth, she didn't want to know the details. She suspected it had something to do with the failed campaign for sheriff, but she also suspected there was more to it than that. The man had always put her off. Not just because of the campaign, but because of the sleazy article he'd written about her past, and the irritating way he was always—before now, anyway—hanging on Regina's every word.

Since he'd been fired, though, Sidney had been spending a lot of time drinking at Granny's and at the Rabbit Hole. Emma had been forced to "escort" him home one night after finding him drunk and raving in the middle of Main Street at midnight. He'd gone down a rabbit hole of his own, apparently, which was why she was skeptical when he came to her office with a manila envelope, claiming to have David Nolan's "real" phone records.

"As opposed to what?" Emma said. "His fake records?"

"That's right," he said. "The records you have are falsified." He handed her the envelope. "These are the true phone records."

"You're telling me that the police have the wrong records," she said. "And you, the former newspaper editor, have the right records?"

"That's right."

Emma took it and looked at the paper inside. It resembled the official records she'd subpoenaed from the phone company, but there was one telling difference: Glass's version showed an eight-minute call between David and Kathryn an hour after Kathryn had last been seen.

Emma tried to think it through. Had Glass manufactured these? If so, to what end? And what was the other possibility? That she had in fact been given falsified records by the phone company? If that were true, who had done it, and why?

"Why would you expect me to take this one as the real version and the other as the false?"

"Because I don't have an agenda," Sidney said.

Sure you don't, Emma thought.

Problem was, when Emma went down to the phone company herself to straighten out the mix-up, she discovered that Glass's records were accurate, and the original copy she'd received—through the mayor's office—was incorrect. That was the difference. The original records had gone through Regina's office. And they'd changed on their way through. She asked around to find out how such a thing could happen, but they couldn't explain it and neither could Regina's office.

Sidney Glass had come to her with good information. That was interesting. And for whatever reason, it looked as though Regina was trying to push her away from David as a suspect.

She liked David, even though he'd been such an idiot about the affair. But she couldn't let that keep her from doing her job, and with the phone record, it only made sense to bring him in for some questioning. There was no body—not yet, anyway, but Emma knew that a few days going by with no leads was a bad, bad sign for a missing person. So on the night of the Miners Day Fair, when most of the town was distracted, she discreetly approached David and asked him to come down to the station. "I'm not arresting you," she told him, "but we need to talk about that day."

David came willingly, although he was adamant about his innocence. Emma expected nothing less and went easy on him during the interview. He said he couldn't explain the phone record, and that there had to be a mistake.

"You don't understand, Emma," he said. "This whole thing—this has pretty much destroyed me." He shook his head, rubbed his eyes. "If there was just some way to have done it all better, you know?"

"Sometimes life is just messy no matter what you do," she said. "But, David . . . I shouldn't say this, but I'll say it: I believe you. I don't think you had anything to do with this. I don't know where she is or what happened, but I don't think it was you."

"Thank you," he said. "I appreciate that. A lot."

"I do think you might want to get a lawyer, though," she said.

The worried look came back.

. . .

REGINA SHOWED UP in the office an hour later, wanting to know where Emma was with the investigation. For the moment, it seemed as though their personal war was on hold. Emma had never seen Regina so concerned for something other than herself. She, like David, was legitimately broken up about Kathryn's disappearance.

"Nothing new," Emma said. "I'm sorry to say."

"Why did you have David Nolan in?"

Emma looked at her, surprised. "Were you staking out the station, Regina?" she said.

"I saw him come out," she said and shrugged. "And now I want to know what you're thinking. It's the chain of command and I'm within my rights."

Emma shook her head. The woman knew everything about the town. It was inhuman.

"I was asking him about the phone records. He apparently—"

"Pocket-dialed Kathryn the night she left, yes," she said, nodding. "I was informed of the erroneous record."

"That's a bit of a leap," Emma said, "but I'm not coming to any conclusions."

"Ms. Swan, please. He had nothing to do with it."

Interesting, Emma thought. Regina's pulling for David. She didn't know what it meant. Not yet.

"And you're so sure because . . . ?"

"Because I know him. And I know this town. Perhaps you have an advantage as an outsider, as someone who can see things anew, but I've been mayor here for a long time and I have a sense for these things."

Emma didn't like how adamant Regina was.

Regina stood. "The point is that I'd like to see some more urgency coming out of this office. Perhaps a little more creativity. What about this new stranger in town? What about carjackers? What about Gold? Have you talked to him? I want you to find my friend. It's as though you haven't even looked."

"We all want to find her, Regina," she said. "Just be patient. I'm good at finding people. Sometimes it's tricky."

· · ·

AFTER THE HUNTSMAN released her and she fled into the woods, Snow White had little more than the clothes on her back. It was hard going as she forged a new path, all alone, without the help of a single friend, and she lived hand-to-mouth and slept in the woods for weeks, counting on the generosity of strangers to get through the days. She was just getting the hang of life as a fugitive when something new changed everything: snow.

And cold.

And wind.

And ice.

She had been doing all right in her first weeks on her own, scavenging and begging for what food she could, sometimes finding a kind peasant who'd let her sleep in the barn. The Queen and her men had begun printing wanted posters and distributing them across the land, though, and she knew that the kindness of the people would only go so far. If she exposed herself much more, someone would turn her in.

One night, when the temperature had dropped considerably, Snow found herself shivering and stumbling through the woods, thinking for the first time that this—all of it—might be the death of her. She'd escaped the Huntsman only to have become invisible. Not the worst thing in the world when you were on the run, but the problem with being invisible was that no one could help you, either.

She couldn't feel her hands or her feet when she saw, at the top of a hill, a small farm and a little light in one of the windows. She stopped beside a tree and watched. A young man was at the window, and he was talking with someone. Thirty feet from the main house, there was a chicken coop. Chicken coops, she knew, tended to be excellent places to sleep. Warm, free of humans, and full of eggs. She was so cold, and seeing that whoever was in the window was distracted by the young man, she decided to risk it, and ran through the snow toward the coop.

Once inside, she crinkled her nose at the smell of the chickens, who clucked and stirred at their new guest. The rooster seemed mildly disturbed by her presence and put on a show atop some hay, but soon he settled down as well, and Snow tucked herself into a corner of the coop. She fell asleep almost immediately.

. . .

SHE DREAMT OF HER FATHER, and the time before Regina, when her mother had only just died and he took her to the shore to play castle on the rocks. It was a memory—a cherished memory—but in the dream, there was more: Her father was happy, looking out at the water, and when Snow turned to look where he was looking, she saw her mother rise up out of the waves, a smile on her face. She held her arms out to Snow, and the weight of all the sadness lifted. They would be together again, if only for a day, if only here.

She turned to her father. "It's Mommy!" she cried.

He nodded. "Yes!" he said. "Go to her!"

Snow looked back at her mother, who was twenty feet out into the sea. Worried, she looked back at her father. "I can't get to her!" she cried.

"You can!" he cried. "You have to swim!"

"But I'm afraid!"

"It doesn't matter!" cried her father. "She's dead anyway! And so am I!"

Snow woke up with a start, the image of her father's wryly smiling face still lingering behind her eyes. It was dawn and the chickens were restless again.

Her stomach growled, and Snow sat up and looked at them. "I'm sorry," she said to one of them, "but you have something I need."

She moved around the coop and collected a couple of eggs, not wanting to take so many that the owners would be in difficult straights. She gently placed them into her satchel and was about to leave when she heard something.

Footsteps.

Someone was coming.

She darted to the back corner of the coop and crouched

down behind some crates, knowing that she could very well meet her end here and now. It wouldn't take the Queen or any of her men. Just an angry farmer.

Someone came inside, and Snow pulled herself into a ball. In so doing, though, her cloak scraped against the wooden wall, and she closed her eyes, knowing the noise had given her away.

"Hello? Who's there?"

A woman's voice.

Snow's initial vision of an angry farmer with a pitchfork changed into someone else. A girl. Someone kind. Perhaps.

She took a chance.

Slowly, Snow rose up from behind the stack of crates. A young woman, pale-skinned, wearing a red cloak, stared back at her.

"Who are you?" the girl in red said.

"I'm sorry," she said. "I was stealing eggs. I'm so sorry."

The girl smiled.

"Well. You're the most honest thief I've ever met."

"Only two," she said, and held them up. "I was just so hungry. And it's so cold outside."

"Did you spend the whole night out here?" the girl asked.

Snow nodded.

"Did you not know there was a wolf monster on the loose?"

Snow looked concerned. "I thought I did hear something," she said. "But I should—I should be going. I'll leave these." She looked for a place to put the two eggs.

"No, no, it's fine," said the girl. "You can keep them. I don't care. What's your name?"

"My name?" Snow said. "My name is Margaret. No . . . it's Mary. Mary."

"That's quite a name," the girl said. "Can I call you Mary?"

Snow White nodded.

"Come on, you can stay with us, I'm sure it will be fine," said the girl. "My name is Red." She led the young woman out of the coop and into the snow. "I just have to draw some water from the well. But tell me, I don't understand. What are you doing out here?"

They walked across the snow toward a well, and Snow White ignored the question and instead said, "What is this monster?" She helped Red with the bucket then, and together they lowered it down.

"It's Wolfstime. Killer wolf out there. Big as a pony, but a lot more bloodthirsty. It's been stalking the whole area pretty regular. It kills cattle and— Hang on. This pulley sticks sometimes. If you can just . . ."

Snow White had taken a few more steps and stood atop a ridge. Red joined her, and Snow couldn't help but put her hand up over her mouth. All around them the bodies of the men were strewn like broken dolls. The red of their blood stained the white snow.

. . .

RUBY AND GRANNY had been bickering and fighting for weeks. As so many in the town passed through Granny's Diner as a part of their day, it was no secret that the two women were having trouble. And it was no surprise when, after an argument about a Saturday night shift, Ruby up and quit the diner, leaving Granny to fend for herself in a full house.

"Long time coming," people mumbled.

"Can't believe it didn't happen sooner."

Emma and Mary Margaret watched uncomfortably as the whole argument went down. At the end of it, Ruby stormed out and screamed that she was leaving town and heading to Boston. Granny didn't respond, and when Ruby was gone, she acted like she didn't care one way or the other.

"Yikes," Emma said. "Things are not good on the home front, I guess."

"They've always been at each other's throats," said Mary Margaret, turning back to her hot chocolate. "I don't know why."

"I'm sorry, I'm being glib," Emma said. "We were talking about David."

"I just want to be sure he's okay," Mary Margaret said. "I shouldn't, but I can't help it."

"He's okay. He's shaken up, he's worried people think he has something to do with it. But he's okay."

"Is there any word on Kathryn?"

"None. I have nothing. I was just about to go back to square one and think it through from the start of the time line. I'm at a loss."

"Did you check with Boston again?"

"She's not there, if that's what you mean."

"I don't understand how a person can just completely disappear," said Mary Margaret. "Right from her car. What happened? Did she evaporate?"

They left the diner ten minutes later; Emma had seen that Mary Margaret's mood deteriorated dramatically after that part of the conversation. Emma was worried about her friend, but she knew, too, that she probably shouldn't be seen socializing with her so much. Mary Margaret was perhaps a bit too naïve to realize it, but she wasn't clear of suspicion, either. To Emma, Mary Margaret seemed so innocent, so unaware of the dangers in the world. She was independent, but sheltered at the same time. It was an unusual combination.

It was cold, and Emma was hugging herself as they came around the corner. Both she and Mary Margaret were surprised to see Ruby standing at the bus stop.

She had one small suitcase with her and was looking down Main Street furtively.

"You do know no buses ever come," Emma said to her. "Where are you going?"

"Away" was all Ruby said.

"We overheard the fight," said Mary Margaret. "All of us did, I guess."

"Yeah, well that just means you overheard the truth. I'm sick of her and I'm sick of that diner. And I'm sick of Storybrooke. I'm going to Boston."

"Nothing's going to happen tonight," Mary Margaret said. "You're worked up, it's freezing. Stay with us at our place for the night, think this through. Get a good night's rest."

Ruby looked at both women. It didn't take long for her to nod in agreement.

"Okay," she said. "One night."

• • •

GRANNY, RED'S GRANDMOTHER, welcomed Snow into the cottage with a tough-minded generosity. Snow liked her immediately, even though she seemed like she could be prickly. Red immediately told her about what they'd found outside, and the three went back out.

Granny looked grimly out at the scene near the well, and with the full light of the morning, she went to town to sound the alarm. Soon tens—if not hundreds—gathered at the town hall for a meeting to discuss what was to be done. What the locals here called "Wolfstime" was nearly finished, apparently, but now the mayor was infuriated, as a half dozen of the town's strongest men were dead. A good many of the people, men and women both, were hungry for vengeance. There was talk of another hunting party to go looking for the wolf that very night.

Snow White wondered just what she'd happened upon. A part of her thought it might be best to steal away in the night, but there was the threat of this wolf. And what's more, she knew that while people were distracted with their own problems, they wouldn't worry much about her.

"The one thing I know is that last night was the VERY LAST MASSACRE!"

The crowd cheered its approval. Many stood and cried, "Kill the beast!"

"Had I stayed with the party for just ten minutes longer, I would have been among the dead!" cried the mayor. "And had I doubled back? Perhaps I would have been able to slay the beast!"

"You surely would have failed," said a voice.

Snow looked to her left, as did Red. Granny had been the one to say it.

Snow could see that Red was mortified by her grandmother's comment. She noticed Mayor Tompkins scanning the room, looking for the source of the remark. His eyes lingered on Red's, and he smiled at her. Red looked away.

Hm, Snow White thought. Something's there.

"This creature is more powerful than you can imagine," said Granny. "Stronger, smarter. You wouldn't have had a chance, Mayor. Stay inside, lock your doors, hide your children, forget your livestock! That's my advice!"

Granny's advice was greeted with derision and boos.

"We've heard this from you before, Widow Lucas," said the mayor.

"Aye, you have," said Granny. "But I haven't told you how I know."

The crowd went silent. Granny stood.

"Nearly three score years ago, I was a child with six older brothers as big as oak trees, all of them veterans of the second Ogre War. And my father, the biggest of them all. Come one Wolfstime, he decided to go out and take on the wolf. A different wolf back then, of course, but just as fearsome. They did it for me. They went out there to protect me." At this point Granny nearly broke down, and Red reached up and took her hand.

Granny continued: "I was supposed to be asleep, but I crawled out on the roof and lay down in the thatch to watch. They had the beast surrounded, the seven of them, with spears all pointed in at it. Then it started. . . . It was lunging. Not at the men, but at the spears, grabbing with its teeth, breaking the shafts. They stabbed it with the splintered ends, but it didn't matter. It tore their throats so fast that not one of them got a chance to scream, or pray, or say good-bye."

The crowd remained rapt. Granny gave them a long look, remembering.

"It looked at me with black eyes that didn't even seem to be there. They were holes in the world. And then it walked away. You ever see a wild animal just turn its back and walk away like you don't matter? If this wolf is like that one, there is no defeating it. It has already won just by existing in our world. You don't kill it. All you do is hide."

Granny released Red's hand, reminded her to wear her hood, and told the two girls that it was time for them to leave.

It was only midday when they returned to the cottage, and Granny—exhausted from her night awake—told Red and Snow that she needed to lie down. "Don't go far," she said. "And don't be outside anywhere near dark. Promise me?"

"I promise," said Red.

Once Granny had closed the door of her room, Red took Snow's hand and said, "Come on."

. . .

MARY MARGARET WAS TIRED of waiting around for things to happen.

The next morning, while Ruby and Emma still slept, she packed a bag and went out to the woods at the edge of town, intent on finding Kathryn.

She remembered how Emma had ordered them to move in a long line when there had been hundreds of people to help. Alone, though, it was harder to come up with an efficient system. She parked her own car where Kathryn's had been found, double-checked her compass, and decided that she was just as likely to find something walking in a random zigzag as she'd be following any type of rules. She headed out into the forest.

She searched for two hours, being sure to check back and reorient herself at her car every now and then. As she searched, she thought about David, and Regina, and who in town was even capable of harming Kathryn. David? It was impossible. She didn't doubt that Regina had it in her to do something like this, but for what reason? Mary Margaret couldn't see it. And that meant the culprit was someone who seemed normal and safe, some kind of sociopath. She thought of Dr. Whale, or Sidney Glass. She could make any—

She stopped in her tracks.

David was standing ten feet from her, his eyes glazed over.

"David?" she said, walking toward him. "What are you doing out here?"

It was strange—he didn't seem to recognize her. He walked past her and said, as he went by, "It's me."

"I know it's you. You don't look right."

"I'm looking for her."

"David, listen to me," Mary Margaret said, falling in behind him. "Emma doesn't really suspect you, no matter what she said. Kathryn is okay, she's somewhere. We just have to—"

"I'm looking" was all he said.

Mary Margaret stopped, and David continued on, zombie-like.

"David?"

"I'm looking," he said again. "I'm looking."

• • •

HENRY SAT WITH RUBY in the sheriff's station, ticking down a litany of job openings in Storybrooke, hoping to help Ruby find new employment. Emma was at her desk, going over Kathryn's disappearance in her head, but she wasn't getting anywhere. She listened to her son being helpful. He suggested sales; Ruby said she wasn't interested. He suggested being a bike messenger; Ruby said she was a klutz. "There's nothing I can do, really," Ruby said. "That's the whole problem."

"I'm sure there are things you can do," said Henry. "Maybe you just don't know about them yet."

"All I've ever done is work at this diner," she said. "There's got to be more to life."

The phone rang, and Ruby picked up. After listening for a moment, she assured the caller—Ms. Ginger—that the "foot-steps" she was hearing were Archie's dog, Pongo, and not a prowler. Ms. Ginger thanked her and she hung up.

"I just wish I had skills," Ruby said. "Anyway."

Emma smiled.

"Seems like you have some."

Henry and Ruby each looked over a shoulder. Emma shrugged.

"Look, you need work, I need some help around here. I have it in the budget. Why don't you come on board as the of-fice manager?"

"Oh no," said Ruby. "I couldn't do police work."

"I just mean answer the phones and help out, that kind of thing," Emma said. "You won't have to shoot anyone."

"Oh."

"I need someone. Whaddya say?"

Ruby thought about for it a moment, then smiled and nod-ded. "I say okay," she said. "Thank you, Emma. Thank you for giving me a chance at something."

"My pleasure," she said. "And your first job can be to go over to Granny's and pick us up lunch. I'm starving and I don't have time."

"Done."

Ruby grabbed her purse and went to the door. Before she could reach for the knob, however, the door swung open, and Mary Margaret, looking frazzled, burst into the room.

"I just saw David in the woods," she said. "He's looking for Kathryn."

"She's not out there," Emma said, shaking her head.

"Something is wrong with him," she said. "He's . . . confused. And disoriented."

. . .

RED LED SNOW WHITE into the forest, and the two talked about Granny's story, and the wolf. Snow was glad that Red didn't seem too interested in her path and wasn't asking any questions, and so she let her new friend talk about being stuck under Granny's wing. Red told her all about Peter, too, and how the two of them planned to be together.

"Is that the boy you were talking to at your window last night?" Snow asked.

"You saw that?"

"I was hiding in the woods," she said. "I heard your voices. He seemed cute."

Red smiled mischievously at her. "He is," she said. "We're in love. We're going to be together, but we have to get away from here."

"Why?"

"Because there's nothing here for either of us," she said. "We belong in a big city. A castle. A court. We're not meant for the dirt. It's violent and dangerous and small-minded here."

Snow had quite a lot to say about how violent and dangerous and small-minded things could be at court, but she held her tongue.

"What's Peter like?" asked Snow.

"Brave," she said. "Charming. Strong. Smart."

Snow smiled, looking at Red's face as she listed the qualities of her lover. Snow wondered if she herself would ever meet someone who made her feel that way. She hoped so.

"I'm worried that he's going to try to hunt the thing tonight, though," Ruby said. "And that he'll get hurt. Which is why *we're* going to track it down right now."

She gave Snow another mischievous grin, this one meaning something completely different.

"What?" said Snow. "We can't—"

"Oh, come on, it'll be fun," said Red. "And besides, we're safe in the day. It doesn't have its full powers until the middle of the night." She laughed, and Snow was shocked—and a little impressed—by how cavalier she seemed to be. She liked this girl.

"I'm a good tracker," Red said. "I know how to find it. So we'll catch it in its den or in its cave, then we'll be able to lead the hunters right to it."

"I don't know," Snow said. "It seems dangerous."

"Come on, Mary!" said Red. "Live a little."

If you only knew, thought Snow.

They crossed an open field, trudging through the snow, and Red explained how to look for tracks. They scanned the ground in likely spots for nearly an hour. Snow would occasionally call Red over and point to this or that divot, and Red would disabuse her with a "That's a deer," or a "Dog, for sure." Snow was growing tired, and her feet were freezing, by the time Red called to her and said, "Now, here are some monster wolf tracks."

What Red pointed to seemed large enough to be the tracks of a dragon. Snow White could hardly believe her eyes.

"And look, look at this," said Red, leading her in the direction the tracks went. "Look at how far apart they are."

"How big is this thing?" Snow White said, gaping at the length of the wolf's stride.

"Big," said Red. "Really big. Come on."

. . .

THEY FOLLOWED THE TRACKS for a quarter mile. For a period, the wolf seemed to have been running somewhere, but as they climbed a hill—and Snow said, "Aren't we getting close to the cottage again?"—the tracks were less spread apart. The two were also confounded when the size of the paw prints seemed to decrease.

"Is it shrinking?" Snow said, both of them hurrying along.

"I don't know. I—" Red stopped and pointed. "Look."

The paw prints weren't shrinking. They were changing shape.

"What kind of a monster is this, Red?" said Snow White.

She asked because it was plain: The tracks had become boot prints. Mid-stride, the wolf seemed to have turned into a man.

"One that's not just a wolf," Red said.

They continued to follow the tracks over the hill and back down into the valley. Neither woman spoke, even as the cottage came into view.

The tracks led directly to Red's window.

"I don't understand," said Snow. "Who else was at your window last night? Besides Peter?"

Red, her hand up at her mouth, said nothing.

"Red?"

"No one," she said. "Just Peter was here." Eyes wide, she looked at Snow White. "Peter is the wolf."

. . .

WHEN RUBY RETURNED with the sandwiches, Emma looked at her and said, "Leave those wrapped up. Mary Margaret had to go. We're going to look for David in the woods."

Ruby looked surprised, and Henry glanced up at Emma and gave her one of his coy, knowing grins.

After Emma had calmed Mary Margaret down and sent her home, Henry had opened up his storybook and shown her the story of Red, and said, "She's always struggling with feeling worthless, see? *Look*. You have to actually let her do things. She can track, even. See?"

"There's a real investigation going on, Henry," she said. "Someone is actually missing and in trouble. I don't want you getting too caught up in the curse stuff right now."

"But all I'm saying is that Ruby can help," he said. "I know her."

"Okay," said Emma. "Fine."

And so she asked her to come along.

. . .

EMMA AND RUBY ARRIVED at the edge of town, where Kathryn's car had gone off the road, and they headed north, into the woods. There was no sign of David anywhere, and it was only a couple of hours until dark.

"Not good," Emma said. "If he's out here somewhere, and something's wrong with him . . ."

"What would be wrong with him, though?" asked Ruby, looking out into the trees.

"I don't know," said Emma. "A holdover from the coma? I don't get it, either. All I know is Mary Margaret seemed pretty shaken up."

"I shouldn't even be out here," said Ruby. "I'll probably just screw this up, too."

Emma liked Ruby, and wanted to ease her anxieties, but she also didn't have time for this, and regretted bringing her out here. Ruby was picking her way through the rough terrain like someone who'd never been in the woods, and even more distressing, she seemed more preoccupied with her own problems than with the task at hand. Emma took a breath and kept herself from suggesting that Ruby go back to the car. Two bodies out here were better than one.

"Wait."

Emma turned and looked at Ruby, who was looking out into the forest.

"What?"

"I hear him."

"Really?"

"Yes. Or . . . something. I know where he is." She looked at Emma. In her eyes Emma saw something completely different. Something . . . hungry. "Don't you hear it?"

Before Emma could respond, Ruby took off. She was running through the forest, hell-bent on something. "Hey!" Emma cried, running after her. "Wait! Where are you going?"

"He's over here, come on!" Ruby yelled, over her shoulder.

They ran, Emma more and more behind. She was out of breath and about to take a break when she finally saw Ruby, in the distance, come to a stop and fall to the ground. "What?" Emma cried. "What is it?"

But Ruby didn't have to answer, because soon Emma could see for herself. David, unconscious, lay in a heap, curled up beside the trunk of a silver maple.

. . .

"HE'S BRUISED, dehydrated, scratched up, everything you'd expect," said Dr. Whale. "Cut on his head is superficial, that didn't cause this. He's dealing with a mental health problem."

They were at the hospital. Emma and Dr. Whale stood outside of David's room. David was awake, but he was claiming to have no memory of going to the woods. Emma didn't like it one bit, but for now, there wasn't much she could say.

She and Dr. Whale went back into the room. "We'll figure this out," Emma said to David. "Hang in there."

"It's like none of it happened," David said. "I mean I know it did, because you're telling me. But it sounds about as real as one of Henry's stories right now."

Emma turned to Dr. Whale. "How . . . functional could he be during one of these . . . episodes? I mean he talked to someone during this one."

"Anything's possible," said Dr. Whale. "People in similar states, say from sleep medication, do all kinds of things. Cook, talk, drive cars." He shrugged. "It's very hard to say."

"You want to know if I could have made that call," he said, looking at Emma. "Or more. I get it. You think I kidnapped her. Maybe even killed her. And that I don't even know it."

"Take it easy, David," said Dr. Whale. "No one is saying that."

"We're just trying to figure it out," added Emma.

"That would explain it, though," David said, looking forlorn. "That would explain why I didn't seem like I was lying to you. Because I didn't know."

"Stop talking right now, David." Emma didn't need to turn—the loud and abrasive voice was one she knew all too well. Regina. "Why are you here?" it continued, and Emma presumed it was now directed at her. "Why doesn't he have a lawyer present? Have you even read him his rights?"

"No," said Emma. "Because he's not under arrest. We're talking."

"Right."

"Why are you here?" Emma asked.

"Because I'm still his emergency contact," said Regina.

"I thought that changed to Kathryn," said David, confused.

"Yes, well," said Regina. "She's currently missing, and so it reverted to me." She went to the bed. "I'm here to offer support, and protection, if you need it." She looked at Emma. "Why don't you concentrate on finding her?"

Why is she so intent on defending him? Emma wondered.

"Maine is big," Emma said.

"This room is covered," Regina snapped back. "Now get out there and find her."

● ● ●

IN THE WAITING ROOM, Emma called Ruby. Something had occurred to her.

"I need you to go out and check something for me," Emma said. "Right now. The last time David had one of these little dreamwalks, he ended up at the toll bridge. I'm wondering if we might get lucky. You need to go and check it out. Right now."

"Me?" said Ruby.

"You were great out there in the woods, Ruby," Emma said. "You can do this. Call me if you find anything. Take my car. The keys are on my desk."

Emma was back in the woods shortly after having received the call from Ruby, who had certainly found something. The forensics team wasn't too far behind. Ruby, who had been given a cup of coffee, sat in the VW, looking a little dazed. After taking a last look at the box that Ruby had uncovered by the river, Emma walked up the steep grade and got into the car on the passenger side. "You did good," she said. "Again."

"I'm not so sure I wanted to do good," Ruby said.

"I know," she said. "But this is a big break."

Emma wasn't exactly pleased to have the vision in her head, either, but she meant what she said. They could move forward now, once they got the lab work back. The contents of the box . . . well, she could understand why Ruby had screamed into the phone.

She reached over, took Ruby's hand. "Thanks," she said. "For today."

Ruby nodded and tried to muster a smile.

Emma could think of nothing more to say.

. . .

THOUGH PETER HAD PROTESTED, Red had told him that she believed he was the wolf, that he had to be restrained, and that she would stay with him through the night. In order to fool Granny, then, Snow White agreed (against her better judgment) to wear Red's red cloak and pose as her in her bedroom, just in case Granny decided to check up on her.

The two women said their good-byes, and Snow, wearing the cloak, fell asleep in Red's room.

Granny came calling sometime past midnight.

"Red, dear," Granny said. "I need you to get up. I—"

Snow, wide awake, did her best to stay hidden in the sheets, but Granny, no one's fool, noticed something was amiss. She reached for Snow White and turned her over. When she saw that it wasn't Red, her eyes went wide. "What have you done?" she whispered.

"We didn't mean any harm," protested Snow.

"Where is she?" Granny said, with so much urgency that Snow felt a jolt of nervous energy. She sat up on the bed and explained about Peter.

"She's with that boy?" Granny said. "Right now?"

"Yes," said Snow.

"Dear gods," said Granny. "Come, show me where." She reached for her crossbow. "Now, girl!"

. . .

THE TWO HURRIED OFF into the night, Snow struggling to keep pace with Granny. She seemed to know something—what confused Snow, though, was the comments she kept making about "that poor boy."

"You don't understand," said Snow. "He is the wolf. We saw the tracks. The wolf is also a man."

"He isn't the wolf, girl," said Granny, grunting her disapproval.

Snow stared at her, realizing the implication.

Red. Red was the wolf.

It seemed obvious now, but for some reason, it hadn't ever seemed . . .

"You knew this?" Snow asked, still moving quickly behind Granny.

"Of course I knew. Her mother was one, too, before a hunting party killed her. I thought maybe Red didn't get it, but when she was thirteen, it started. I paid a wizard for that cloak, and it keeps her from turning, but she doesn't wear it, and she's found some way out of the house."

"Why didn't you tell her?"

"I didn't want her to have that burden. It's a terrible, terrible burden."

They reached a farmer's fence, and Granny stopped, waiting for direction from Snow White. Snow pointed.

"You're one, too, aren't you?" Snow said.

"Aye" was all Granny said, sniffing at the air. "I have her scent now. Silver-tipped arrows will stop her. We're approaching from downwind, so we have a chance."

They did, but young Peter did not. By the time they arrived, Red, fully turned, had already slaughtered her love. Snow White threw the cloak over her and Granny was saved the tragedy of having to shoot her own granddaughter, but for Red—who only realized the truth as she awoke to find herself covered in blood, being lifted into the arms of Snow White and Granny—the tragedy had already taken place. Perhaps she would have preferred a swift death by silver-tipped arrow, at least in that particular moment. She cried out when she saw Peter, deceased. She cried out even more when she realized she'd been the one to do it, and that her plan had been the thing to kill her love.

But there was no time to lament. There would be decades and decades to lament. In that moment, Granny and Snow had to get her to a safe place. Because even as she cried and reached for Peter's lifeless body, they could hear the approach of the hunting party.

"Get her home, get her safe," said Granny, once they were all moving. "They're too close."

Snow and Granny locked eyes, and Snow understood. Granny could control the wolf inside. And she was going back. To protect them.

"I'll see you there," Granny said. "In the morning."

Needless to say, Granny survived.

The hunting party did not.

HAVING HEARD that David had been found and had returned to work, Mary Margaret went to see him at the animal shelter. He was safe, that was true, but he was not okay.

Not in the least.

She found him pacing about the back office. "I don't know what's happened. I can't be sure of anything, Mary Margaret. I might have killed her for all I know."

"You didn't kill her. You don't have it in you," Mary Margaret said. "And besides, she's going to turn up alive. Just wait."

He shook his head in frustration. "Why would I have called her?" he asked. "That doesn't make sense."

"There has to be an explanation," Mary Margaret said. "What if—"

The door to the shelter opened, and David went out to the entryway. A moment later he reentered the office. Emma was behind him.

She gave a nod to Mary Margaret.

"We found something by the river," she said. "Near the toll bridge." She gave David a heavy look.

"What is it?" David said.

"I don't know how else to say this, so I'm just going to say it," Emma said. "There was a human heart inside of a jewelry box. We think it's Kathryn's."

Mary Margaret clutched the arm of the chair, felt the room grow dim. She closed her eyes and gathered herself. David had sunk down and now leaned against his desk, completely deflated. "I must have done it," he said, near tears. He held out his wrists. "Cuff me."

Emma looked at him.

"Do it!" he said.

"I can't, David," she said. "There was a fingerprint inside of the box. It wasn't yours."

David and Mary Margaret looked at her, confused. Emma turned to Mary Margaret.

"It was Mary Margaret's."

CHAPTER 12

HEART OF DARKNESS

FEW DAYS AFTER SNOW WHITE CONSUMED the potion that made her forget Prince Charming, she was holed up with the seven dwarfs, her memory blank. The dwarfs were realizing that the memory loss had some side effects. Snow was not . . . herself. She was furious, in fact. All the time.

Furious with everything and everyone. And she didn't quite know why.

Grumpy had a guess.

After a morning of watching her attacking bluebirds with her broom, he went to the other dwarfs and told them that they had to do something.

"Like what?" said Sneezy.

"I don't know," he said. "Something. We have to talk to her."

And they did. The dwarfs agreed with Grumpy that it would be most helpful to Snow if they all sat down together and discussed the matter. As a group. Friendship, it was agreed, and a safe place for discussion, were crucial elements to a successful intervention. They made the plan, invited a special guest, and when they were ready, Grumpy went to Snow's room and asked her if she might come out to the kitchen.

"Why?" she said defensively. "I'm happy here."

"There are some people here," Grumpy said, "who'd like to talk to you."

Snow looked confused, but she finally relented.

In the kitchen, however, she took one look at the serious faces of the gathered dwarfs and turned on Grumpy. "What is this?" she said.

Grumpy held up both hands and said, "Sister, sister. We're your friends. We just want to talk."

"Talk about what?"

"About how you've been acting," he said, "since you drank that potion."

"The potion is not the problem," sneered Snow. "The real problem is that I'm living with a bunch of dwarfs when the woman who killed my father is prancing around in my castle, living my life. And this happens to be the same woman who tried to have me murdered, too. Am I mad? Yes. I'm furious."

"It's not fair to take this out on your friends," said Jiminy Cricket, who had joined them for the conversation.

"You're right," said Snow, lost in thought. "You're absolutely right."

"Progress," muttered Jiminy to Grumpy.

"I should be taking it out on her," Snow White said. "By killing her."

. . .

IT WAS AWKWARD, to say the least, when Emma booked Mary Margaret. She took her picture and did the appropriate paperwork, even though Mary Margaret proclaimed her innocence throughout. Emma told her she was only doing her job and that the fingerprint was hard evidence. Maybe she was innocent, but Emma knew that playing favorites now would have dire consequences down the line. She wasn't going to endanger Mary Margaret by acting hastily. It would come down to figuring out what had really happened to Kathryn. And for that, she would need time.

To make things more difficult, Ruby had quit, made up with Granny, and gone back to work at the diner, which meant that Emma was alone again at the office and had few people she could talk to about the case. Few people she liked, at least.

Regina, who'd called and said that she wanted to be a part of the interrogation, showed up a few minutes after the booking was complete. Mary Margaret consented and said that she didn't need a lawyer.

"Why would I?" she asked. "I'm innocent."

As Emma asked questions, Mary Margaret kept her composure and revealed a key new piece of information: The box was her jewelry box. She didn't know how it had ended up buried beside the river, and she definitely didn't know how a heart got into it, but the jewelry box was hers. She said she wasn't going to pretend it wasn't.

Outside, while Mary Margaret remained in the interrogation room, Emma and Regina discussed her answers.

"No one is accusing Ms. Blanchard of being a bad person," Regina said. "But she's a woman who's had her heart broken. And that? It can make you do unspeakable things."

• • •

GRUMPY HAD NEVER THOUGHT of Snow White as the violent type, but watching her disarm and assault one of the Queen's

Black Knights was nothing if not impressive. They were five miles from the hovel, and he had followed her, knowing that to march into the Queen's castle would be suicide for Snow White, but not quite knowing how to stop her. The Black Knight had appeared on the road and tried to intimidate her, but she would have none of it. Quickly, effortlessly, she swept the knight's feet out from under him with the mining pick she'd taken from the hovel, interrogated the knight as to the queen's location, mocked him, and sent him on his way.

She was trying to put on the knight's abandoned armor when Grumpy emerged from the forest and said, "Are you crazy? You think that that 'disguise' is going to fool anyone?"

"What are you doing here?" she said. "Did you follow me?"

"Yes, I did," he said. "Because I don't want to see you get killed."

"I won't," she said sternly. "And besides, the Queen deserves to die."

"That might be true, but justice doesn't always care what's deserved," he said. "You're this angry because you've forgotten."

This stopped Snow for a moment. "What do you mean?" she said eventually.

"I mean I have a better idea," said Grumpy. "We go to Rumplestiltskin and get your memory back."

．　．　．

EMMA LOCKED MARY MARGARET back up in the cell, told her she'd be out of the office for a few hours, and headed back to their apartment to search the place.

Mary Margaret's claim was that someone had broken in and stolen her jewelry box, but when Emma examined the locks on both doors, she found no sign of forced entry. There were only two keys—hers and Mary Margaret's. Something wasn't right.

She searched Mary Margaret's room but came up empty. She was moving on to her own room when she heard a knock at the door.

Noon on a Monday, she thought. She checked her gun, left the safety off.

"Who is it?" she called through the door.

"It's me!"

Henry.

"What are you doing here?" she said to Henry, after she'd pulled open the door. He came in, beaming.

"It's kinda like the first time we met, isn't it?" he said.

"Why aren't you at school?" Emma asked.

"I'm sick."

"You are not sick."

He sighed and tossed his backpack on the couch. "I wrote notes," he admitted. "But I have to help you. Mary Margaret isn't guilty. This is really important for Operation Cobra."

"This isn't Cobra, I keep telling you," Emma said. "This is real life."

"It's the same thing."

Emma shook her head. "Fine," she said. "You're sick. You can help me search this place, then."

"What are we looking for?"

"I don't know yet," she said. "Anything strange."

She went back to her room and started rooting around near the window, checking for signs of a forced entry there. About five minutes passed. There's nothing here, she thought. And that's because no one—

"I think I found something!"

Emma went out to the living room and found Henry on the floor, pulling at the vent beneath the coffee table. She frowned, moved the table aside.

"There's something down there," said Henry.

"I see it." She brushed him out of the way, studied the grate. She went to the kitchen then and got a screwdriver. It took her a minute to unscrew and lift the grate. When she did, the ceiling light illuminated the rectangular hole, and she could see the outline of the object.

"My god," she said.

Henry said nothing.

Emma pulled a Kleenex from the box on the table, reached down, and pinched the blade of the hunting knife, making sure not to let the handle touch anything.

"Go to Granny's Diner," she said. "Stay there until I come get you." Emma squinted. Was that blood on the blade?

"But I—"

"Go, Henry," Emma said.

Then, a little softer, as both of them looked at the knife, she added: "Go right now."

. . .

ACROSS TOWN, back at the sheriff's office, Emma looked sadly at her friend through the bars. "We have the weapon now," she said. It was bagged and in the evidence locker. Things were looking bleak for Mary Margaret.

"But in the heating vent?" she cried. "I don't even know how to open that."

"Then someone broke into our house and planted it there."

"Do you not believe me?"

"I believe you, Mary Margaret, but I need some evidence pointing in the right direction. So far it's all been pointing the wrong way."

"What are you saying?" said Mary Margaret, sinking back down to the bench in the jail cell.

"I'm saying that it might be time to hire a lawyer," Emma said.

"An excellent idea!"

Both Emma and Mary Margaret turned to see Gold standing in the doorway, his cane held delicately in both hands. He nodded hello.

"What are you doing here?" asked Mary Margaret.

"Offering my legal services," Gold said, coming into the room. "I can be very persuasive. Ask Ms. Swan. I found myself in that same seat not long ago, and now, look at me. A free man."

"It helps to have a judge in your pocket," said Emma.

"It does, actually, yes," he said. "But Ms. Blanchard, I've been following your case, and I believe you'd be well-advised to bring me in as your counsel. Immediately. I, too, can have you free of that cell quite soon."

"What she needs is for me to have space to do my job, Gold, not—"

"No one is stopping you," said Gold. "I'm simply offering to help—"

"Please go."

Both Gold and Emma looked over to Mary Margaret.

"I think you should reconsider, Miss Blanchard," said Gold.

"I wasn't talking to you, Miss Gold," she said, turning a steely gaze to Emma. "I was talking to the sheriff. I'd like to speak to my lawyer now. In private."

Emma eyed her curiously, shrugged, and turned to Gold.

"Okay, you win," she said to Gold. "I hope you have her best interests at heart."

"Of course I do," he said, smiling at Mary Margaret. "I have for some time."

They talked for fifteen minutes. By the time Mr. Gold left, Mary Margaret was feeling much better. Was Mr. Gold trustworthy? Absolutely not. But she knew that he was an enemy of Regina, and she felt sure Regina was trying to frame her. And so in this case, her enemy's enemy was her friend.

She was only alone in her cell for a minute. Emma came back in and nodded at her, but didn't ask about Gold. She didn't have time to ask about anything, actually. A few minutes later, David showed up.

Mary Margaret watched in silence as David requested a few moments alone with her. Emma sighed and looked over in her direction.

"You're popular right now," she said. "You mind?"

"No," Mary Margaret said. "I'll talk to him." Of course she would. David was her only other advocate in town.

Emma turned back to David. "You can have ten minutes."

"I need it to be alone."

She nodded. "Okay. I'll go get a coffee," she said. "Again. Ten minutes."

Emma left them. David took a breath and went to the cell, where Mary Margaret waited hopefully, hands on the bars.

"You came," she said.

"I needed to talk to you," he said. "I did call Kathryn. I remember. We talked. She told me— Mary Margaret, she told me that she wanted you and me to be together. She gave us her blessing."

"She did?"

He nodded.

"There's more, though," he said. "I remembered something else."

Mary Margaret waited, still hopeful. David could barely bring himself to say what he said next.

"I remembered something you said once," he said, "about wanting to kill her. I need to ask you if you had something to do with Kathryn's disappearance."

They stared at each other. Mary Margaret could not believe what she was hearing. Regina was supposed to be the liar; Regina was supposed to be the one making things up. This—this made no sense.

"When your phone records came back, when I found you wandering in the woods, when everyone thought you killed Kathryn . . . I stood by you. I never once doubted you. But now that everything is pointing toward me . . . You actually think I am capable of that?"

David reached for the bar. "I just don't know anymore."

"Get out," Mary Margaret said. "You are unbelievable, David."

"But I—"

"Get out of my sight."

. . .

MARY MARGARET SPENT a terrible night in the cell, tossing and turning. She knew one thing: Whatever was happening, Regina was behind it. She didn't have evidence and she couldn't prove it, but she knew. For her, it would be a matter of finding the hard facts. And in the meantime, she needed a few—only a few—to keep the faith.

Emma was growing more and more concerned that she wouldn't be able to find a way to free her friend. The lab results had come back and confirmed that the heart was Kathryn's. It was now a murder investigation. She, like Mary Margaret, believed Regina was somehow behind it, but so far Regina had bested her at every turn. So she went to the man she'd come to think of as the equalizer.

"I need your help, Mr. Gold," Emma said to him. She was standing in his pawnshop, and he was behind the counter, a wry smile on his face.

"Do you?"

"I do," she said. "I think Regina is behind what's happening with Mary Margaret. I just can't prove it."

"And how can I help?"

"I don't know how to handle her," she said. "I just don't."

Gold smiled. "Quite an act of humility," he said. "I admire that, Ms. Swan. And you're right to be wary. She is a dangerous woman. Very dangerous."

"So tell me," Emma said. "Tell me how to beat her."

CHAPTER 13

HAT TRICK

MMA AND GOLD TALKED FOR TWO HOURS, developing their plan. When Emma felt ready, they headed back to the jail, intent on filling in Mary Margaret.

One problem: Mary Margaret wasn't there.

Henry greeted them outside the sheriff's office, where he was sitting with his book, leaning back against the door. "Your plan is amazing!" he said when he saw them.

"What plan?" said Emma. "What are you doing here?"

"I came to talk to Mary Margaret, but then I realized what was going on so I decided to wait for you."

Emma frowned at Gold, and the two of them went past Henry and into the office. A bolt of cold dread passed through Emma's body when she looked at the empty jail cell.

"It appears Miss Blanchard has taken matters into her own hands," Gold said. "What an interesting development."

Henry had come in behind them.

"Henry," Emma said. "What did you do?"

"I didn't do anything," he said. "I thought *you* did it. Isn't this your plan?"

"No," Emma said. "But it might be someone else's."

"Either that, or she escaped on her own," said Gold.

"The arraignment is at eight a.m. tomorrow," Emma said, going to the cell to examine the door. "She's a fugitive now; she's in trouble."

"Then you have until eight a.m.," Gold said. "To find her."

"What can I do to help?" asked Henry.

"Go home, kid," Emma said. "This is getting way too serious for you to be caught up in it."

"Miss Blanchard's future is already in jeopardy, as you know," Gold said, looking placidly at Emma with his penetrating eyes. "But I should also remind you that if you're caught aiding her, yours may very well be, too."

"I don't care," Emma said, gathering her things. "I'd rather lose my job and help my friend."

"Even if it involves a miscarriage of justice?"

"Even if."

"How interesting," Gold said. "Friendship."

"Haven't you ever had any friends, Mr. Gold? It changes things."

"Yes," he said. "I've heard that."

"Then you understand."

Gold nodded at this. Emma couldn't tell if he respected it, questioned it, or just found it amusing.

. . .

IT WAS LATE, but Emma decided to have a look around near the toll bridge. She didn't know where Mary Margaret had escaped to, but without help, she couldn't have gone very far, and hiding in the woods was just as likely as anything else. The bridge meant something to her. Maybe she would head there.

Emma took the Bug and made her way toward the out-skirts of Storybrooke, worried for her friend. Distracted by her thoughts, she was not paying attention when she ripped around a tight corner and nearly hit a man.

She only glimpsed him for a second as he lurched off the road, diving away to avoid being run down.

Emma stopped the car, got out, and ran back to him. In the bushes she found a man she'd never seen before, sitting up-right and clutching at his ankle. He nodded and said, "Hello. Nice night for a walk." He was tall and lanky, Emma saw. Hand-some in an unusual way, and dressed more formally than most in Storybrooke.

"I'm so sorry," Emma said. "Are you hurt?"

He used a tree to help himself stand, then tried to put some weight on the ankle. It didn't look like it would hold up too well.

"Let me give you a ride home, at least," Emma said.

"I'm fine, I'm fine," he said, waving her off, gimping back toward the road. "It's really no problem." But it obviously was a problem, and he struggled getting just a few feet.

"How far is your house?"

"About a mile," he said. "That way."

"You can't make it a mile," she said. "Come on. Let me drive you; it'd be silly not to."

He sighed and seemed to see the light. "Okay," he said, "fair enough. What's your name?"

"I'm Emma Swan," she said, holding out her hand. "I'm the sheriff. I don't think we've ever met."

"The sheriff!" he cried, smiling. "No, I don't believe we have. I don't get out much." He shook her hand. "But it's good to meet you. My name's Jefferson."

. . .

EMMA WAS SURPRISED when Jefferson pointed out his driveway—an old private road she'd never even noticed before, not far from the very edge of town. They crept through the woods about a quarter mile before coming to a wrought-iron gate and, once through, to the home itself. It was impressive, to say the least. Classical, regal, enormous, and lit up like a Christmas tree. Emma couldn't quite believe what she was seeing. The man lived in a mansion in the middle of nowhere. He looked down on Storybrooke like a lord. How did she not know this guy?

She helped him to the door, and when he invited her in, she agreed. She had to admit: She was curious. Not wanting to get into any details about Mary Margaret, she had told him that she was out looking for a lost dog. He seemed to accept it.

"You must have a big family," she said, which was her way of saying: How could anyone need this much?

"No, it's just me here," he said, limping into the foyer.

Emma followed him, and they entered a large, plush living room.

"This search you're undertaking," he said. "You're out here looking for your dog, is it? I believe I can be of some assistance. I know you have your fancy GPS devices and what have you, but I'm something of an amateur cartographer. . . ." He was rustling around now at a rolltop desk, and when he turned, he was holding a rolled-up map. He limped past her again and unfurled it on the top of the piano. "This has great detail of these woods," he said. "Please use it."

"Huh," Emma said, looking at the map.

"Can I get you anything to drink? Some tea to warm up?"

Emma was transfixed by the map, not just because of its incredible detail, but because of the artistry of it. She started studying the areas she knew, remembering her various encounters. It would have been nice to have had this when they were looking for David. . . .

She looked up. Jefferson was gone from the room, but she could hear him in the kitchen, clinking cups together. He reappeared a few minutes later with a tray of tea. "I thought you might like to warm up before the search," he said.

Emma distractedly took a cup. "This map is incredible," she said, sipping at the tea. "You're very talented."

"Thank you," he said. "It's one of my hobbies."

"And what is it that you do for a living?" she asked.

"Oh, this and that," he said. "Many things." He eased himself down onto his couch. "Come, come," he said. "Have a seat."

Emma glanced once more at the map, then went to the couch and sat down. Maybe it was the stress of the last few days, maybe it was the lack of sleep, but she was suddenly feeling tired. Very tired.

"I really should be going," she said, sinking into the couch. Drowsily, she looked at Jefferson. "I should—"

"You're welcome to stay as long as you like."

Inexplicably, she dropped the cup of tea. It tumbled to the carpet. She stared down at the wet stain, shook her head. Usually I would try to clean that . . . , she thought.

"It's really fine," Jefferson said, and his voice stretched across the room.

She frowned, squinted over at him. All of him was stretching.

"Who . . . ," she tried, but something went wrong. She rolled off the couch, onto the floor, only vaguely aware that she'd been drugged . . . that he had . . .

"Who are you?" she managed, but the world—all of it—was going gray.

· · ·

SHE DREAMT OF A MAN—a father. A father and his daughter.

It was only the two of them.

The father was bold, confident, and powerful. But he was hiding, too. Hiding from the Queen.

He and the daughter played.

They were safe.

They were safe until the Queen came back.

· · ·

WHEN SHE WOKE, she was alone.

She was in the same room, facedown on the couch, her hands bound behind her back. It took her a moment to remember. When she did, the adrenaline started to rush. She was in trouble. Maybe big trouble. Emma managed to squirm her way to the edge of the couch and twist enough to see that the teacup she'd dropped was still there. Watching the door—she didn't know where Jefferson was—she got herself up into a sitting position, slid down to the floor, and managed to knock a throw pillow down on top of the cup. With her shoe, she crushed the teacup. She picked up one of the shards and went to work on the tie that was biting at her wrists.

She was free in a minute.

Once she was up, she looked around the room for a weapon—her gun was in her car—and settled on an iron poker from the rack beside the fireplace. Could she run? Sure. But that felt wrong. She was about to go hunting for psychos when she noticed the telescope at the window, pointed down at Storybrooke. She checked the door once more and looked into the eye of the telescope.

She shuddered.

The sheriff's office, in perfect focus.

Jefferson had been watching her.

She took a breath and decided not to think about the implications of that discovery. Instead, she crept toward the hallway, poker held like a sword.

She came to a half-open door. She heard the sounds—metal on metal—before she got there, but what she saw through the crack made her eyes go wide: the silhouette of Jefferson in a darkened room, sharpening what appeared to be a large pair of scissors.

She stepped back and took a breath. She was about to burst in when she heard a different sound.

A whimper.

Coming from down the hall.

She decided to investigate, and backed away from the room Jefferson was in, unsure if it was wise to give up the element of surprise. But the whimper came again, and she couldn't ignore it. She turned and went to another closed door. The sounds seemed to be coming from behind it.

Quietly, carefully, she twisted the knob and pushed open the door.

In the center of the room: a chair. Little else. On the chair, hands bound, gag in her mouth, eyes screaming in terror: Mary Margaret Blanchard.

Emma rushed into the room, set the poker down, and immediately pulled the gag out from Mary Margaret's mouth. "What are you doing here?" Mary Margaret whispered.

"I should ask you the same thing," Emma whispered back, moving to the rope that bound her wrists. "Who is this guy?"

"I have no idea," she whispered back, eyeing the door.

"I was in the woods, running, and he just grabbed me and brought me here."

"Are you hurt?"

"No—are you?"

"No," Emma said. "How did you get out of the jail?"

"Someone planted a key under my pillow," Mary Margaret whispered. "I thought about it, thought I was in trouble if I stayed there. I don't know. I panicked."

"Who put it there?"

"I don't know."

This guy, Emma thought in a flash. It made perfect sense— and on top of that, he'd been watching the jail. But why would he want both of them here?

She pulled the rope through and the last of the knot fell apart. Then she leaned down and got to work on Mary Margaret's feet, also bound, saying as she worked, "All I know is we gotta get out—"

"Emma!"

"Hello," came a cool, disturbing voice from the doorway. Emma spun. Jefferson stood, silhouetted by the hallway light. He was holding a gun. Her gun.

"I found this out in your car, hope you don't mind," he said. "Blades can be very messy."

"I already called for backup," Emma said.

"You haven't called anyone," he said. "No one knows you're here. And so now you're going to do what I say. Tie her up again."

Emma tried to see a way out, but she couldn't yet. She needed time. So she nodded her head. "Okay," she said. "Just take it easy."

"Make it tight," Jefferson said. "Very tight."

JEFFERSON LED EMMA BACK to the room where she'd seen him sharpening the scissors. Once inside, he flipped on the light, and Emma was dazzled by what she saw.

Hats.

Many, many hats.

They were all top hats, all black, and each occupied an individual, backlit shelf. In the middle of the room was a long table covered in bolts of cloth, scissors, clamps, and stencils—this was the room of a hatmaker.

"I don't know who you are," Emma said, turning to face him, "or what you're doing, but if you hurt her, or me, you're not going to get away with it."

"Hurt her? I'm practically saving her life."

"What does that mean?"

"She was trying to leave Storybrooke," he said. "You know what happens to people who try to leave Storybrooke, don't you?"

"Yeah," Emma said. "They leave."

"No, they don't," he said. "Bad things happen to them. The curse."

Emma shook her head. "Bad things. A curse? You sound like Henry."

"If he's talking about the curse, than he's a smart kid," he said. "You should listen to him."

Okay, Emma thought. He's insane.

"The look on your face betrays your thought," he said. "I know how I must seem to you. But let me tell you a story."

"Okay," said Emma, thinking that it was good to get him talking. Get him talking and keep him talking.

"Once upon a time," he said, "there was a man who lived

for only one thing: his daughter. They lived together in the woods, and he found a way to make ends meet by doing some cobbling here and there, selling wares at the market. They didn't have much, but they had enough."

"Sounds lovely," Emma said.

Jefferson smiled a sarcastic smile. "It was," he said. "But in stories like this, it never lasts, does it? Of course this man had a past, and of course the past caught up with him. Finally."

"What was he?" she asked. "A retired pimp?"

"No," he said. "He was someone who owned a very special, very powerful item. And he knew how to use it. He had worked for a bad, bad woman long before, and one day, she came to his house and told him she needed his services. This item he had, you see, could open up a doorway to another realm, and she needed to get somewhere. To Wonderland, in fact."

"Wonderland?" Emma said. "I didn't see that one coming."

"Of course you didn't," he said, "but the man did. You see Wonderland is a place where all forms of exotic magic are possible, and this woman needed something special. She needed to get back something she'd lost, and it was there, being guarded by the Queen of Hearts."

"What was the cost?" Emma said.

"What?" The question seemed to catch him off guard.

"The cost?" Emma said. "There's always a cost."

"Right," Jefferson said. "Yes. Well, initially this bad woman promised that his daughter would always be safe. But the cost, as you so rightly point out, was far higher than he expected."

"What happened?"

"He was trapped," said Jefferson. "She betrayed him, got what she came for, and left him in Wonderland."

"He couldn't get home to his daughter?"

Jefferson shook his head very slowly. "No," he said. "He couldn't." Emma saw real pain in his eyes. This guy, she thought, is completely insane.

Just as she thought it, Jefferson looked up at her and smiled. "He was driven mad, you see," he said. "While there. Because he couldn't get back."

Emma waited.

"So what happened?" she said.

Jefferson nodded. "Of course. You'd like to know the ending. Any good story has a good ending."

"He never got back?"

"I need you," Jefferson said, "to make me a hat."

Emma looked at him. He was watching her as though he expected her to know what he meant. "What?"

He pointed the gun around the room, then pointed it at the hat on his own head. "What do you think?" he said. He laughed.

"I'm sorry, but you kidnapped me so I could make you a hat?" Emma said.

He put a hand on her back and led her to a bench, then went around the table to the other side, all the while holding the gun on her.

"That's right," he said.

"You don't have enough?"

"Mine don't work," he said. "That has always been the problem. But you have magic, and that's what this world is lacking."

I see, Emma thought. The hat had something to do with that portal. In his story.

"I have been stuck here for decades trying to manufacture a hat like my old hat—a hat that has magic, and a hat that can transport me back to Fairy Tale Land. I've thought it through, you see. This land has no magic, but *you* have magic, Emma. Which means that you can make a hat that works."

"I don't know how to make a hat, let alone a magic hat," Emma said.

"Try."

She looked at him. He did not seem well. In the woods, at least, he'd had the appearance of sanity, but now—well, something was coming unhinged. Emma was afraid. Both for herself and for Mary Margaret.

She picked up the scissors and reached for a bolt of cloth.

"You do know there's no such thing as magic," she said. "Right?"

"Of course, of course," he said. "That's what every ignorant person in this world seems so sure of." He laughed. "Except, that is, when someone needs a personal miracle of their own. Am I right? Then the people of this world *loooove* to believe in magic."

"Why do you keep saying it like that?" she asked. "Are you not from this world?"

"Of course I'm not," he spat, irritated by the question. "I'm stuck here, but I'm not from here. Didn't you listen to the story?"

"And where are you from?"

"I'm from where everyone else in this godforsaken town is from." He pointed the gun emphatically as he said it. "And I've been separated from my little girl." He shook his head. "There are curses, Ms. Swan, and then there are *curses*."

Emma decided to play along.

"I thought everyone was here now, though," she said. "Isn't your daughter here? Somewhere? That's an improvement, isn't it?"

"She's here, yes," he said, looking forlorn. "She doesn't re-member me. She lives with another family. She—"

The doorbell rang.

Jefferson's neck snapped around, and he looked toward the hallway. "Stay here," he said, and he stormed out. Emma heard him locking the door from the other side.

She looked around the room, knowing she had to make some noise. This was her chance. Maybe her only chance.

. . .

SHE HEARD HIM talking to someone at the door for a few min-utes. She couldn't scream, though—it could put Mary Marga-ret in danger.

Emma felt the wind go out of her sails when she heard the sound of August's motorcycle starting up. Soon the grumble of the engine faded, and Jefferson came back in. "Almost!" he cried, and he laughed as he said it. She watched him clap a few times. "But not quite," he said.

Not yet, she thought.

"Back to work," he said. "You and your friend Snow White won't be leaving until you make it work and get me home."

. . .

SHE WORKED ON THE HAT THEN, for what felt like hours, doing her best to re-create the contours of the other hats he'd made. She had no idea what she was doing, but she knew there would be another opening. Somehow. Somewhere. He was too emo-tional, too unhinged, to pull off a rational kidnapping. She just needed to be patient, and to keep probing.

A few hours later, past dawn, she saw her opening.

Jefferson left the room and returned with the telescope

she'd looked in the night before. As he set it up near the window, he giggled to himself, then said, "You don't believe me, do you?"

"About what?"

"About Grace?" he said, now scanning Storybrooke. "I'll show you."

She set down the scissors, knowing he still had the gun in his hand. "Okay," she said, going to the window.

"There she is," he said. "Look."

Emma looked. In the light of the morning, she could see through the kitchen window of a small room. There, a young girl sat at a table, eating breakfast with her parents.

"You think this is your daughter?" she asked.

"I know it is," he said. "Here, she's called Paige."

Emma recognized the girl, actually—she had seen Henry talking to her outside of school. Her name was in fact Paige.

"She's called Grace in your world?" she asked.

He looked at her skeptically. "The world you don't believe is real?"

Emma shrugged. She knew now—this was the way to get to him. To believe. "I guess I'm not sure anymore," she said. "I know that I want to believe. According to Henry, the woman in there is my mother. I wish that were true. Is that enough? I'm not sure. But I'm open to it."

He nodded and came to the telescope. He looked out the window. "You're open to faith, then," he said. "And let me tell you, you have to be if you're separated from your child."

Emma smiled sadly. "I know a thing or two about that."

She went back to the table, and Jefferson took another step toward the window, his hands clasped behind his back. "So you know sometimes you have to believe, because it's the only way you can stay sane."

"Maybe."

Emma took a step toward the telescope.

"So now you understand why I need that hat to work," he said, gazing at the home where his "daughter" lived.

"I do," Emma said. "I do."

He was about to say something more, but he didn't have a chance. Just then Emma hit him in the head with the telescope, and he crumpled to the ground, unconscious.

Emma grabbed her gun and went straight for Mary Margaret. She burst in and began to untie her. "What happened?" Mary Margaret was saying, more nervous now than she'd been before. "What— Emma. Emma!"

But the warning came too late, and Jefferson was too fast. He punched Emma and she went careening, the gun flying from her hands. He pinned her to the floor, raving at her. She grabbed at the only thing she could get her hands on: his scarf. When she pulled it free, she was horrified to see a long scar spanning the entirety of his neck.

He threw her down, reached over her head, and retrieved the gun.

"Off with her head . . . ," Jefferson said then, a maniacal smile on his face.

He pointed the gun.

Emma thought: This is my death.

And then in slow motion, something swung. Mary Margaret was free, brandishing what looked like a war hammer.

No. A croquet mallet.

She hit Jefferson in the center of the back, and he stumbled forward and dropped the gun. When he turned to face Mary

Margaret, she was ready for him. Emma, stunned, watched as she kicked him hard in the center of the chest, and he went flying backward, arms windmilling.

Directly into the window.

The glass shattered, there was a last cry from his lips, and suddenly Jefferson was gone.

Both women ran to the window.

It was a long fall because of the house's perch on a hill. Emma, looking down, expected to see a gruesome scene.

But instead, there was nothing. No body.

Just a top hat.

. . .

OUTSIDE, EMMA AND MARY MARGARET looked for any sign of Jefferson. It was morning now, and the sun was crawling up over Storybrooke. Emma was exhausted.

"Who was he?" Mary Margaret said quietly, hugging herself, looking out at Storybrooke.

"A lonely man," Emma said. She smiled at Mary Margaret. "Maybe the better question is how long have you been a black belt?"

"I don't know what came over me," she responded, looking up at the broken window. Her eye seemed to catch something else, though, and she said, "Emma, look."

Emma looked where she was pointing and saw her car, hidden under a tarp, parked behind a garage.

"So, Sheriff," Mary Margaret said. "I guess you'll be taking me back now?"

Emma sighed. "Run," she said.

"What?"

"I won't stop you."

"That's not going to help anything."

"I'm not so sure your arraignment will help anything," Emma said. "What's important is that you choose. You get to choose, not them. You're my friend, and in my life, friends have been my family." She put her hand on Mary Margaret's shoulder. "I mean that. I'm not going to abandon you."

Mary Margaret smiled.

They walked up to Emma's car and pulled off the tarp. "Everyone thinks I killed Kathryn," Mary Margaret said, "but I didn't. Still, I think we can beat this. I don't want to run."

Emma nodded.

"Good choice," she said.

Her friend Mary Margaret wasn't out of the woods, not by a long shot, but as they rode back toward town, Emma felt a strange new peace wash over her. Neither woman spoke. Mary Margaret looked out the window, her forehead leaning against the glass as though they were on a family road trip, and they were both coming to the end of a long journey. She believed her friend. She believed in her innocence, and she knew that Mary Margaret wasn't capable of harming Kathryn. They were in this together, for better or worse.

"So you think," said Mary Margaret, not turning to look at Emma, "he was crazy?"

Of course was what she wanted to say, but she knew that Mary Margaret was asking about something bigger. Emma had entertained the idea, if only for a moment, that it was all real, that Henry's stories weren't stories, but histories. Part of her longed for it to be true, but her better sense told her it was foolish. For the first time, though, Emma considered how desirable it would be for Mary Margaret to believe she had a daughter, and a true love, and a whole history that meant love in her life. Probably pretty appealing.

"I do," Emma said quietly.

"Yeah," Mary Margaret said, finally turning to look at Emma. "Me, too."

PART THREE

LOST AND FOUND

CHAPTER 14

THE STABLE BOY

HEY GOT MARY MARGARET TO THE COURT-house in time, and not long after that, Emma was locking her back into her cell, her heart heavy. Things had not gone well—the judge had determined there was enough evidence to proceed with the murder trial. Mary Margaret wasn't saying anything. As of now, she was still on the hook for Kathryn's murder.

"We're both exhausted," Emma said. "You sleep. I'm going home to sleep. I'll see you again in a few hours."

Mary Margaret nodded, her head down.

"Have faith, Mary Margaret," said Emma. "Have faith."

Emma walked slowly down Main Street, her head fuzzy, her body used up after the adrenaline and excitement of the night at Jefferson's mansion. Rather than tired, though, she felt tense and worried—she doubted she'd be able to sleep. She considered taking a walk, she considered heading back to the toll bridge in search of new evidence. Anything to spring Mary Margaret. But when she saw Henry sitting in the diner, having a morning cup of hot chocolate before heading off to school, she smiled and went inside. Sometimes the real world was too much.

"Hey, kid," Emma said. "You're a sight for sore eyes."

"I know what you're doing here," said Henry. "You came for story time."

"Maybe so," Emma said, nodding at Ruby for a cup of coffee, and as Henry dug around in his book, Emma thought back to that moment with Jefferson, when he asked her to accept it. To believe that all the stories were true. She'd believed for a second while she pretended. And it had felt good.

"Have you ever wondered," said Henry, "why Regina really hates Snow White so much?"

"Yeah," Emma said, not bothering to correct him and call Mary Margaret by her actual name. She was more interested in asking Henry about Jefferson, or the Mad Hatter, but she didn't have it in her to encourage him. She was fine with him telling her stories, but the other way around made her the Mad Mother.

"It goes back a really long way," Henry said, pointing to an illustration in his book. "It goes back to when Regina was a girl, when she was in love with a stable boy."

"Regina knows how to love?"

"Ha-ha," Henry said, but it wasn't a laugh, and Emma thought: I am being too glib with this kid's heart. Regina had raised him, after all. It wasn't as simple as Emma wanted it to be.

"So what happened with this stable boy?" she said. "And what does it have to do with Snow White?"

"Regina's mom was really, really mean," Henry said, "and she had magic. She started out as a peasant and married this rich lord guy, and she was determined for her daughter to be a queen one day. To have the ultimate power. And then one day, Regina was out riding and this little girl shot past on a horse, totally out of control. Guess who it was?"

"Hmmm," said Emma. "Snow White?"

"Yes!" Henry cried. "And Regina saved her, and Snow White's father, the king, was so happy that he proposed to Regina."

"Uh-oh," Emma said. "Which meant the stable boy was screwed."

"Kind of," said Henry, showing her a new picture: This one showed a young couple in a stable, both of them terrified, staring at an evil-looking woman. "Except Regina tried to say no and stay with the stable boy, and her mom killed him right in front of her."

Emma frowned. "Jesus," she said. "That's awful. This book is really for kids?"

"It's for whomever."

"I don't get why Regina would hate Snow White, though," Emma said. "What's the connection?"

"Snow White accidentally told Regina's mom about the stable boy," Henry said gravely. "That's how the mom found them up there. So Regina always thought that her one true love ended up dead because of Snow White."

"That's . . . incredibly sad," said Emma.

"I know. And do you know what makes it even worse?"

"What?"

"Regina didn't tell Snow White that Daniel ended up dead. Snow White never even *knew* how bad it was."

She had more questions—Whatever became of Regina, then? What happened next?—but she was distracted by a commotion outside of the diner. A few people were running down the sidewalk, and a crowd seemed to be gathering across the street. Emma squinted and stood. "Hold on, Henry," she said, and she jogged to the door and headed across the street.

There were about twenty people gathered around something, but Emma couldn't see what. "What's happening?" she said, coming up to them. "What—"

She stopped short and stared, amazed by what she saw.

It was completely impossible.

But somehow, it was happening.

Kathryn, ragged and skinny and staring up at all of them, her face and clothes covered in dirt, was sitting in the middle of the alley.

Alive.

. . .

THE AMBULANCE ARRIVED a few moments later, and Emma sent Kathryn on to the hospital. Before going herself, she had a quick errand to run. She went right to the police station.

Mary Margaret was asleep on her cot when she came in, but she stirred when Emma closed the door. "What is it?" she asked, seeing Emma stride up.

"You're free," Emma said. "I'm dropping the charges. Kathryn is alive."

"She's—what?" Mary Margaret said, sitting up, still groggy. "Can you even do that?"

"I don't know," Emma said, "but I'm doing it."

"How is she alive?"

"She's alive because she was never in danger," Emma said. "Not any real danger, anyway." It was a hunch, but the hunch was developing in her mind.

She opened up the cell and Mary Margaret stepped out. "Get home, get some rest, clean up. I've got a whole lot of questions. But one thing's for sure: You didn't kill anyone."

"But you knew that already," Mary Margaret said.

"Yes," she said. "I did."

Across town, Emma arrived at the hospital as Dr. Whale finished checking over Kathryn. David was there, sitting outside her room. He did not look well.

"How is she?" Emma asked.

David looked up and nodded at her. "I think she's okay, I don't know," he said. "This whole thing . . ." His voice trailed off.

"How are you?"

"I don't know," he said. "Happy. Sad. Overwhelmed. I'm just so relieved she's alive."

"That seems honest," Emma said.

"Do you—do you know how Mary Margaret is doing?"

"She's okay. She's relieved, too, obviously. But I think she's been pretty traumatized by all of this. As you might imagine."

"I want to talk to her," David said.

"I know" was all Emma said in response.

"So what do I do?" David said, when he realized she wasn't going to offer any more.

"Maybe right now, the best thing is just to do nothing," Emma said. She left unsaid what the two knew to be true: Mary Margaret didn't want to see David. Not after he'd so easily lost faith in her.

David nodded.

He got it, Emma knew. He probably didn't want to think about it, but he got it.

She went into Kathryn's room.

Dr. Whale was saying something to Kathryn, and after a moment of listening, Emma realized he was talking to her about his watch. ". . . still the only Swiss watch with no Japanese parts, and it costs more because—"

What is it with this guy? Emma thought.

He stopped when he realized Emma was standing in the room.

"Sheriff Swan," he said. He gestured toward Kathryn. "She's awake, as you can see."

Emma ignored him, went to Kathryn's bedside.

"Kathryn, I'm Emma Swan," she said. "We met at David's homecoming party."

"I remember," Kathryn said. "You're the sheriff. And roommates with Mary Margaret." Emma heard some tone there. Not great tone.

"That's true," she said, "but I'm not here to play favorites. I don't want to take a lot of your time, but if you can remember what happened to you, or if you can help us in any way . . ."

Kathryn nodded.

"I don't remember much," she said. "I had a car accident. I remember the air bag going off. The next thing I knew, I was in the dark, in some basement. I didn't see anyone, but there was food and water. After that, I don't know. I guess I was drugged."

Dr. Whale nodded. "We're still trying to flush it out of her system," he said. "But she was. Definitely."

"I woke up in a field near the edge of town and just started walking," Kathryn said. "That's all I can tell you."

"You never saw anyone?" Emma asked. "You didn't hear a voice, smell any perfume? Cologne? No details at all?"

"Nothing. I wish I could help, especially since . . . while I was gone, everyone thought I was dead? Is that right?"

Emma looked at Dr. Whale. "Who's been gossiping?" she said.

Whale shrugged.

I do not like this guy, Emma thought.

"I figured she needed to know," he said. "She'll read about her heart in the paper eventually, right?"

"Excuse me," said Kathryn. "My heart?"

"You don't have to worry about the details right now," Emma said quickly, not quite knowing how to explain to the woman that her heart had been found in a box. "What's important is that you're safe."

"Although we do now know that somebody had to have doctored those DNA results."

"DNA results?" Kathryn said. "What are you talking about? I really don't understand."

"Don't worry," said Whale. "Yours is still right where it's supposed to be. The police found a heart and it was believed to be yours."

Great, Emma thought.

Kathryn, looking aghast at this detail, turned back to Emma. "Who would do this?"

"Somebody trying to frame Mary Margaret," Emma said. "We don't know who. Yet."

Kathryn shook her head. "Why?" she said. "Why would anyone do such a thing?"

"We don't know," Emma said.

. . .

THAT NIGHT, the party celebrating Mary Margaret's release was very well attended. Even August was invited.

As Emma sipped some punch and watched August mingling, she wondered about the odd man who'd come to town so recently. She could not figure him out.

She came over just as Henry and Mary Margaret came together. Henry told her that he had a card to deliver. It was from the entire class of children at school, and it read, "We're so glad you didn't kill Mrs. Nolan."

"Why thank you so much, Henry," Mary Margaret said, taking the message in stride. "Please tell everyone I'll be back soon."

"I also got you a bell," he said, handing her a little box. "For the class."

Emma smiled. When she looked up, Gold was watching her, and he nodded to the corner of the room. She walked over.

Emma decided to lay it all out for him: "I don't know what you've been doing with Regina, but I know this whole thing isn't as clean as you're pretending it is. You two somehow manufactured this. I don't know how, or why, but I know something is going on."

"What would possibly make you think I had any agreement with Regina?"

"I don't know," Emma said. "Call it a hunch."

"Hunches are not evidence," Gold said, "and you are a sheriff."

"Were you the one who made Kathryn appear out of thin air?"

"You speak as though I have magical powers," Gold said.

"Sometimes it seems like you do," Emma said.

"I don't understand," Gold said. "Are you proposing that I was both working with Regina and against her?"

"I don't know," Emma said. "Maybe you were working diagonally."

"Perhaps," said Gold. "It's always hard to tell with me, isn't it?"

"Yes. It is."

"Let me ask you a different question entirely," he said.

"What do you think of this stranger? This August? Do you trust him?"

Emma looked over at him. So did Gold.

"I'm starting to."

"His full name is August Wayne Booth," said Gold. "It's obviously a false name."

Emma was silent for a moment, and then she said, "Writers use pseudonyms. I'm not worried about August."

"So you do trust him, then."

"I don't know if I trust him," Emma said, "but I trust him a whole lot more than I trust you."

"Oh, you should trust me more, Ms. Swan," Gold said. "I always follow through with my agreements."

"You always say that, too," Emma said.

"I do," said Gold. "Because it's true."

. . .

THE NEXT MORNING, Emma was at the diner, trying to enjoy a quiet cup of coffee for the first time since Mary Margaret had been released. She didn't know why, but she didn't feel as relieved as she'd expected to. Sure, her friend was out of danger, and Kathryn was safe, but she'd seen too much, and sensed too many backhanded dealings, to really feel as though Storybrooke was "cleaned up." If anything, she now knew how broken it was. And if she didn't know any better, Sidney Glass, former editor of the *Storybrooke Daily Mirror*, was drunk again at eight in the morning. He was in the corner booth.

She shook her head, hoping he wouldn't do anything that would require her to take him to jail. He claimed that Regina had fired him because of the election, but Emma suspected she still didn't know the full story. What she did know was that

Sidney had it bad for Regina. She'd suspected before, but some of his ravings during those late-night arrests, were about "her" or "that woman." Glass never quite revealed who he was talking about, but it was pretty obvious to Emma, especially after he'd so willingly been Regina's lapdog. The two seemed to have had a falling out, but Emma didn't trust him and she never would.

Unfortunately, Glass saw her soon after she saw him, and he stumbled over to her booth and sat himself down.

"Mr. Glass," Emma said. "Probably not the best time to be drunk."

"Every time is the best time to be drunk," Glass said. He nodded once, as though confirming this idea to himself.

"What do you want?"

"I want to explain to you," Glass said, "that this town has all sorts of secrets."

"Not news to me," said Emma. "But thanks."

"I'm not so sure you know about all of them," Glass said. "Don't get cocky."

"Let me guess," said Emma. "You're about to tell me about more of them."

"One, maybe," Glass said. "One or two. I know what you're thinking: Regina did something to that girl. And I know what else you're thinking: Gold has something to do with it, too. Am I right?"

Emma said nothing, just stared back at him.

"Looks like I am."

"I'm just glad she's safe, Sidney," Emma said, getting to her feet. "I hope you stay safe, too." She dropped a couple dollars on the table, and Glass looked at them blankly.

"Hope springs eternal," said Glass, still staring at the bills. "It has to."

"Hope is fine," she said. "But I like evidence. And truth."

He nodded at this. "One more thing, Ms. Swan," he said.

"Okay."

"Things are about to change," he said, "again. You'll get your truth. But there's another piece of information you need to have."

"Are we talking about Kathryn again?"

Sidney shook his head. "No," he said. "We're talking about skeleton keys."

Emma raised her eyebrows.

"I'm listening," she said.

"There is a set," Sidney said. "Regina has them. They open every door in this town."

"That's ridiculous."

"I know," he said, "but that doesn't mean it's not true."

"Why are you telling me this?"

Sidney sighed, looked back at the table. "I don't know, Ms. Swan. I'm conflicted."

"About what?"

"About a lot of things," he said. "I'll see you soon."

. . .

MARY MARGARET had had almost no time to think since she'd been out of jail, and she spent the day after the party cleaning up, resting, and doing her best to process what the last few days had been like. David was on her mind. Of course. The way he'd so glibly betrayed her, the way he was always balking. She had shown him so much faith, so many times. She'd given him so much trust. And what had he given her in return? Hesitation. Doubt. Suspicion. She knew she would have to talk to him, but she didn't know when it would be, or what she would say.

David forced the issue, however, by showing up on the sidewalk outside of her apartment that evening.

She came out at dusk, and he went to her before she could close the door.

She had almost no reaction when she saw him. She felt empty, looking at his face.

"Go away," she said finally.

"I have to talk to you."

"So talk," she said impatiently. She began to dig in her bag.

"I need to apologize."

"Yes, you do."

"I get it," David said. "I didn't believe you and I should have believed you."

Mary Margaret exhaled and stopped digging in her purse. The words came easily, actually. The message was so simple.

"I will never forget that moment," she said. "When the world blows you backward, and the one person you thought would be there to catch you is gone."

"I'm so sorry," David said.

"You should have believed me," Mary Margaret said. "I don't care how the evidence looked."

"I'm human," he said. "It was a good setup. I made a bad mistake. I didn't have faith."

Mary Margaret shook her head and looked past David, up at the clock tower in the center of town. "Sometimes I think there are forces trying to keep us apart."

"What kind of forces?" David asked.

"I don't know," she said, shrugging. There were people she could name, yes, but maybe that was too easy? A story she was imposing on a relationship that just didn't work? "All I know is that every time we get close, something seems to poison us. We have good moments. I don't want them to be replaced with bad moments. That feeling."

"But, Mary Margaret," he said. "I—I love you."

But the words were not powerful. They didn't mean what they could have meant.

"I know," Mary Margaret said. "And that's what makes it so sad."

. . .

EMMA WAS EXHAUSTED. She'd spent the last few days just on the cusp of some kind of insight—incredibly close to seeing the truth, but frustratingly unable to get to it. Nothing about the heart in the box made sense anymore, save for one explanation. Regina. She didn't understand motive and she didn't understand means. But she understood the person.

It was about four o'clock when Regina herself walked into the station. Emma was surprised to see her, and was even more surprised to hear what she had to say:

"You're about to receive a major break in your case," Regina said, "but before you do, I want you to understand all of the circumstances that led up to this."

"I can't wait."

Regina nodded. Emma couldn't believe it. So many months of conflict with this woman, and now, here she was, turning herself in. She didn't trust it, but that didn't mean she wasn't delighted.

"Sidney," Regina called, turning toward the door. "You can come in now."

Emma's delight turned to confusion as she watched Sidney

Glass, head down, come into the room. Regina waited for him with an outstretched arm, as though she were a mother bringing her son to the neighbor's house to apologize.

"Okay, Sidney," she said to him. "Tell the sheriff what you told me."

Sidney looked up, sheepishly.

What in the hell is going on? thought Emma.

"I did it," Sidney said.

Emma waited.

She looked at Regina, back at Sidney. "You did what?" she said.

"I—I kidnapped Kathryn," he said. "I held her in the basement of an abandoned summer home by the lake. I bribed a lab tech to get me the heart from the hospital and used the same person to doctor the lab results."

Emma was stunned. She had nothing to say.

"And the other thing," Regina said, prompting him again.

"I borrowed some skeleton keys from Regina and planted the knife in your apartment."

"My keys," Regina said, shaking her head. "I can't help but feel personally violated about that part."

Emma finally found her voice. "And you want me to believe that you did this . . . for what reason?" There was no way it was true. She reflected on seeing Sidney the other morning at the diner. There was something between these two. Whether it was unrequited love, a financial arrangement, whatever. There was something.

"My plan was to be the one who rescued her," he said flatly. "That way I would have a big story I could use to get back in at the paper. Write a novel, turn it into a movie." He shrugged. Did she see a grin on his face then? "It was my way to get famous, I guess. It was dumb. It was— I know it sounds crazy."

"Oh, I don't know about crazy," Emma said. "False. It sounds false to me."

"I have maps to the house. Downstairs in the basement you'll find chains and everything. Lots of fingerprints, evidence everywhere." He was tearing up now.

"Can I talk to you?" Emma said to Regina. Emma stood. "Sidney, you stay in here."

She walked out of the office, and Regina followed. After closing the door, she turned to the mayor, arms crossed, and said, "That was the biggest load of crap I've ever heard."

"I'm sure that's not true," Regina said.

"That poor man. I know you're behind this, and I understand that you own this game, and him, and you've got a rigged system in place. But I am about to start playing a different game entirely, Regina. And it's one you're going to lose."

Regina opened her mouth to respond, but Emma was riled up now, and she cut her off.

"All I care about is my kid, Regina. That's it. I don't care what happens to you and I don't care what happens to me. You are a sociopath. You tried to take away someone I love, and now I'm going to take away someone you love."

Regina took a step backward. Emma had the satisfaction of seeing her understand. Regina reached up and took hold of a charm around her neck, began to twist it. She's scared, Emma thought.

"I'm taking back my son, Regina," Emma said, "and there's nothing you can do."

CHAPTER 15

THE STRANGER

IT WAS THE DAY MARY MARGARET WAS TO return to work. That morning, Emma was surprised when August stopped by the apartment to install a new, intimidating-looking deadbolt on the door. Henry had apparently suggested it; the two of them had been spending time together. And despite his mysterious entry into town, and the way he had of grinning at her whenever she said anything, the man was growing on her. She also thought it wasn't the worst idea in the world to have a better lock. The incident with the planted knife was still weighing on her.

Emma's next step—she'd decided last night, after her confrontation with Regina—was to hire Gold to build a custody case against Regina. With the resolution to Kathryn's disappearance came a little more clarity. Emma was here for Henry, and she was here to raise him right. Henry living in Regina's home just didn't make sense anymore. The woman was evil. There was no other way to say it.

"Are you ready?" Mary Margaret asked. "To take care of him? If you win?"

Emma looked at her, didn't answer. Instead she turned to the door.

"It looks like it belongs in a castle," Emma said, looking at the enormous lock once August was finished installing it. He looked proudly at the door, then nodded.

"No one is getting in this place," he said.

Just then, Henry's voice squawked to life on Emma's walkie-talkie. "Code red! Code red! Operation Cobra emergency!" he yelled.

"What is it?" Emma said into the walkie-talkie.

"Meet me at the sheriff's station!" Henry cried.

Emma raised an eyebrow and looked at Mary Margaret. "Duty calls," Mary Margaret said. "Good luck."

August left with Emma, and when they were outside, he asked if it would be okay if he came along. Emma, hurrying down the sidewalk, gave him a funny look. "Why?" she said.

"I thought you didn't believe in any of that Operation Cobra stuff," he said, struggling to keep up with her. More of the limp. She'd seen it a few times already. She wasn't sure what to make of it.

"I don't," she said, "but it's a way to connect with Henry."

August nodded. "You know that a custody battle with Regina isn't going to do anything, right?" he said.

"You came over to install a lock, not give advice."

"You need to look at the big picture, Emma," he said. "That's the only way you'll understand what you're up against with Regina."

"Yeah, new guy? How's that?"

"It's not something I can tell you," August said. "Take the day off. Let me show you."

"What will you do?" she asked. "Take me on a magical mystery tour?"

"No," he said. "Not at all. But I'll ask you to take a leap of faith."

"Yeah? Are we going to go drink some more water?"

"No. Something serious this time. Something important."

Emma stopped walking, and he did, too.

"Who are you?" she said. "Really?"

"Just a concerned citizen."

"Right, August. Right."

They didn't speak the rest of the way. Emma was over his cryptic comments and would have preferred him to simply come clean and tell her what he knew. Because he did know something. At this point it was tedious.

When they reached the sheriff's office, they found Henry at Emma's desk. He had his book in front of him and was studying it carefully.

"What's the emergency?" Emma said to him.

"There's a new story in the book!" he cried.

Emma went over, looked at it. "How is that possible?"

"Somebody must have added it while it was lost," Henry said. "I don't know. Maybe it's somebody trying to tell us more about the curse."

"What's the new story about?" Emma asked.

Henry looked at August, then looked back at the book. "Pinocchio," he said. "It's about Pinocchio. But it's not done."

"Come on, Henry," Emma said. "I'll walk you to school." She gave August her best "time for you to go" look and helped Henry gather his things. "You can tell me about it on the way."

. . .

"AUGUST IS PINOCCHIO," Henry said. "Isn't it totally obvious to you?"

"Um," said Emma. "No."

"Why do you think he's limping?"

"Because his leg hurts?"

"No," Henry said, shaking his head. "He's limping because he's turning back into wood. Now that he's stuck in a world where there's no magic."

Emma nodded. "That's right. We're in the land without magic."

"Right," Henry said. "So he's in trouble."

He explained the basics of Pinocchio's story, and it all sounded familiar to Emma—marionette, Geppetto, whale, et cetera—until Henry got to the part where the Blue Fairy asked Geppetto to design a magical portal wardrobe to evade the Evil Queen's curse.

"Hold on," Emma said. "This story joins up with the other stories?"

"Of course, they all do," Henry said. "And they needed Geppetto to help make the wardrobe that would save you and save Snow White and protect the two of you from the curse. But Geppetto snuck Pinocchio inside right before you to get *him* to safety, too. He made Pinocchio promise to take care of you."

"I see," Emma said. "Just little baby Emma and little baby Pinocchio."

"I think he was a little older than you."

Emma sighed. "Sure, kid," she said, patting him on the shoulder. "I have noticed a couple gray streaks. You're right."

. . .

EMMA DROPPED him off and headed back to work, taking a moment to smile at Mary Margaret. Mary Margaret smiled back, and as she left, she said to Henry, "Did you have a nice walk with Emma?"

"She never believes any of my stories," he said. "But yeah."

Mary Margaret nodded, trying to think of something to say to Henry to ease his mind about his book. She felt guilty for being the one who gave it to him, but he got so much joy out of it. She didn't know if it was better or worse that he had it.

"Oh crap," Henry said, looking through his backpack. He looked up at Mary Margaret. "I forgot my lunch at home."

Great, Mary Margaret thought.

"No problem," she said. "We don't start for fifteen minutes. Let me have the office call your mom." She sent him inside, and Mary Margaret waited outside, fantasizing about all the angry things she might say to Regina.

The mayor approached the school a few minutes before the first bell rang. Mary Margaret watched her coming.

"I see that you're back," Regina said to her.

"Yes," she said. "Imagine that."

Regina showed no reaction to this, and after a moment of studying Mary Margaret, she said, "Miss Blanchard, is there some kind of problem?"

"Not anymore," she said. "Although someone did go to a lot of trouble to make it look like I did something horrible. But they failed." She smiled curtly. "So I'm fine."

"Are you insinuating something?"

"Yes," Mary Margaret said. "I am. But I forgive you. Even if you can't admit what you did—I forgive you anyway." She shook her head, frustrated at Regina's implacable gaze. "Your life must be filled with such incredible loneliness if your only joy comes from destroying everyone else's happiness. It's so sad, Mayor Mills, because despite what you think—it won't make you happy. It's simply going to leave a giant hole in your heart."

Mary Margaret thought she saw something—some flicker—behind Regina's eyes. But it soon disappeared.

"Have a nice day, Miss Blanchard," Regina finally said. "I'll see you again soon, I'm sure."

She left just as the bell started to ring.

. . .

EMMA WENT STRAIGHT to Mr. Gold's pawnshop after she left the school. She was intent on following through with her plan to get custody of Henry once and for all. She was scared that it would disrupt his life, and she knew that Regina would put up a fight, but there was something about the way she'd acted last night—perhaps she'd let slip a part of the façade and showed, for a moment, her truest colors?—that made it no longer possible to delay. There was one lawyer in town she knew could win against Regina, even though she didn't trust him. She had few options.

Inside the shop, Mr. Gold was behind his desk, looking through some papers. "Ah," he said, seeing her come in. "Ms. Swan."

"I have to save him, Gold," Emma said. "I have to get Henry away from Regina."

He nodded thoughtfully.

"I must admit," he said, "your intentions are admirable. Removing Henry from her custody after what we've seen her do to Mary Margaret does seem like the best course of action." He nodded to himself. "However," he added, "I can't take the case."

This was not what Emma was expecting to hear.

"How can you say that?" she said. "You know what Regina did."

"Yes, but we can't prove it," he said. "I'm sorry, Ms. Swan, but I've made up my mind," he said. "Now, if you'll excuse me, I'm just about to leave."

Emma put a hand down on the desk in front of him. "Change your mind," she said.

"I know how to pick my battles," he responded. "This is not one we can win."

"Why are you suddenly scared of her?"

"I'm not scared. I'm afraid I'm simply not the person who can help you beat Regina. This time."

She was furious, but there was always something with Gold—always a trick. The way he was smiling, she realized he was implying that somebody else would help. Somebody, perhaps, better suited.

And then she saw it.

"I guess you're not," she said.

.   .   .

SHE WENT STRAIGHT to the inn, asked Granny for the room number, and was soon pounding on August's door. She heard some movement inside, and after a minute, he opened it. Emma's first thought: He looks haggard.

"Take it easy, take it easy," he said. "Is everything okay?"

"No," she said. "It's not. I'm just about out of options."

"Just about?" he said, cocking his head.

"You said that if I want to beat Regina, I have to see the big picture. Do you remember?"

He nodded.

"Well. I need to see the big picture." A little grin crept across August's face. "Show it to me."

"Okay," he said. "I will."

They took his motorcycle. Soon they were tearing down the road out of Storybrooke, Emma holding his waist, her helmeted head pressing against his leather jacket. As they crossed the town line and headed toward the interstate, Emma realized that this was the first time she'd been out of Storybrooke since the night she'd arrived with Henry. How was it possible that her world had been so overturned? That her life had become something else entirely? Henry's warnings about leaving Storybrooke rang through her head, but she discounted them. She didn't know where they were going, but August apparently had a destination in mind. Fifteen minutes later they were cruising at eighty back toward Boston, August expertly weaving past the slower vehicles. What was it about this man? He knew something. She knew he knew something. Whatever it was, she was about to find out.

. . .

WITH AUGUST DRIVING, it did not take them long to get to the outskirts of Boston.

August piloted them down a forgotten road, and soon they were back in the woods, still far from the urban population of Boston. He slowed as they approached a dusty old diner on the side of the road; Emma couldn't even tell if it was operational.

August stopped, and Emma got off the bike and removed her helmet. "What the hell," she said, looking at the diner, "are we doing?"

"Revisiting history."

"Can you stop screwing around, please?" she asked. "I'm

not a character in one of your books. Tell me what we're doing here."

"I think you know," he said. "I think that's why you're so upset." He nodded toward the diner. "You've been here before."

Emma squinted at the diner and tried to remember any time in the last few years she'd been here. August watched her for a moment, then reached into his jacket and pulled out a folded newspaper clipping.

The headline read SEVEN-YEAR-OLD BOY FINDS BABY GIRL ON SIDE OF HIGHWAY.

"You see the diner in the background?" August asked. "That's this one. This is where that boy brought you."

She looked back at the diner, but she didn't have to. She knew that they were the same. And that he was telling the truth.

"You brought me to the place I was found," Emma said defensively. "Big deal. Why?"

"This is my story, too. Yours and mine—it's the same story."

"How is that?"

"That seven-year-old boy who found you?" He nodded once more. "That was me, Emma." He pointed to the picture of the boy. "That was me. "

. . .

EMMA FOLLOWED AUGUST in silence as he led her through the woods. Being here made her think of her parents' choice to leave her. She had been dumped, like garbage, by the people who were supposed to take care of her. This walk was stirring up the old rage, which she'd worked so hard, for so many years, to suppress.

"Why are we in the woods?" she asked August, mostly to distract herself from the growing cyclone in her stomach.

"The answers are all out here," he said. "Right where I found you."

Emma stopped walking. After a moment, August glanced back, saw her, and turned as well. He reached out and braced himself with the trunk of a tree.

"You're not that boy," Emma said. "You know how I know? I wasn't found in the woods. I was found by the road. Near that diner."

"Why do you think that?" asked August. "Because you read it in the newspaper? Did it ever occur to you that maybe the seven-year-old boy might have lied about where he found you?"

"It occurs to me that you've been lying to me," she said. "About everything. And that I've been eating it up because I'm vulnerable, and you know that." She shook her head. She was not going to cry in front of him, no matter what this place was doing to her. "I'm done listening."

He took a pained step toward her. "When I found you," he said, "you were wrapped in a blanket. It was white with purple ribbon around the edges. And the name 'Emma' was embroidered along the bottom of it.

"That wasn't in the article, was it?" August asked.

Emma told herself he could have found it; he could have seen it in the apartment.

"No," said Emma, "but it's not very convincing. Why would you lie about where you found me? All the way back then?"

"To protect you," he said plainly.

"Protect me?" she said. "Protect me from what?"

August took a breath, then went back across the trail to the big tree. It was no different from any of the others around, at least not on first glance. Emma watched August as he went to it, though, and she could see, once he was there, that the middle of the tree was hollow.

"No one could know where you really came from," August said.

"I came from a tree?"

"You know the stories from Henry's book, right? You know about the curse in those stories, and how you play a role in them. Am I right? It's true, Emma," August said. "All of it. We both came into this world through that tree. Just like we both left the last world through a wardrobe."

"I get it," Emma said. "You're Pinocchio. That explains all the lying." She nodded. "You're the one who added that new story to the book, aren't you?" she said. "And actually, I see. You're the one who replaced the whole book. After the first one was lost." She shook her head. "You're nuts, aren't you?"

"I needed you to know the truth."

"The truth is that you're out of your mind. And you're not even a good liar, August. Why not put an ending to the story?"

"Because this?" he said, opening his arms. "This is the ending. We're writing it. Right now. You and I."

"How does it end?" Emma said.

"With you believing me," he said pleadingly.

Either that, Emma thought, or with this guy chopping off my head and burying me out here.

"It's not going to happen, August," she said, "so just drop it."

"Just—just trust me," he said. He was getting frustrated, something Emma didn't like to see. "Touch it. The proof that you need will reveal itself to you. Just touch it. How hard is that?"

"Why are you doing this?" Emma said. "Why do you care so much that I see whatever truth it is you want me to see?"

August nodded and looked down. "Because I promised my father that I would protect you," he said, "when we came through to the other side." He took a breath and looked back at her. She was surprised to see tears in his eyes. "And I failed you. I left you."

"What do you mean?"

"I left you at the foster home," he said. "I promised I would stay with you, and I left you."

Emma didn't know why, she couldn't explain it, but this made her tear up as well. She did everything she could to hold it in.

"I'm so sorry, Emma," he said. "I—I ran away. I didn't like it there. I was afraid. But I should have stayed with you."

Emma could think of nothing to say, and she instead looked at the hollow tree.

"Isn't it worth just giving it a shot? Indulge me. Take a leap of faith. Touch the tree."

Emma looked again at the tree. It would be so simple. She kind of wanted it to be true. She did. More than anything.

She stepped toward the tree. After one last look at August, she reached out and touched it.

She closed her eyes.

She waited.

Nothing happened.

After a few seconds, Emma opened her eyes. August was eagerly awaiting a report. "Do you see it?" he asked. "Do you remember?"

Whatever he thinks, Emma realized, he's not lying. He believes this. All of it.

"What did you see?" he asked.

"Nothing," she said.

"That's not possible," he said, coming to the tree, touching it as well. "You were supposed to remember. You were supposed to believe."

She felt the weakness of all those emotions drain out of her, and her old steely self returned. Her gaze hardened. Her shoulders tightened. "I don't," she said, turning away from the tree. She started walking back toward the diner. She had another thought, though, and turned back.

"You wanted me to get answers," she said. "Well, I think I just did. I'm done, August. With you. With Storybrooke. With all of it."

He followed her; she could hear him struggling to keep up as he crashed through the bushes. "Emma, wait," he said. "You don't understand. This isn't how it was supposed to be—"

His speech was interrupted by the sound of him falling, and Emma turned to look as he cried out. August lay on the ground, holding his leg in pain. He clenched his teeth and looked at her.

"What is wrong with your leg?" she asked flatly.

"I was supposed to be there for you," he said. "I was supposed to be brave for you. I wasn't. For that, I'm sorry."

"What in the hell are you talking about?" Emma asked. "Do you still think you're my guardian Pinocchio?"

He shook his head at her sarcasm, then leaned back against a tree trunk. He looked defeated. Thank God, Emma thought. Maybe now we can go.

"You don't believe," he said.

"If you think getting me to feel sorry for you now is going to change anything, you're wrong."

"I'm not screwing around here. Whatever you believe or don't—this is real, Emma. I'm sick. I'm dying." He took a few breaths, and his eyes glazed over. "You ever been to Phuket?"

"What does that have to do with anything?" Emma asked.

"Beautiful place," he said. "An amazing island. The perfect place to lose yourself, you know?" He scratched at his beard. "That's where I was . . . when. When you decided to stay in Storybrooke."

"How the hell did you know, or would you know, that I decided to stay there?"

"Because at eight fifteen in the morning, I woke up to a shooting pain in my leg. That's eight fifteen at night in Storybrooke. Does that time sound familiar?"

Emma waited. She didn't know where this was going, but she was ready to not believe whatever he said.

"That's when you decided to stay. When time started moving forward there again. I should have been there for you, but I wasn't. And because I was halfway around the world, I got a painful reminder of how far I had strayed." He got himself back up to his feet during this speech, and now he leaned down to the cuff of his pants. "If the tree won't make you believe, Emma, maybe this will."

He pulled up the bottom of his trousers, showing Emma his hairy white shin.

"Are you still ready to deny it?"

"All I see," Emma said, "is your leg."

August looked down, his eyes wide. "You don't see that?" he said loudly. "You don't see that I'm turning back into wood?"

It was confirmed. The man was crazy. And what did that make her? She was out here with him. She had reached for that tree, hoping to see something. Wanting to believe. But nothing good ever came from wanting to believe. All it meant was that you'd miss the truth.

"You just don't want to believe it," August said.

"That's not true," she said. "But either way, why is it so important to you that I do?"

"Because the town—everyone—needs you, Emma. It's your responsibility to save us."

"My responsibility? You're telling me I'm responsible for everyone's happiness? That's crap. I didn't ask for it and I don't want it."

"Right now. Not so long ago, you didn't want Henry. Then he came to you, and now you're fighting like hell for him."

"For him, yes. Because that makes sense. He's my son. And that's all I can handle. I'm not even doing a good job of it. Now you want me to save everyone else?"

August just stared back.

"Take me back," she said. "I'm done."

. . .

IT WAS DARK by the time Emma returned to Storybrooke. She barely said good-bye to August when he dropped her off at her apartment, and after a moment's consideration, she didn't even go in to gather her things. She had her car, she had her keys, she had the clothes on her back. What else had she ever needed?

She drove the Bug to Regina's mansion, parked on the street, and grabbed her walkie-talkie from the glove compartment. "Code Red," she said quietly. She took a breath and said it again, this time louder: "Code Red, Henry."

"Emma!" he cried. "What's wrong?"

The light was on in his room, and she smiled up at it, imagining him in his bed, excited to imagine another step in the plan unfolding. This would be hard.

"I need to talk to you," she said. "I'm outside."

A second passed, and she saw his face in the window. "It's about you and me," she said. "Can you come down?"

"Sure."

He did, and when he got to the car, they sat in silence for a few moments.

"Henry," she said finally. "Have you ever thought about what's keeping us here?"

"The curse," he said immediately. "That's what's keeping everyone here."

She shook her head sadly. "You once told me that I'm different. That I can leave."

He nodded.

"Then aren't you different, too?" she asked. "Because you're my kid?"

"Yeah," he said. "Why?"

"I need to ask you something, then," she said. "Okay?"

He waited.

"Do you want to get away from Regina? Come live with me?"

An enormous smile appeared on Henry's face. "More than anything," he said.

This is right, Emma thought. This feels right.

"Good," Emma said. "Then buckle up."

"Why? Where are we going?"

Emma put the car into gear. "We're leaving Storybrooke."

CHAPTER 16

AN APPLE RED AS BLOOD

T HAD ALL HAPPENED SO FAST—SNOW, HER memories of Charming erased, had been intent on finding the Evil Queen and killing her once and for all, and only moments after Charming had finally awoken her to her love, and to clarity, George's soldiers hauled him away. It was as though they were doomed to be apart; forces conspired to keep them away from each other. Just when he found her, she lost him. She wasn't going to let it happen again.

She had an army.

And this time, she was going to find him.

Her army was, admittedly, not of the traditional sort. She had the seven dwarfs, Red, and Granny. They had traveled to King George's castle with the aim of rescuing the prince. They hunkered down to make their final preparations. Snow again scanned the gates with her spyglass, then pressed her back against the stone wall, behind which they were all gathered.

"There's a half-dozen soldiers on each parapet," she said.

"We're going to need air support," said Granny.

"Air?" said Grumpy. "I know just the person who can help us. Someone who owes me a favor."

Before Snow could ask him what he meant, they heard a rustling in the nearby trees. The dwarfs and Snow all drew their weapons, but were glad to see Red emerging from the forest. "Don't shoot," she said. "It's only me." Snow saw a dried trickle of blood near her mouth and decided it was best not to ask whose it was.

"What did you learn?" she said.

"Your prince is still alive," said Red. "And the Queen is here."

Snow felt elated by the news, but wary of the Queen's presence. Storming a castle protected by King George's men would have been hard enough. The Queen, and her magic, presented a new layer of difficulty.

"It's a trap," said Granny.

Snow nodded grimly.

"We can't stop now." She imagined him inside, chained up, at the mercy of two exceptionally cruel people. "But I'll understand if any of you want to turn back," she said. "I can't ask you all to risk your lives."

She looked at the dwarfs, one by one. She looked at Granny and Red. No one moved.

"Okay then," she said. "There's no time to waste." She turned to Grumpy. "Grumpy? That air support would be lovely."

He smiled. "Did I ever tell you about the time I fell in love with a fairy, and we made a plan to run away together? Man oh man," he said. "It was something else." He nodded at his friends, said, "We'll be back," and hustled off, into the woods.

"Why is the Queen doing this, do you think?" Red asked Snow, sitting beside her against the wall.

"Because of a mistake I made as a child," Snow said. "My father was supposed to marry her, but she loved someone else. A stable boy named Daniel."

"What happened?" Red asked.

"They kept their love a secret, but I found out," Snow said. "I broke her trust and let the secret out. And because of that . . ." Snow sighed. "Daniel had to run away and their chance of love was ruined."

"He left her?"

Snow nodded sadly. "She never saw him again."

"I guess I never thought of the Evil Queen as ever caring about love," Red said.

"She did once," Snow said. "And I destroyed her chance at happiness. Now she wants to destroy mine."

. . .

EMMA AND HENRY SPED through town and were nearing the edge of Storybrooke before Henry spoke up again. "I don't want to go," he said. "What about—what about my stuff?" He looked in the backseat, saw Emma's small bag. "Is that all you have?"

"All I need." Emma nodded. "We have to get away from here. From her," she said.

"No, no," Henry said, shaking his head. "Stop the car."

She hadn't heard him like this before; he tended to get excited, yes, but right now he sounded afraid. Emma wasn't sure this was the right thing to do.

"You have to stay in Storybrooke," he said, "because of the curse. You have to break the curse!"

She shook her head, knowing he was close to tears.

"No, I don't," she said. "I have to help you. Those are different things."

"But you're a hero!" he cried. "You can't run! You're supposed to help everybody."

She thought of August's argument out in the woods. It was

the same thing. Help others before you help yourself. But Emma had never lived that way, and she wasn't about to start now.

"Look, kid," she said. "I know it's hard for you to see it, but I'm doing what's best for you. That's what you wanted when you brought me to Storybrooke. That's what I'm doing."

"I want you to do what's best for all of us," Henry said, almost arguing with her thoughts. "I thought you were believing. I thought you were starting to get it."

"Henry—"

"You weren't?"

"I don't know what I was doing. But now I see it clearly. The problem is the place. This place. Storybrooke."

"But the curse," he said, shaking his head. "You're the only chance to bring back the happy endings . . ."

There was nothing she could say, so she didn't bother trying to comfort him. He would figure it out eventually. She watched grimly as they approached the sign marking the edge of Storybrooke, thinking, for the first time, of what their lives might look like in Boston. They could—

"Henry!" she cried.

It happened fast. He reached over and yanked the wheel to the side, and it was all Emma could do to keep the Bug from rolling. She corrected the steering, hit the brakes, and whipped the wheel back the other way to make up for their momentum to the right. The Bug spun but didn't roll, and they came to a stop perpendicular to the road.

She looked at Henry. "What are you thinking?" she said. "You could have gotten us both killed!"

But her heart stopped her from saying more. He was crestfallen. Tears in his eyes, snot bubbling out of his nose, he strung together a series of fragments: "...We can't go... please...please don't make me...Everything is here...your parents...me...your family...we can't go. Don't make me go." He hung his head, and Emma reached over, pulled him toward her. This wasn't the way. It wasn't going to work like this. She'd have to find another way.

"Okay," she said. "I'm sorry. We're not going." She shook her head. "I'm sorry."

. . .

AFTER A FEW MOMENTS, and after Henry calmed down, Emma turned the car around and headed back to Storybrooke. She dropped Henry off at home and went back to her apartment. Inside, she found Mary Margaret in the kitchen, making breakfast.

"I thought you'd left," Mary Margaret said when she came in.

Great, Emma thought. Now she's pissed, too.

"Mary Margaret—" Emma began.

"But it was hard to tell, seeing as you didn't bother to say good-bye." She looked up from the toaster and took a step toward Emma, her anger rising. "Do you remember when I left? When I ran? What you said to me? That we had to stick together. That we were like family?"

"Yes," Emma said. "I'm sorry. I shouldn't have left."

"That's right, you shouldn't have. Why, after everything, would you just go?"

Emma sighed. "I don't want to be sheriff anymore. I don't want people relying on me. I don't want this." She shook her head, feeling more defeated than she had since she'd been here.

"What about Henry?" Mary Margaret asked.

"I—I tried to take him with me."

"You abducted him?"

Emma had never seen Mary Margaret this angry. She had no defense against her accusations, either.

"I want what's best for him."

"And being on the run is what's best? It sounds like it's what's best for you, Emma. I thought you'd changed."

"You thought wrong," Emma said.

"Well, regardless," Mary Margaret said, "you've got to do the right thing for him now."

"And what's that?"

"I don't know. You're his mother." She gave Emma one last angry glare. "Figure it out."

. . .

SNOW WATCHED THE CASTLE wall through the spyglass until she heard the signal: a piercing wolf's howl. That was it. Now was the time.

She turned to Grumpy. "Do it," she said.

He nodded, and she watched as Happy nocked an arrow and Grumpy lit the lanolin-soaked rag wrapped around the arrowhead. The arrow lit, Happy drew it back and launched it up into the night sky.

That was the signal.

"Let's go!" Snow cried. She and the dwarfs, along with Granny and Jiminy, ran toward the castle walls.

As they ran, Snow heard the first bombardments coming from their "air support": The Blue Fairy and a cadre of her companions swarmed down from the sky and began peppering the castle and its guards with multicolored fireballs.

"Go, go!" Snow cried, and soon they reached the castle

walls. Above, the soldiers were all preoccupied with the fairies. Snow nodded to Granny, who shot a grappling claw up over the wall. The metal gripped the stone, and Snow nodded. So far, so good.

She, the dwarfs, and Granny all climbed the dangling rope, and one by one, they reached the lowest parapet. Snow surveyed the scene. All of the guards had flocked down to the central courtyard and were shooting up into the sky.

"Come on," Snow said.

They hustled down a set of stone stairs and soon reached the courtyard. Just as they did, Snow felt a hand on her shoulder, and turned to find Red there behind them. Snow nodded. They were at full strength. She could see, a hundred yards in the distance, the doorway where she guessed Charming was being held. A dozen guards blocked their path.

This time, she didn't have to give the order. The dwarfs were out front, their pikes raised, all of them screaming with the rage of battle. Snow, Red, and Granny were not far behind.

The guards never saw them coming.

It took only a minute to dispatch them all, distracted as they were by the aerial bombardment. Beside her, Snow felt Red expanding in size, and then she heard the wolf version of her friend cutting through the terrified guards. She concentrated on her own fight with an overweight, armor-clad man, who was too slow to stop her flurry of quick strikes with her short sword.

"There!" Granny cried, just as the guard she was fighting fell. From the east, another dozen guards were streaming into the courtyard. "Now's your chance!" Granny said. "We'll hold them."

Snow nodded and ran for the doorway, taking the stairs by twos, remembering the way from her last incursion.

At the top of the stairs, she reached a long, dark corridor. The torches had been extinguished. She looked down the hallway, breathing heavily, listening for any sound. I am alone, she thought. She took a step.

When she did, King George stepped out from a doorway halfway down the hall. He drew an enormous sword and pointed it at her head.

"Hello, my dear," he said. "Going somewhere?"

Snow took a step forward, holding her measly sword out. This man, she thought, has caused me much misery. She had to get past him, she knew that. But she was terrified.

When she was ten feet from him, she saw movement near George's feet. Before she realized what she was seeing, George cried out in pain.

Jiminy, a tiny sword drawn, was stabbing at George's calf.

"Ha!" he cried, and stabbed again.

George attempted to slice downward, but Jiminy was too quick. He danced to the other calf and stabbed there. This time Snow cringed at the attack; she saw a small spurt of blood shoot out from George's leg, and he crumpled to the ground.

Snow ran up. "Good job," she said, kicking George's sword aside. "Come on."

"Snow!" came a cry. "Snow White!" It was Charming. His voice was coming from a chamber at the end of the hall.

"He's here," she said. "Go tell the others." Jiminy nodded and hopped off, back toward the stairs.

Snow took another breath, then walked toward the sound of her beloved's voice. The Evil Queen was still somewhere, and Snow was wary of a trap. Sword held high, she cautiously stepped into the room.

And she saw him.

He was standing in an alcove, his hands bound, looking at her with both hope and fear in his eyes.

She ran toward him. "My love!" she cried. "Charming!"

It was only after she'd approached, though, that she realized that they'd been had. The image of Charming was only that: an image. He was in a mirror. Which meant that he was not, in fact, here in this castle. The Evil Queen had taken him away, back to her own home. She put her hand on the glass of the mirror.

"The Queen took me to her palace," he said sadly.

"But I'm rescuing you," she said.

"Snow," he said, shaking his head. They were both crying now.

"Is this going to be our life?" she asked. "We take turns finding each other?"

"We will be together. I know it," he said. "Have faith."

She heard the sound of the Evil Queen's muted laughter and watched as green smoke filled the mirror, clouding over her love. The laughter become louder, and soon Snow was looking at a haughty, happy Regina.

"Let him go," Snow said. "Your fight is with me." She could not believe that the betrayal of Regina's secret, so long ago, still drove the woman. She knew how powerful love could be, but she couldn't imagine vengeance—this much vengeance—no matter what happened.

"Exactly my thought, old friend," Regina said. "Have you ever heard of a parlay? We break off this messy fight and have a little talk, just you and me. Come unarmed."

"Fine," Snow said. "Where do I meet you?"

"Where it all began," said Regina.

Snow knew exactly what she meant.

. . .

EMMA HAD ALREADY GONE to Archie's office, only to find the OUT TO LUNCH sign up on his door. Considering the town, that meant pretty much one option: Granny's.

She found him alone in a booth, eating a grilled cheese sandwich and tomato soup.

"You got a minute?" she said, sliding in across from him.

He dabbed at his mouth. "Of course, Emma," he said. "Of course."

Emma told him the story of what Henry had done the night before, in the car. Archie listened attentively, and when she was through, he said, "He grabbed the wheel?" He shook his head. "He must not have considered the consequences."

"That's just it," she said. "I think he did. I think he would rather die than leave Storybrooke."

He nodded. "Children like stability and structure. Change means no one's going to be there to take care of them."

"I want to be there to take care of him," she said. "But it's easy to say it. Harder to do it."

"Let me ask you a question," he said. "As this war between you and Regina rages on, who is really getting hurt?"

She knew the answer; she didn't need to say it out loud. How much of this could the kid take?

"But isn't it good for him to be with me?" she asked.

"Emma, all personal feelings aside. And even professional feelings. I'm afraid you just don't have a case for getting custody."

"I'm his mother."

"You are. So is Regina. And, well, the court's gonna look at how he's been doing since you came into his life."

"And he's happier, isn't he?" Emma said hopefully.

"Maybe," he said. "But objectively? He's skipped school. Stolen a credit card. Run away. Endangered himself. Repeatedly. So, in the eyes of the law . . ."

"What about in your eyes?" she asked. "What do you think?"

"You know, a while back I told you to engage him on his fantasy life, and perhaps . . ." He sighed. "Perhaps I was wrong. He's been retreating further into it."

"So you think he's better off with Regina," she said.

"I didn't say that."

"Do you think," Emma asked, "that she would ever hurt him?"

"No. Never," Archie said. "Everyone else, sure. But not him. Her actions, right or wrong, have been defensive. I'm not judging here. But in many ways, Emma, your arrival woke a sleeping dragon."

She found it to be an odd choice of words.

"So tell me," she said finally. "Honestly. Is Henry better off since I got here?"

"I don't think it's a matter of being better off," he said. "It's a matter of this conflict needing to end. If you two are going to be in his life, you have to figure out the best way to do that. Plain and simple."

Yup, Emma thought. Plain and simple.

"Okay," she said. "Thanks, Doc." She slid out of the booth.

"Are you all right?" he asked her. "You look like you're in pain."

"Not me," she said. "Just my conscience."

. . .

SHE LEFT THE DINER in a daze, oppressed by her own emotions. What had she done to Henry? What had she done? It all seemed so cocksure now, so bold and reckless. This was a boy, her son, who did not have the capacity to navigate this much conflict and change, and here she was, just inserting herself into his world. It turned out that she was the dragon of the past. In this case, she was the Evil Queen.

She stepped off the curb, transfixed by this horrible thought, and was almost run over by a pickup truck. It honked and hit the brakes, and Emma stumbled backward, still in a daze.

"Emma!" she heard from across the street. Mary Margaret was running toward her. "Are you okay?"

Emma looked at her and nodded.

"I'm so sorry," came another voice—the driver of the truck. "I didn't see you!"

Emma looked in his direction. It was David. Perfect.

"Are you okay?" he echoed, rushing up to her.

"It's fine," Emma said, snapping herself out of it. "I wasn't looking. I'm totally fine."

She felt David and Mary Margaret flanking her on either side. David put an arm around her. "We'll take you to the hospital," he said. "You're not well."

"Does anything hurt?" said Mary Margaret.

"Guys. No. Seriously." She shucked them off. "I'm okay."

She stormed away. She had to find Regina.

· · ·

KING GEORGE'S CASTLE WAS THEIRS. King George himself was locked in the dungeon, and Snow, Granny, Red, Jiminy, and the dwarfs were together in George's war room, planning their next step. That's what they thought they were doing, at least—Snow didn't need a plan. She knew her next move. She was going to meet with the Evil Queen, unarmed, and end this conflict once and for all.

Of course her companions didn't want her to do it.

"You're too noble for your own good," Red said, watching Snow remove every hidden weapon and piece of armor from her body.

"I'm not. But enough of you have risked your lives because of something that's between the Queen and me. I won't let anyone else get hurt because of me," said Snow. "I'm not asking. I thank you all for your support, and I love each and every one of you. But this is something I have to do. Alone."

She pushed past the dwarfs, looked back at her friends once more, and smiled. They were her family. They were strong. They believed in her. She loved them.

"I don't trust the Queen," said Red.

"I know," said Snow. "Neither do I."

She smiled one last smile and walked out the door.

. . .

IT WAS NOT A LONG TRIP. Snow left at dawn, and an hour before dusk, she was approaching the estate where Regina had grown up, and where Snow had spent so much time as a little girl. So much had happened since those days! And she was here again. So much stronger than she had ever been. So much more in possession of herself. Even after her father had died—after Regina had killed her father—Snow White had been unable to see the forest for the trees and had been too scared and too intimidated by the size of the world to push back against it, to demand justice, to unseat Regina when she deserved to be unseated. Right then and there. In a strange twist of fate, it had taken all of this—her time alone as a bandit, her friendship with Red and the dwarfs, and her love for Charming—for her to really come into herself. For her to be able to confront the Queen now. Funny how things tended to work out.

She tied her horse at the front of the estate and went on foot to the stables, where she knew Regina would be waiting for her.

And she was. Snow saw her on the top of the hill, watching as Snow approached. Snow walked resolutely, her head up, her eyes locked on Regina's.

"Hello, Regina," she said once she'd reached her.

Regina looked down the hill. "Do you remember when I ran down your runaway horse?" she asked. "Do you remember when I saved your life?"

"Of course," said Snow. "It all looks the same."

"Not quite," Regina said. "This is new."

Snow looked to where Regina was pointing—a mound of grass with a simple marker. She realized what it was. "A grave?" she asked.

"A grave," Regina repeated. "Daniel's grave."

"Daniel?" Snow asked, suddenly realizing the true extent of what she had done as a child. "I thought he ran away."

"Ran away? I told you that to spare your feelings. Out of . . . kindness," Regina spat. "But he died. Because of you."

Years. It had been years that she'd assumed that Daniel was somewhere safe. This changed everything.

"I'm . . . so sorry," Snow said. "I was very young, and your mother—"

"—ripped his heart out in front of me. Because of you. Because you couldn't keep a secret."

"And you," said Snow, "killed my father, and took him from me. Haven't we both suffered enough?"

"No," said the Queen.

The word hung in the air between the two women. After a moment, then, Regina withdrew a red apple from a black satchel. "Did you know that apples stand for health and wisdom?" she said, admiring it.

Snow did not like the look of the apple. Not one bit. "Why do I think it would kill me if I ate it?" Snow said warily.

"It won't kill you," said Regina. "No, what it will do is far worse. Your body will be your tomb, and you'll be in there with nothing but the dreams formed of your own regrets." The Queen smiled at the apple.

"You're going to force me to eat it."

"No, of course not," said Regina. "That would be barbaric. And it wouldn't work anyway. The choice is yours. It must be taken willingly."

"And why would I eat it?"

"Because if you refuse the apple, then your Prince Charming will be killed."

She had known it was coming, but hearing the Queen say it made her imagine his death, and along with that came a glimmer of the feeling. Agony. Years—decades—of agony. It would not be worth it to live like that anyway. She was trapped.

"As I said, the choice is yours," said the Queen.

"I take it and he lives?" Snow said. "That's the deal?"

"That is the deal."

Snow nodded, took a breath. "Then congratulations," she said. "You've won."

Snow took a step forward and took the apple, and without another moment's hesitation, she bit into it.

She chewed slowly, looking at the Queen, waiting for the

pain to come. And when it did, it came all at once, rushing over her chest. She dropped the apple; she felt her eyes go wide and her legs quiver. Regina smiled through it all.

The last thing Snow saw were blades of grass; the last she heard was a quiet laugh from the Queen.

. . .

EMMA STOPPED on the middle of Mifflin, gathered herself, and approached Regina's home. Before she pressed the doorbell, a thought struck her: It's not just Regina's home. It's Henry's.

Regina answered the door wearing an apron and holding a spatula. She looked genuinely surprised to see Emma.

"We need to talk," Emma said.

"Yes," said Regina. "I imagine we do. Come right in." Emma remembered the first time she'd been here, which was the night she arrived in town. Everything looked the same, and yet virtually everything had changed. From the kitchen, the smell of something—pie or some other pastry—filled the whole first floor with a warm, inviting scent. She didn't trust the feeling it evoked.

"Look," Emma said to Regina, who was waiting patiently. "This isn't easy. But I think this—whatever it is between us— needs to end."

"At last, something we can agree on," Regina said dryly.

"I want to make a deal. About Henry."

"What kind of deal?" Regina said cautiously.

"I'm leaving town," said Emma.

"What?" Now Regina looked absolutely befuddled. Emma enjoyed catching the woman off guard, although this time it was bittersweet.

"This? What we're doing? It's a problem." Emma pointed

from Regina to herself. "I'm going to go. But there are conditions. I still get to see Henry. Visit, spend time. Whatever. And you promise not to hurt anyone again. Not David, not Mary Margaret. No one."

"I never hurt anyone," said Regina.

"Then it's an easy promise to make," said Emma.

Regina looked dubious. She crossed her arms. "Do you expect me to believe you're really giving up?" she said.

"I'm not giving up," Emma responded. "I'm doing what I've always done. I'm doing what's best for Henry. The only way for us to stop fighting is . . . for us to stop fighting."

"You're right," Regina said. "It has to end."

"So then let's make it easy," Emma said. "I go back to Boston. You get Henry."

"And you still get to see him. You're still in his life."

"Let's be honest. We both know the world where I'm not in his life no longer exists," Emma said. "There's nothing anyone can do about that."

She took a deep breath, then nodded. "Fine," Regina said. "You're right. Would you mind following me for a moment?"

Regina led Emma into the kitchen, where the temperature was a little higher. The place, Emma had to admit, was a real home. A clean, safe home. The lights were bright, and when Regina went to the oven, Emma watched as she pulled out a crisp, steaming apple turnover. There is no chance in hell, Emma thought, I could cook something like that.

"So what exactly are you proposing, then?" Regina said.

"I don't know. Just that we'll figure it out in good faith as we go."

Regina nodded. "However," she said. "He is my son."

"Yeah," Emma said. "All I want is your word you'll take

good care of him. And no one—not him, not this town—will get hurt."

Regina nodded. "You have my word."

Emma stared at her; she could always tell when someone was lying. She looked at Regina for a long time, trying to see if she was being honest.

"What?" Regina finally said.

"Just seeing if you're telling the truth," said Emma.

"And am I?" Regina asked.

Emma nodded. "We have a deal."

Seeing Regina smile was a strange experience. Had Emma seen it before? "Ms. Swan?" Regina said. She held out the turnover, now inside a box of Tupperware. "Maybe a little something for the road?"

Emma shrugged. "Why not?" she said, taking it.

"If we're going to be in each other's lives, we need to be cordial, don't we?"

Emma nodded.

"I do hope you like apples."

. . .

IT TOOK HENRY fifteen minutes to arrive at Emma's apartment after she'd called him on the walkie-talkie. She waited at the kitchen table, a cold cube of dread in the pit of her stomach, imagining how she was going to tell him that her time in Storybrooke was over.

When she opened the door, he took one look at her face and said, "Is everything okay? You sounded strange over the walkie."

He came inside, and Emma remembered the way he'd so brazenly entered her apartment in Boston. The same laser-guided initiative. She loved that about him.

"Henry, yesterday . . . when I tried to take you away . . ." She crossed her arms. Do not cry, she thought. "You were right. I can't take you away from Storybrooke. But I can't stay here, either."

Henry looked back at her, trying to figure out what she meant. "I don't get it," he said finally.

"I have to go, Henry," she said.

There. It was out. The hardest part was over. An arrow through the heart did not do the feeling justice. Something in her was dying.

"Go?" he said finally. "You're going to leave Storybrooke?"

"Yes," she said. "I talked to Regina. I made a deal with her. I'm still going to be able to see you. I just won't be here . . . every day."

"NO!" he cried. "NO! You can't trust her!" His tears were coming again, which pulled at her own.

"I have to, Henry. This is what's best for you."

"You're just scared," he said. "This happens to all heroes right before the big battle. It's just the low moment before you fight back."

She shook her head. "This isn't a story. This is reality. And things have to change. You can't skip school anymore. You can't run away. There are consequences. You can't— You can't keep believing in this curse."

He looked back at her, eyes wide, shaking his head. "You really don't believe, do you?"

"This is how it's going to be. I made a deal. I used my super power. She was telling the truth. She's going to take care of you."

"Maybe she will, but she wants you dead," Henry said.

This surprised Emma.

"Henry, come on," she said.

"She wants you dead, because you're the only one who can stop her."

"Stop her from what?" Emma said, raising her voice. "What is it that's she's really doing? Other than fighting for you?" She took a step toward him, meaning to hug him. "This whole thing has gotten out of hand."

She put a hand on his shoulder and knelt down to him. She thought he would pull away and fight, but he didn't. He buried his face in her chest, sobbing. It was unbearable. She felt him stiffen then, and his head came up. He was looking at something over her shoulder. She looked, too. It was the apple turnover.

"Where did you get that?" he asked.

"Regina gave it to me," Emma said. "So what?"

He sniffed the air. "Is it apple?"

"So?"

He went to the counter and pushed it away. "You can't eat it," he said. "It's poison."

"What?"

"Don't you see?" Henry said. "The deal? It was all a trick. To get you to eat this. To get rid of you once and for all. This is exactly how she got rid of Snow White, except this time, you don't have a Charming here to come wake you up."

It was terrible to hear him going down this path again. Archie had been right—he'd retreated into it. Her presence here was hurting him. "Why would she do that after I told her I would go?" Emma asked.

"Because as long as you're alive, wherever you are, you're a threat."

"You have to stop thinking like this."

"BUT IT'S THE TRUTH!" he yelled. She had never heard him so loud.

Emma reached for the turnover. "Fine," she said. "I'll prove it to you." But when he saw what she was doing, Henry snatched the turnover before she could get it, and held it in front of his own mouth.

Like a threat.

"What are you doing?" Emma said.

"I'm sorry it's come to this. You might not believe in the curse, or in me," Henry said. "But I believe in you."

He took a big bite.

Same difference, Emma thought.

Either way, he'd know for sure.

She waited.

He chewed and swallowed.

"Do you see?" Emma said, after she thought that enough time had gone by. "You want some ice cream with that, or can we get back—"

Before she could finish the sentence, Henry dropped to the floor.

She ran to him, grabbed his little shoulders, shook him. "Henry?" she said. "Henry?"

Panic gripped her after she took his pulse. He was not messing with her. Almost no heartbeat.

"Henry?" she cried again, her voice trembling.

One thought kept circling her mind: This is not happening.

"Henry!" she cried. "Henry!"

CHAPTER 17

A LAND WITHOUT MAGIC

HE HOSPITAL. SCREAMING. FRANTIC CRIES. Dr. Whale's harried questions.

More doctors. Trying to stabilize Henry.

Tears.

Emma ran alongside the gurney, her eyes full of tears, as they carted her son into the ER. She was unable to think. She could barely answer their questions. She tried to tell Dr. Whale about the turnover, to tell him that Henry had been poisoned, but none of it made sense, none of it sounded right. She sounded like a raving lunatic, and Dr. Whale insisted that Henry had not been poisoned. He could find no evidence.

"Is anything different?" Whale said. "You have to think, Emma. What's happened in the last few hours?"

Frustrated, she grabbed Henry's backpack from the gurney, pulled it, and began riffling through its contents, looking for any ideas. Soon, however, the backpack spilled all over the floor, and Henry's things were everywhere. Emma, tears in her eyes, began to look around. "I don't know," she said. "I don't know."

Whale, frustrated also, went back to Henry.

And just then, Emma saw Henry's book.

Magic, she thought. It's not poison. It's magic.

She remembered Henry's words from that first day: "All the stories in this book actually happened."

She touched the book. And as she did, she remembered . . . more.

She remembered . . .

Her mother, handing her to her father.

Her father, fighting the Queen's men as he held her.

The wardrobe, and being gently set inside.

The woods, waking up . . . with August.

Emma blinked as the images flashed over her.

All of her life, Emma had been a skeptic. She'd been the person who poked holes in other people's logic, the person who saw through the illusions that trapped everyone else. It was what made her good at her job, and it was what had gotten her into (and out of) so much trouble along the way. This time, though, it was different. This time, she'd been the one living in a dream world. Emma, the realist, had been utterly wrong.

It's all real. All of it is real.

All of it.

The gurney and the team of doctors reached a set of doors, and as they pushed Henry through, down the hall, they all heard a withering shriek. Everyone stopped and looked up. Regina, in a panic, was running toward him. "My son!" she cried.

Emma's eyes narrowed. If it was real, than Regina was behind it all. And if Regina was behind it all, it was time to kill Regina.

"You did this," she said, grabbing the woman by the collar and pushing her into a door. The door gave way, and the two of them ended up inside a storage closet. Regina didn't know what had hit her.

"What in the hell are you—"

Emma punched her. The rage of the last weeks flowed through her shoulder and her fist as she struck the blow, and Regina's head banged back into a shelf. She tried to hit Emma back, but she wasn't fast enough. Emma grabbed Regina's arm and pushed her again, back into the shelf.

"Stop this," Regina sputtered. "My son is—"

"Your son is sick. Because of you," spat Emma. "That apple turnover you gave me? Henry ate it."

Regina's eyes showed Emma a new kind of terror. Something she'd never seen, quite honestly.

"What?" said Regina, wilting before her.

Emma stared back at her, letting the truth sink in.

"It was . . . it was meant for . . . you." Regina barely got the words out. Emma was holding her up, and she guessed that Regina would probably fall if she let go.

"It's true, isn't it?"

"What are you talking about?"

Emma slammed her against the shelf one more time.

"It's true, isn't it?"

Now Regina understood.

"Yes," she said. "It is."

"Why would you do this?" Emma cried. "I was leaving town. Why couldn't you just leave it alone? It would have been okay!"

Regina shook her head. "Because as long as you're alive, Henry will never be mine," she said.

"He's not going to be anyone's unless you fix this," Emma said. "Wake him up. Turn off the magic."

"I can't," Regina said, shaking her head.

"Why not?"

"That was the last of the magic in this world," Regina said. "It was supposed to put you to sleep. That would have been it."

"So what's it going to do to him?" Emma asked.

"I don't know," Regina said. "Magic here is unpredictable."

Emma stared. "So he could die?"

"Yes," Regina said. "Yes."

"Then what do we do, Regina?"

Regina straightened up as well, nodding, thinking it through. "We need help," she said. "There is one other person in this town who knows about this. Who knows about magic."

Emma knew who she meant. There was only one possibility.

"Mr. Gold," she said.

Regina nodded.

"Actually," she said, "he usually goes by Rumplestiltskin."

. . .

"CAN WE TALK?"

Mary Margaret looked up toward the voice. She had a fresh cup of coffee in her hand, and she nearly spilled it when she saw David coming toward her. He was looking contrite, although that didn't mean anything. She was tired of having a man who had to apologize for himself. All the time.

"I don't think there's anything left to say," she said. She went toward her car.

"I was wrong."

Mary Margaret stopped. She looked back at him and sighed. She couldn't stay away. No matter how hard she tried.

"About you," he said. "About me. About everything."

"I'm listening," she said.

"I didn't believe in you," David said. "And I wish I had a good reason why—but—well, it's like I keep making the wrong decisions, and I don't understand how it keeps happening." He shook his head, frustrated. She didn't say it, but she could relate. "Ever since I woke up from that coma . . . my life hasn't made any sense. Except for you. And what I'm feeling—it's love, Mary Margaret. And it keeps pulling me back to you."

She tried to imagine a version of David, one that had been driven by love all these months. Through every bumbling decision. It wasn't easy, but she supposed she could see it. In a way.

"That may be," she said. "But I'll tell you what I've felt since you came into my life. Pain."

"I know," he said. "I'm sorry."

"Why are you here, David?"

"Because Kathryn put a down payment on an apartment in Boston," he said. "She's not going to use it. But I am." He looked at her sadly. "Unless you can give me a reason to stay here."

She looked at David for a long time.

"I can't," she said finally. "I'm sorry."

She walked to her car and got in, not wanting him to see her face. How many times had that happened? Too many.

Her phone buzzed again, as it had several times this morning. She had ignored it up until now, but she looked this time, mostly to distract herself. Eight missed calls. All from Emma. She called up her voicemail and put the phone to her ear.

"Mary Margaret," came Emma's frantic voice. "It's Henry. It's Henry, I don't— Something is wrong. Something is wrong."

. . .

IT WAS TRUE that Emma hadn't known what the day would bring once she decided to leave Storybrooke. In her wildest imagination, however, she hadn't come up with this: working together with Regina. The two of them were on the way to Gold's shop. They hadn't spoken since they'd left the hospital, and Emma had no plans to say anything to Regina now. She hated her, of course. But she had to work with her.

"Do my eyes deceive me," said Gold, once they were both at his counter, "or is that the look of a believer?" He could tell, apparently. Something about her had changed.

"We need your help," said Emma.

"Indeed you do," he said immediately. "It seems quite the tragic ailment has befallen our young friend." He pointed to Regina. "I told you magic comes with a price. Always."

"Henry shouldn't have to pay it," Regina said.

"No, you should," said Gold. "And you will, no doubt. But alas, for now, we are where we are." He smiled politely and folded his hands.

"Can you help us?" Emma said.

"Of course I can," he said. "True love, my dear. That's the only magic powerful enough to transcend realms and break any curse. Luckily for you, I happen to have bottled some."

Regina looked incredulous, Emma saw. "You did?" Emma asked Gold. Apparently this wasn't a joke. Gold had a bottle of love somewhere.

This new world, Emma thought, is going to take some getting used to.

"Indeed," said Gold. He looked toward Emma. "From strands of your parents' hair, I made the most powerful potion in all the realms. So powerful that when I constructed the dark curse, I put one drop on the parchment. As a little safety valve."

This made sense to Emma, actually. She didn't know much about magic, but she knew a back door when she saw one. "That's why I'm the savior," she said, almost relieved that it wasn't about religion, or a prophecy, and was simply about the manner in which a lonely old man had constructed a spell. "That's why I can break it, too."

"Now she's getting it," Gold said.

"I don't care about breaking the curse," said Emma. "I just want to save Henry."

"Which is why it's your lucky day," Gold said. "I didn't use all of the potion. I saved a little. For a rainy day."

"Well, it's storming like a bitch. Where is it?"

"Where it is is not the problem," Gold said. "Getting it is what should worry you. It's not gonna be easy."

"Enough riddles, Rumple," said Regina, and Emma was startled, for a moment, hearing her refer to him by his "real" name. "What do we do?"

"You do nothing," Gold said. "It has to be Ms. Swan."

"He's my son, it should be me," insisted Regina.

"All due respect, but it's her son and it has to be her," Gold said. "She's the product of the magic, so she must be the one to find it."

"I can do it," Emma said. She knew it was true. If it was about saving Henry, she'd be able to do it. Everything that had happened had led to this.

"Don't trust him, Emma," Regina said, turning to her. She put her hand on Emma's arm. Hearing her own name in Regina's mouth was also disorienting, but the hand on the arm—a brief compassionate touch—was totally surreal.

Emma pulled her arm away. "What choice do we have?" she said.

"You expect me to believe that you saved a dollop of the most powerful magic in the realms, which also happens to be the only magic left in this place, and you're just going to give it to us to save Henry?" Regina shook her head. "No. He's up to something."

"Maybe I'm fond of the boy," said Gold.

"Why would you be?"

"Why? Why? You didn't come to me for a why, Regina. You came to me for a how. And that's what I'm providing. Now then, if you'd be kind enough to stop wasting what little time your boy has left, we might accomplish something."

Emma knew he was right. "Okay," she said. "Where is it?"

"With an old acquaintance," Gold said, looking at Regina. "Someone quite nasty."

Regina and Emma both waited for him to spit it out. Instead, he knelt down and retrieved a long wooden box from down at his feet. He brought it up and set it on the counter in front of the women.

"Tell me, Regina," said Gold. "Is your old friend still in the basement?"

"No," Regina said. "You twisted little imp. You hid it with her?"

Emma looked from one to the other. None of it made sense.

"Not with her," Gold said. "In her. I knew you couldn't resist bringing her over. The perfect hiding place!" He cackled.

"Who is 'her'?" Emma said

"Someone you should be prepared for," Gold said. He opened the box. Emma looked down and saw a long, gorgeous, golden sword. "Where you're going, you will need this."

"What is that?" she said, looking at the gleaming weapon.

"Your father's sword," said Gold.

. . .

EMMA NEEDED to have two final conversations: one with her son, who wouldn't be able to talk back, and another with a man made of wood.

Henry had stabilized, and she was allowed to be at his bedside. The many machines around him beeped and clicked as they monitored his vital signs. Emma held his hand.

"You were right, Henry," she said after a few moments of sitting with him. "About the curse. This town. All of it. I should have believed you. I'm sorry."

She stared at him. His eyes were closed. She listened to the sound of the machines humming.

Henry's book was in her lap, and she picked it up and set it on his bedside table.

"For when you wake up," she whispered.

Storybrooke was dark and quiet as she made her way back downtown, to Granny's B&B. She knocked at August's door for a long time, wondering if he had skipped town, before she heard a faint moan coming from within. It was all she needed to hear. She launched herself at the door once, twice. After hurling her shoulder against it for the third time, she heard a crack, and the lock gave. She entered the room.

August was in his bed. And now she could see it: He was turning into wood. His arms were both already a deep, grainy brown, and the wood, like a disease, was creeping up his neck. He looked terrified; all he could do was shift his eyes.

"No," Emma said, going to him. "No no no no no."

"What's happening to you?" she asked sadly, stroking his hair.

"You can see it now," August said. "You believe."

Emma nodded. "Yes," she said. "I do. But how . . . how can I stop this?"

He spoke slowly, deliberately, staring into her eyes: "Break. The. Curse."

"I'll try," Emma said. "I promise. But first, I have to save Henry. And I need your help."

"No, you don't," August said. "You don't need my help. You don't need magic. You don't need anyone's help."

"I do," she said. "This is all too much. I—I just talked to the Evil Queen and Rumplestiltskin about going on a quest for magic. I have this gold sword; I'm supposed to—to—I don't know. Who the hell knows? I can't do this, August. No normal person can."

"You're not normal," he said, smiling. "You're special. All you have to do is believe."

"But I told you already, I do believe," Emma said.

"Not in the curse," he said. "In yourself, Emma."

She stared at him. The wood had made it up to his lips now, and she held his head, hoping that it didn't hurt. He said it one more time: "Believe in yourself. That's real magic."

And he was still.

. . .

SWORD IN HAND, Emma walked to the clock tower. Regina was waiting for her at the door, which was padlocked. Without a word, Emma strode up to the lock, struck it with the hilt of the sword, and the thing clanked to the ground, broken.

Emma gestured. "Lead the way."

They entered a small library with stone walls. Emma's eyes were drawn to one object in particular: an enormous mirror. Regina went directly to it and touched the glass, and when she did, the mirror jerked sideways, revealing a passageway.

More movement then. Underground machines hummed to life. A frame rose up from below, settling into the open space. Emma realized that it wasn't a passageway at all. It was an elevator shaft.

"Okay," Regina said. "Get in."

"After you," Emma said.

"It's a two-man job," Regina said, shaking her head. "I have to run the elevator from up here. I lower you down. And besides," she added, "you're the one with the sword."

"I'm supposed to trust that you're not lowering me down into the pit of doom, then?" Emma said.

"I don't think you have a lot of choice, Ms. Swan."

Emma thought of Henry, lying in his hospital bed. Regina was right.

"What is down there, Regina?"

"An old enemy," Regina said. "Her punishment was unique. She's been down there for twenty-eight years, trapped in another form. She doesn't want to hear from me."

Emma took this in, not believing that she'd heard the whole truth. "Okay," she said finally. "I'm going down there, but let's be clear about something, 'Your Majesty.' I know who you are now. What you've done. Whom you've hurt. Whom you've killed. And there's one thing you need to know before we go any further." She gave Regina a long, cold stare. "The only reason you're not dead is because I need your help to save Henry. And if he dies? So do you."

Regina nodded brusquely. "Let's get on with it."

Emma stepped into the elevator then, and Regina slowly lowered her down.

It took two minutes, and the lower she went, the darker things got. When the elevator finally settled onto the ground, Emma could hardly see anything. Looking up, she saw just a faint square of light where she'd begun. She was deep underground.

She stepped off the elevator into a smoky cavern. It was hot, too—not at all what she'd expected. Her light caught something, causing a glimmer, and she stepped out across the rocky floor. She knelt in front of something—something big. Something glass. It took her a moment to figure it out. It was a coffin. Somewhere in the back of her mind, she thought that it matched up with the Snow White story. What was it? Hadn't Snow White been in a glass coffin?

Emma stood and took a breath. She looked around.

And then she saw it.

At first, she thought it was another light, someone else shining a flashlight at her. But it wasn't.

It was an eye.

A yellow eye.

All was still, though, and Emma took a tentative step forward and reached out toward the blackness beside the eye. Her hand touched something that wasn't stone.

What in the hell is this? she thought.

It was scaly, warm. She rubbed her hand along it.

And then the walls began to move. She heard a grunt, and then a roar. She stumbled backward, eyes wide, realizing what this was: a dragon.

It came to life with a screech and a ball of flame.

MARY MARGARET FOUND the book in Henry's hospital room, but there was no sign of Emma. Whatever was wrong, she was out there, somewhere, taking care of it. This was why Mary Margaret loved her friend so much; Emma knew how to fight back. That had been missing, in Mary Margaret's own life, for a long time. She admired it.

Dr. Whale had explained the situation, and now Mary Margaret decided that the least she could do was stay with Henry, to be with him through this. She could read him a story.

And she did. She told him the story of how Snow White had sacrificed herself to end the conflict with the Queen, and how she'd fallen into a magical slumber because of the apple. Charming, meanwhile, had escaped from the Queen's dungeons, and with the help of Rumplestiltskin, he was able to finally locate his true love once again. She was not well when he found her. Not at all.

"When Prince Charming saw his beloved Snow White," she read, "there in her glass coffin, he knew all that was left was to say good-bye. He had to give her one last kiss. But when their lips met, true love's kiss proved more powerful than any curse. A pulse of pure love shuddered out and engulfed the land. As her eyes opened, it was clear, no matter what, that they would live happily . . ."

Mary Margaret paused, took a breath. She was crying. It had just . . . happened.

She went on: ". . . happily . . . ever after."

She closed the book, then closed her eyes. It was all such a fantasy. It didn't work like that, did it?

"I'm sorry, Henry," she said, taking his hand. "I gave this

book to you because I knew . . . I knew life doesn't always have a happy ending. But I thought . . . I thought that that was just not fair."

She squeezed his hand, remembering how David—John Doe then—had woken up after hearing a story about love. And for a second, she believed it was happening again—she heard a beep from one of the machines and looked back at Henry hopefully. However, the beeps then became urgent, and sounded more like warnings. Nurses began to rush into the room.

"What's happening?" she said.

Dr. Whale burst in. "He's crashing," he said. "You have to leave."

Mary Margaret found herself in the hall, her hand over her mouth, her heart pounding. Nurses and doctors huddled around Henry; she couldn't see anything. But she could see the concern in the eyes of the doctors and hear it in the sounds of their voices.

Henry was dying.

. . .

THE DRAGON BURST UP into the air and showed Emma its full, terrifying form. Wings spread, it shrieked down at her. It was almost too big, and too frightening, and too shocking for her brain to even admit that it was real. Which didn't much matter, at least for the first pass: Her body took care of the self-preservation. She ran, changed direction, and dove as the dragon swooped down over her, raining fire down at her heels. This bitch is pissed, Emma thought, getting to her feet.

Overhead, the dragon was circling, and she ran to the other side of the cavern, where she saw a good outcropping of rock.

She dove under it just in time, feeling the heat of the flame against the skin of her cheeks. This time, the dragon didn't swoop away.

It landed.

Emma turned, eyes wide, and looked at the growling creature, which was not ten feet from her. She feebly held the sword up, but it was heavy and ungainly. She sensed that the dragon was amused.

"Screw this," she said.

She dropped the sword, pulled her gun, and started to shoot.

After firing into the heart of the thing, there was no sign that the bullets had even caused a tickle. It lunged at her, and she ran to the other side of the cavern, the dragon snapping its huge jaws just behind her head. At the far wall, she steadied herself.

She changed her aim and fired at the head in a tight pattern near the nose. She could see small geysers of blood erupting when each bullet hit, but again, they seemed to have little impact.

"Really?" Emma said aloud.

As she did, she saw that the dragon's chest now seemed to be glowing orange. She figured she was going to have to dig that potion out of it.

The sword was on the other side of the cavern, back where she'd dropped it. She tossed the gun aside, visualizing the move she'd have to make to get the sword. The dragon turned to face her. She smiled at it. Then went straight for it.

The dragon seemed confused by Emma's charge, and was late shooting a long plume of fire at her; so late that she made it past, and made it under the legs of the huge beast. She dove for the sword and felt it in her hand. The dragon, confused, slowly turned around, screeching in frustration.

It rose up then, ready to turn her into a pyre.

Emma waited as long as she could.

And then she threw the sword.

The blade struck the beast directly at the glowing spot on its chest, and the dragon screamed an ungodly scream, its wings flapping in agony. The scream, however, did not last long. All at once, the tremendous creature exploded into a ball of flame and ash.

Emma hit the deck and waited for the hot wind to pass over her. When all was again quiet, she approached what was left of the body—really just a pile of black crud. She sifted around for a moment, but the potion wasn't hard to find. A white jeweled egg, the perfect carrying case for a love potion. Emma collected it, found her sword, and headed back to the elevator shaft.

Breathing heavily, still not really admitting to herself that she'd just fought a dragon, Emma yanked the cord and yelled up the shaft: "Regina, pull me up!" After a moment, the elevator jerked to life.

Emma studied the egg as best she could as she lurched upward. She'd lost her flashlight somewhere, but the light from above let her see the clasp. She opened the egg up and saw the vial inside, glowing a strange violet hue. So that's what love looks like, she thought.

About ten feet from the top of the shaft, the elevator stopped moving. Emma looked up. "Regina?"

A head peeked over the side.

Not Regina.

"Gold?" said Emma. "What are you doing here? Where's Regina?"

"She had me take over," he said. "You've got the egg, I see!"

She was good at telling when people were lying, but even the worst judge of truth would have been suspicious of Gold, the way he eagerly leaned toward her, awaiting a reply.

"Yeah, I got it," she said. "Pull me the rest of the way up."

"I can't," he said. "The elevator is broken. You're going to have to climb the rest of the way."

Emma looked down at her pants and her pockets, trying to think of some way to secure the egg for the climb.

"It's too fragile, you can't climb with it," he said. "Toss it up to me, then climb."

"No way, Gold," she said. "Just hold your horses."

"Henry doesn't have the time, Ms. Swan."

Emma looked up, and sighed. She had to trust him. She didn't like it, but she had to.

She tossed the egg.

Gold caught it, looked at it for a moment, nodded at her, and disappeared.

"Gold?" she said. "Gold?"

Nothing.

He was gone.

• • •

IT TOOK HER TEN MINUTES to get up out of the elevator, and another five to get to the hospital. She didn't even consider going after Gold. She went to Henry. What August had said—*you don't need magic*—had circled through her mind the entire time she climbed, like a dragon in her head. Yes, maybe all of it was real, and yes, maybe there was some crazy logic to the curse, but she knew one thing: She loved that kid. She loved him more than she loved herself. She'd never cared about herself enough to know that she was capable of giving love to someone else, but she knew now. And so she went to him. To Henry. To family.

The mood was grim when Emma entered the ER, and her heart shuddered when she saw Mary Margaret's face. To her right, Regina. (Now she knew why she'd left the library and left her at the bottom of the shaft. She'd come to watch over her son.) Behind them, Dr. Whale and the nurses. All of them looked somber, broken. Mary Margaret was crying. When Emma realized Regina had a tear in her eye, she knew the worst was true.

"What is it?" Emma managed. She and Regina kept staring into one another's eyes. Emma knew that right now, it was like looking into a mirror. They'd fought for so long, but now . . . they were two mothers.

"We did everything we could," say Dr. Whale.

"I'm sorry," said Mother Superior, who was flanking him. "You're too late."

Shock. Pure, unadulterated shock. Emma's eyes glazed over as she walked past them and into Henry's room. She barely heard Regina saying, "No, no, no," over and over again. She heard a faint ringing in the back of her head. All she saw was him. His beautiful face. His eyes closed.

"Henry," she muttered, dropping to her knees at his bedside. She put a hand on his chest. "Henry," she whispered. She didn't care if he was alive or dead. "I love you."

She leaned forward, closed her eyes, and kissed him on the forehead.

She felt it right away: A shock of energy pulsed out of her

and into him, building itself up from a core of energy deep within her chest. The force of it made her eyes come open—it was pain, but it was the pain of love, of all the longing she'd felt for the last decades, all of it focused here, on him. Another wave rolled over her then, and this one knocked her backward, to the floor. People—everyone—were thrown back. It was like a hurricane had entered the room.

It took a moment for the winds to die down, and for Emma to get to her feet. When she did, she stared at Henry in disbelief.

His eyes were open.

He was looking at her.

"I love you, too," he said. And smiled.

. . .

MARY MARGARET WANDERED away from the hospital and toward downtown Storybrooke, thinking, of all things, about her name.

Mary.

Mary Margaret.

The words sounded so strange on their own; together, even stranger. She stopped on the sidewalk in front of the diner, squinting in great concentration as a series of very old, very hidden feelings paraded through her heart.

She had used that name before; it did come from somewhere. She remembered a snowy landscape, and then saw the snow red with blood. Bodies. A wolf. And—and her friend. Her friend Red.

Her head snapped up. She looked down the street and saw him coming toward her, a smile on his face. His arms out.

"My prince," she whispered, seeing David—no, *Charming*—coming toward her. "My prince!"

He started to run, and she ran to him. They met in the middle of the street and Snow felt it all come back, then, held securely in his arms. All of it. The bridge. Her father. Regina. Red. Storming the castle. The fairies. The dwarfs.

The curse.

"I knew I would find you," said Charming, lifting her from the ground.

"And I knew I would find you," she responded. He laughed, and they kissed. Everything, finally, was as it was supposed to be.

. . .

THE NURSES AND DOCTORS had all scattered. Some did stick around to gape at Emma and wonder how she'd managed to perform the miracle, but soon, after their memories began to come back to them, and they realized that they'd been living within the mental fog of a curse for twenty-eight years, people scattered, frantically searching the town for loved ones and friends. Emma was right where she was supposed to be.

Regina, surprisingly, had disappeared as well.

Henry seemed to be okay, although he was a little weak. Emma told him about the dragon, and what she'd had to do to get the love potion, and she also told him that Gold had run off with what she'd recovered. "August told me that I didn't need it," she said. "So I knew. I knew it was right to come to you. But what is Gold up to, do you think?"

Henry shrugged, sucking on the straw attached to his little cup of orange juice.

"Whatever it is," Emma said, "it's probably bad for the rest of this town."

Short-term retribution. But then what?

"What is that?" Henry said, pointing out the window.

Emma saw it, too: a purple smoke flowing down the street as though it were water. She stood up and went to the window.

"I have no idea," Emma said. "But I don't like it."

She looked at Henry, whose eyes had gone wide. This time there was no smile, but the amazement in her son's eyes reminded her of the first moment they'd arrived in Storybrooke together, all those months ago. They were eyes of fascination.

"Magic," Henry said. "Magic is here."

She turned and watched the smoke creeping over the town, sensing that her son was right. She knew what it meant. This wasn't over.

In fact, it was just beginning.

With her eyes still on the smoke, Emma stepped back to Henry's bed and let her hand rest on his shoulder. Together, they watched in silence. Was it safe? No. Could she ever get back the life she could have had, or create the life she should have created for Henry? No. She couldn't take any of it back and she couldn't change the past. That was not how life worked. Not in this world, and not in any other world. The best she could do was make the right choices in the present. Here and now.

She would not leave her son again. She would always be there to protect him. Always. She squeezed his shoulder.

Henry, as though he'd heard the vow echoing in her heart, reached up and took his mother's hand.

"Thanks," he said.

"For what?" Emma asked, smiling down at him.

He looked up.

"For coming back."